Simon Maginn w
1961, the young
St Mary's College and at the University of Sussex,
where he studied music. His earlier novels, *Sheep* and
Virgins and Martyrs, have been translated into several
languages. He lives in Sussex.

Also by Simon Maginn

SHEEP
VIRGINS AND MARTYRS

and published by Corgi Books

A SICKNESS
OF THE SOUL

Simon Maginn

CORGI BOOKS

A SICKNESS OF THE SOUL
A CORGI BOOK : 0 552 14250 6

First publication in Great Britain

PRINTING HISTORY
Corgi edition published 1995

Set in 11/13pt Adobe Times by Kestrel Data, Exeter.

Corgi Books are published by Transworld Publishers Ltd,
61–63 Uxbridge Road, London W5 5SA,
in Australia by Transworld Publishers (Australia) Pty Ltd,
15–25 Helles Avenue, Moorebank, NSW 2170,
and in New Zealand by Transworld Publishers (NZ) Ltd,
3 William Pickering Drive, Albany, Auckland.

Reproduced, printed and bound in Great Britain by
Cox & Wyman Ltd, Reading, Berks.

For CHF

Acknowledgements

Thanks to Hugh for explaining the mysteries of the motor bike, Sarah for telling me about limb buds, and Calum for medical assistance. Thanks as always to my editor Averil Ashfield for driving me mad until we got it all sorted out, and sorry about that wax doll. (It didn't work anyway.)

'Victory is neither God's nor the Devil's.
Victory belongs to madness.'

M. Foucault, *Madness and Civilisation*

1

There's something inside me, I don't know what's inside me, I suppose you'd have to call it curiosity. The thing that killed the cat. It must be strong, since cats don't kill easily. It's certainly strong in me. Was, rather.

Most children go through a stage when all they'll say is 'why'. No, not this bus, Martin. Why? Because it doesn't go where we want to go. Why doesn't it? Because it goes somewhere else. Why does it? Because that's where the *driver* has to *take* it. Yes but why does he? And so on. In certain children, what begins merely as an irritating mannerism becomes ingrained, a way of taking on the world. And in a very few cases it can even be turned into a vocation, a calling, or, less grandly, a way of screwing together some money.

I am an investigative journalist. When I say 'am' I mean, of course, 'was'. I'm not anything at the moment. Nothing you could put a name to anyway. What do you call someone who lies in a hospital bed, subject to periodic funny spells in the head, murmuring slightly fuzzy recollections into a tiny tape recorder? Someone who, to speak frankly, isn't always in total control of all his faculties and functions? And when I say 'investigative journalist', I mean, naturally, something

11

far less coherent, less dignified than that. People say 'I am an architect', 'I am a works supervisor', 'I am a psychiatrist'. As if putting a fancy label on it will change the goods. We are what we are, or, in my case, were. I used to go to places, find things out, piece together stories, then sell them to editors and news agencies. I have on occasion been commissioned, which meant that I was trusted with a cash advance for the story. I have been doing this for the last four years, on and off. More off than on, in truth. Only in two of those years have I actually made enough money to pay tax and buy my round like a man.

It is not clear why one story should attract rather than another. I investigated corrupt property deals and graft in one of the grubbier northern Labour metropolitan boroughs, mostly because it enraged me. The politicians abused the trust of the ordinary working people. My grandparents lived nearby, they could easily have voted in these parasites. They were good people, my grandparents, they deserved better. But over and above that, it was a simple saga of innocence betrayed, and it was easy. I went 'undercover' (and how I have always loved that word! Undercover, seedy hotel bars and quick lies to strangers) to expose organized dog-fighting in the North Midlands. The mistreatment of animals enrages me, and the perverting of their simple natures for the debased entertainment of sadistic—

No; again it was a simple, strong story. Good against evil, cowboys and Indians. A news editor once told me that no-one ever wore a grey hat. White or black. That's why I chose that story.

So part of my job has always been to – simplify. Take a complex tangle of human motivations and failings, take weakness, overweening pride, greed, delusion, the need to believe, and assign hats, white and black. That sort of story you can sell. But it's a long, long way from the truth.

2

Fiona and I live in Ealing, which is quite an admission, if you think about it. Ealing. The word has a kind of hollowness, a whiteness about it. It sounds like the cry of some forlorn marsh bird. The light falls flat and straight, and in the middle of it all, on Ealing Broadway itself, is a big, bland shopping centre, imaginatively named the Broadway Centre, where blameless purchases are made by perfectly blameless people. I have been in physical danger a few times in my life, once when I went undercover with the dog-fighters, once when I was all but discovered hiding under the stairs in a house in Clapham. And on those occasions my thoughts have turned to the Broadway Centre, where people, at that very moment, were buying moisturizing cream and Tipp-Ex and prawn sandwiches. It represents, for me, all that is safe and lawful and moderate.

And boring, of course. I would rather crouch under some pornographer's filthy stairs, blinking with fear, listening for footfalls, than wait to pay for my dry-cleaning, safe and sound in the Broadway Centre in Ealing. Or that's what I tell myself afterwards, anyway. All lies, no doubt.

Fiona lies for her living too, in a way. She has

acquired the label of Press and Public Relations Officer in the most bizarre of the London boroughs. She denies the lying, she says PR only works if it's true, it's purely a matter of presentation. We met at a party in Chalk Farm, five years ago, and she moved into my flat a year later. It seems much longer than that, and I have trouble sometimes remembering what it was like when she wasn't there. The time I was there on my own seems shadowy and unreal, provisional.

We met in the queue for the toilet: I, in my penetrating, forensic, journalistic way, asked her what she did for a living, then.

'So what do you do then?'

'Dancer.'

'A dancer, really? Classical?'

'Nah. Exo'ic.'

I took in her figure: five foot nothing and no wood nymph.

'You know, I do, like, cab'ret an' that. For business-men an' that.'

'Oh yes.'

'I got this act, wiv a bo'lle.'

'No kidding.'

'And a dog.'

'Uhuh.'

Someone pushed past and waved, and this five-foot nothing stripper from Luton called out, 'Alison, have you seen Leo anywhere?' in impeccable Oxford May-Ball tones. She turned back to me.

'Do you do anything, particularly?' she asked me in her new voice, 'or not really?'

'Yeah, yeah I do a bit of freelancing actually.'

15

'Oh, a vet are you?'

'What?'

'Lancing. I thought vets did that.'

I looked closely at her, at her brilliant, sparkling eyes and polite smile. I was genuinely unsure if she was serious or not. She certainly looked serious.

'That's right. And I do it free, you see, because of my love of animals, all animals. I'm a Buddhist. I don't need to work, actually, because I'm independently wealthy.'

'Oh really? Who are your people?'

'Urm – '

'Only I don't think I've seen you anywhere. I thought I knew everyone. You can't be anyone very much.'

'Maybe it's you that isn't anyone much. Did you ever consider that?'

'Oooh, 'ark at 'im, Lord bleedin' Muck,' she said, and I realized that she was in fact imitating a rich girl imitating a cockerney lass.

'I bet I can guess what you do really,' I said, go on then, she said, and I said: PR.

'Bugger,' she said, and then it was her turn for the toilet.

We've always got on, I've always been amazed at how easily. We have similar backgrounds, we're both ambitious. She's probably brighter than me, on balance, but not much. I can still fool her, when I want to. Could, rather. I kept on waiting for the major row, the crisis, the drama, but there was none. We got along beautifully, sweetly, right up until just before she left, and even then I understood perfectly why she did it. I would have done the same in her place.

3

Why one story rather than another? It isn't just a matter of good against bad, white hats and black hats. Nor is it solely a question of matching supply with demand with news and features editors. These are just modish poses, the kind of thing someone photographed in monochrome in strong light and cigarette smoke would say. A guy's gotta make a buck, lady.

The story in this case started simple. I was driving through that area of the West Midlands west of Derby and north of Burton-on-Trent. I don't know if it has a name; in my mind it will always be the Badlands. A certain kind of commentator would probably call it post-industrial. It's wide, flattish, open agricultural land, vast farms of rape and maize and wheat, surrounded by the hulks of chimneys and refineries and gravel pits and mines. There are other, older scars, too, disused tramways and railways and cuttings; and before that the geometric traces of the old Roman roads, like the pathways of warrior ants, carving out their impossibly straight lines into the distance. Then the rivers and brooks, innumerable, labyrinthine. The land undulates, and the horizons are vast, topped with an immense, beautiful sky. There are small, quiet towns of identical terraces, two-lane roads which describe long, gradual curves. Crakemarsh and Doveridge, Rocester and Mayfield; Gallows Green, Somersal Herbert; Lads Grave. Every so often you come across a quarry or a complex of brick and corrugated-iron sheds, fenced enclosures, warehouses with smashed windows and tall grasses and young trees around them. Everyone has gone home, defeated, and there has been no reason to dismantle anything, so it stays.

Early summer. I was on my way up to Manchester, and was perversely refusing to take the motorway. And regretting it. I hate the motorway, it makes me feel like a herd animal caught up in some kind of stampede. Panic. So I was ambling north and somewhat west, in my beautiful black Saab, through this hot, scarred, repetitive landscape. There were no other cars around for miles, you could imagine that you were in another country, or another decade, the 1950s perhaps. I was fiddling with the radio. A Tina Turner track – presumably the local 'classic hits' station; a burst of techno – Radio One; some rippling piano figures and a plaintive violin line – Classic FM. And then, incredibly, the sound of a man crying. *Crying*. I had a moment of complete unreality, and for a moment the sound filled the car, too loud, too intense: it sounded like my own voice, my own cries. I grabbed for the volume control, and guided the car to the roadside and parked. Densely packed fields ran away from me in all directions, combed with the tracks of the great machines, tricking the eye, masking the perspectives.

I turned the sound up again. A woman's voice now. 'Caller?'

An unattractive, phlegmy sound, between a snort

and a sniff. The distraught man was trying to stop crying.

'Caller? Do you want to carry on?'

More snortings. Then the man's voice. Inflected, West Midlands, Dudley.

'Yes, I'm. Sorry, I'm.' A little, embarrassed laugh. 'Carry on, I'm.'

Silence, then a new voice, and in my startled condition I thought the voice was coming from all around me, from the neatly combed fields and the long deserted road, from the ground.

'Are you able to talk to me now?'

Not a sympathetic voice, not pitying or comforting, neither was it scolding or impatient. And not exactly the kind of 'expert' voice that you can get on the radio sometimes, telling you how to spot whitefly infestation or explaining about fixed-rate mortgages.

'Can you talk to me now?'

The most obvious quality of this new voice was its control. Measured, gentle, powerful, utterly controlled. And astonishingly seductive.

The distraught man stumbled on, his voice cracked and disfigured by the havoc his grief was playing on his sinuses and Eustachian tubes. A calamity had befallen him, an irrecoverable, unbearable loss; in his bitterness he had harmed a child. He was explaining it as best he could over the phone, to this voice, live on the radio. He came to an abrupt finish, finding that he had run out of words, and there was another pause.

'OK.'

Control. Unbelievable as it seemed, he was about to accept this terrible confession, not merely accept it, but

19

take responsibility for it. He was going to respond to it.

'OK my friend. What we are going to do now, you and I, is speak to the Lord our maker and guide, and present what you have just told me to him, as a gift, as a sacrifice.'

And through my shock at this unforeseen melodrama coming over the air, the almost physical impact of the transaction that had just occurred, was a word, in big, big letters:

STORY!

4

By the time the programme – or I suppose really, *show* is the apposite word – had finished, the man with the seductive voice, who called himself Teacher, had 'helped' five people, four of whom had cried, and I had been parked for nearly fifty minutes. Three cars had passed me in that time. I felt encased in a bubble, I was in the Twilight Zone. I'd never heard this kind of thing on British radio before. That it should happen in this awful abandoned wilderness seemed highly appropriate.

Teacher was no bland US-style God-botherer, in expensive suit and elaborate hairpiece. Throughout the show references had been made to his unorthodox lifestyle. He was no less than the leader of a motor-bike gang, the Sons of the New Bethlehem. They gathered in shopping centres, service-station car parks and the like in this widely-flung constituency, and – his word – 'ministered'. This was a fully-fledged crusade, in leather. People were so amazed by this that they forgot to be sensible and became converts. Some of them went on to be healed.

The presenter of the radio show, a fulsome, patronizing woman with some implausible media name like Gebethny Polporral, invited calls from those 'troubled in spirit'. A caller would be announced: 'Kevin. From Uttoxeter. Go ahead, Kevin, you're through to Teacher.' Kevin from Uttoxeter would then confess, with a greater or lesser degree of accuracy and completeness. If he was found to be evading, he would be nudged by Teacher. What exactly. How often. Tell me how you felt. Tell me why you did that. Tell. When Kevin from Uttoxeter had been reduced to a blubbering, prostrate penitent, Teacher would guide him through a prayer. After that Kevin would be asked how he felt, and he would feel 'better' or 'cleansed'. Teacher would speak, using terms like 'fix', 'repair', 'back on the road'. Melawney Petrollnoch would return to say that Kevin should stay on the line, to arrange a time and a place to meet Teacher, to be healed, if Teacher thought that was needed. One of the 'team of trained counsellors' would then talk to him, make sure that he was all right. Because, of course, it would be irresponsible, not to mention unprofessional, simply to stir such feelings up and then not deal with them. That would smack just a little too much of sensation and the crass exploitation of human misery. At the end of the show Teacher was invited to lead a prayer. This went something as follows:

'Lord. Our lives are pain and trouble. Things don't go right. We try, but sometimes, Lord, we are just as bad as we can be. We can't always get by alone. We tremble in the darkness. But when we turn to you we are cleaned and made good as new.'

And so on.

Need I say that it was compelling? It was compelling. I knew immediately that I needed this story.

And not an interview either, not some meaningless confrontation with this snake-handler, this Teacher, but his *story*. And to get that I would have to go to him as a penitent, as one of the lost.

Undercover. Deep undercover. I was excited. I was hot for it. It was a story worth going after. It would be my biggest story to date. And the hats would be whitest white and blackest black. He was my quarry. My rage, my righteous rage, bubbled up, rich and thick and juicy. I cast around for something to feed it.

5

My Grandma Beale, my mother's mother, lives in Derbyshire. She is a big, cheerful woman in her late eighties. I remember her singing, a wobbling contralto, as she got around on two sticks. She is only occasionally able to walk, and is often now compelled to use the wheelchair she despises. She suffers from rheumatoid arthritis, has done so since early girlhood. My mother was her first child, the first of six; by the appearance of the last, my wicked Uncle Mick, she was reduced to an agonized, immobile shell. Still singing, though. Moving was torment, the journey from sitting to standing was only possible with forward planning and much assistance. Until she married she lived with her mother, able to do only very fine needlework and some lacemaking.

She worked in an ammunition plant during the war, the last war as she called it; on VE Day she went home and took to her bed, where she stayed for the next six months. My Gramp, her husband, attended to her with something like saintly devotion, and she gradually recovered mobility and strength. She went back to needlework, making up dress patterns for a textile firm nearby. She remembered the prototype miniskirt: she queried the design, not able at first to believe that it could possibly mean what it said. When she'd made it up she tried it on, and my Gramp had nearly died laughing.

Then her hands seized up, as if burned in a fire, the only part of her that had been spared so far. My mother and one of her sisters, together with my Gramp, have looked after her since then. She believes that her hands will recover, even if the rest of her never will.

When she was eight, she once told me, she was taken by her father to a healer, the seventh son of a seventh son. Already, at eight years old, the stiffness and pain was apparent, and she could only walk supported. The healer, renowned at the time in rural south Derbyshire, had his hands on her for nearly an hour. He gripped, twisted, pulled. He had bad breath and a harelip. She told me that his dirty fingernails dug into her tender flesh, she was bruised for weeks afterwards. He touched her everywhere. Towards the end of her torture she screamed and her father slapped her, hard, and told her that she was bad, bad, that God had died for her.

And then, for three days, she said, God smiled on her. The stiffness, the swelling, the aching and creaking, all left her and she felt herself to be basking in strong sunlight. She danced, she ran, she swung from trees. It was a miracle, she told me. He was truly a holy man, a saint.

On the fourth day, she fell and couldn't stand up. Her father found her, on the scorched grass beneath a tree, and beat her. God was bleeding on his cross, and she was mocking him! That holy man, that healer, was

25

weeping for her wickedness, and she was crawling on the floor like an animal. He pulled her up and tried to force her to walk. Walk! Damn you! Her screams alerted one of the farm workers nearby, who managed to wrest her from her father's grasp and then broke his jaw with a single punch. This boy carried the little girl home. She lay in bed for ten weeks. She learned to walk, as if from scratch, with sticks. It was like starting again, she told me, like being a baby. She never walked easily after that. And as for dancing, climbing trees – !

But those three days, she said, she had been full of God's grace. He had been smiling on her. And then stopped: he had never smiled after that. She hadn't deserved her miracle, and he had taken it away from her. And when I suggested that the healer had in fact injured her, exacerbated her condition, but given her a powerful autosuggestive 'cure' that had lasted only three days, she touched my hand and explained.

'Sometimes God smiles. Sometimes he doesn't. We aren't to know why, lad.'

A strong, determined old woman. How dared some evil charlatan with dirty fingernails and bad breath handle her, hurt her, and send her away with false hope, a false miracle! How dared he!

And so when I heard Teacher, his seductive voice full of easy forgiveness and special authority, I heard the voice of that seventh son of a seventh son, that—

Feed the rage. I would close him down, this St Marlon Brando. Not because the story was strong and neat and easy, no, and not to slake my curiosity about this freak, this Teacher, to see him, find out if maybe there was something in it, in *him*, but because of my Grandma Beale and her poor hands. Grandma's hands. That was why. At first, anyway.

6

I drove back to London. I had a story to finish, just hack-work really, about the extreme right and organized crime in the East End. I could tie it up in a few days. I was prepared to drop it actually, if it looked like it was going to get in the way. The next story is always the interesting one, the real one. The one you're doing now is just time-filling, no more than a nuisance.

Fiona and I went up West and saw something sexy and ideologically suspect at an art-house cinema. More her kind of thing than mine, though I can't say I object to a bit of sex in a film, as long as it's not too tasteful. Afterwards we strolled round Soho and Leicester Square, hand in hand, like young people, and I bought her a baseball cap with 'I Fuck Like an Animal' on it. Again, more her kind of thing than mine. We went into a pub, and there was a loony in there shouting about the IRA and what he knew about them. Apparently he knew who they all were and that they were really just a cover for Gaddafi or something. I half wanted to ask him about his sources, but that's just the kind of thing Fiona hates, so I didn't. It sounds stupid perhaps but you can never be sure what people know, you really can't. It wouldn't be the first time I'd been put onto a story by a loony in a pub. It was a nutter on the top deck of a night bus who'd first got me interested in the far right in the East End. Nutters get around, and because they're nutters no-one takes them seriously, so they hear things. Unfortunately they tend, in my experience, to be unable to distinguish with complete certainty between what they hear and what they're *hearing*. But that doesn't mean that everything they say is crap.

Finally I came clean and told Fiona that I was about to go off on a jaunt. This was her term for my undercover adventures, my glamour jobs. She asked me if I'd packed my licence to kill, and I assured her that I never left home without it. She needed this kind of banter because otherwise she'd have to take me seriously and accept that I was probably going to get myself into trouble one of these days. Part of the game was that I hinted darkly at the perils and dangers I was letting myself in for and she flicked her hair back and said 'Oh yeah?' in her bored-secretary voice. This way I could let her know that I would be gone for, probably, three or four days, and that I would ring her if I could but that I might not be able to. And she would be able to worry in private and not have to talk about how worried she was.

Fiona regarded my job as some kind of absurd pose, something I felt compelled to engage in because of my gender, like watching *Grandstand* or ogling flashy cars. I think she also believed that I did it, at least partly, to impress her, so she was at pains to make me understand that she was *not* impressed. Not *big*, not *clever*. Some men start fights outside clubs, some men boast about incomes or talk clever about politics. Some men have tattoos, or state-of-the-art hi-fis. I went away to do undercover research. It was something in my hormones, but that didn't mean that she didn't still worry. And now she was pregnant, at last, finally, after three years, she thought I should stop all this Sam Spade crap, as she elegantly put it, and get myself a proper job. Why, she wanted to know, can't you work on a paper again and write court reports. What's so terrible about that?

'Oh, just because of pride, you know, and ambition, details like that. Just because you're pregnant doesn't mean I have to be a failure does it? I don't remember you mentioning that at the time. In fact, as far as I recall, at the time—' She humphed and smiled and gave me patronizing looks. We were close to agreeing that I would stop. Soon. This might be my last job, at least of this kind. It wasn't as if there was much money in it even, and it made us both jumpy.

'So where is it this time?' Weary, but she wanted to know, and she knew I didn't want to tell her. As a rule I am very reluctant to say exactly where I'm going or what I'm doing, partly through bravado. No safety net. Look Ma no hands. But also because I have a sufficiently high estimate of my ideas and abilities to be cautious of being imitated. It has happened.

'Oh for God's sake. Go and get me more bloody Slimline tonic. Try not to get abducted by desperadoes from foreign powers on the way. Do you want some money?'

And, humiliatingly enough, I did.

7

I made contact with the Sons almost by accident.

I had come up by train, since the car could only be an encumbrance if I was going to be there for more than a day or two, and the registration number would make me that much easier to identify, if anyone wanted to try. I had no idea how long any of this was going to take, or under what conditions I would be allowed to get near Teacher. I wouldn't necessarily be able just to drive straight up to the door and park. I might well have to leave the car somewhere and, knowing my luck, it would probably end up getting towed away, and I couldn't allow that to happen. Not to the Saab. So I arrived by train at Derby Station, in brilliant sunshine, and started work.

The first problem, of course, was how to find them. It wasn't as though I could just ring up and ask for an appointment. I went to the radio station, who refused point blank to give out any contact information, on the grounds of confidentiality. I asked to see the producer of the show, and was again politely refused. I visited the police station and with some difficulty managed to gain a ten-minute interview with a detective sergeant who agreed that Teacher was known to them, that they had spoken to him on a number of occasions, that there were no grounds at present for any police interest in him, but that his file was open. Yes, they knew where to find him, if he wanted to be found. No, they couldn't tell me where that was.

First rule of journalism: talk to everyone. I was chatting to a cleaner on my way out of the police station, who'd overheard me talking to the desk sergeant earlier. The cleaner had a brother-in-law, the brother-in-law knew a lad who worked at a service station, at Appleby Magna, just where the M42 ended short of Ashby-de-la-Zouche. The Sons used it often, as a gathering point. They would arrive in twos and threes all afternoon, then roar off together. Sometimes Teacher was with them, sometimes not. The lad had spoken to him many times. The brother-in-law was worried, in fact, that the lad was getting too interested in them. They were, by all accounts, a funny bunch. Religious nuts apparently.

I had to get a taxi to the service station, which felt faintly ridiculous, and made me yearn for the Saab. And once there, what to do? I talked to the woman in the little forecourt shop: she confirmed that the Sons did periodically use the premises, but couldn't say when they might be back. There was no regular day or time. I left my mobile-phone number and offered her cash money if she would ring me when they appeared. She refused the money, but promised that she would ring.

'If you need to see him, then you need to see him,' she said. I thanked her. She called out after me, as I pulled the door open, 'Whatever it is you've got, he'll help you, duck. I know. I'll ring.'

The taxi driver dropped me at a hotel that he said was cheap. While I was rummaging for change he said, 'Listen, this lot that you're looking for. I'd watch out for 'em if I were you. Watch yer back like. You hear stories, you know.'

'What kind of stories?'

'Mate of mine, he knew a bloke, this bloke went off his trolley and tried to top himself. Then he finds out about this lot, on the radio, and goes off to find 'em. No-one never sees him no more. Police just say he must of, you know, done the job properly this time and killed himself, and his body never been found. Maybe.'

'But you don't think so?'

'Who knows what to think really. Could all be completely innocent like.'

'So what does he do, this Teacher? How does he heal people?'

'Well, tha's it, isn't it? No-one knows do they? It's all a big secret. No-one really talks about it. I think there's quite a few round here that're just a bit wary of him, and there's some who think that the police should be doing more, but at the end of the day there's no evidence is there? Who can prove anything against him?'

I gave him his fare, and assured him that I would be careful.

'I'll tell you something,' he said, leaning out of the window as he pulled away, 'he's not from round here. We don't know him. We don't want his kind round here.' I could hardly fail to grasp his implication: we don't want your sort either. It was on the tip of my tongue to tell him about Grandma Beale. Born and

33

bred, pal, know what I mean? But he'd already driven away.

I got the call at eleven thirty the next day. I was trying my luck at the *Derby Evening Messenger*, and getting nowhere. Yes they knew him, yes they'd interviewed him, no they didn't know how to track him down. Oh, and yes, he was several sandwiches short of a picnic.

'Is that Mr Barker?'

'Yes?'

'Mr Barker, yes hello, you asked me to ring you if . . .'

'Are they there?'

'There's five of them here, yes, they're just kind of parked.'

'I'll be there in twenty minutes. Don't let them get away.'

'Excuse me?'

'Thanks for ringing, er, er . . .'

'Sylvia.'

'Sylvia. I'm on my way. Thank you.'

'Yes, all right duck.'

By the time I arrived there were seven. I was struck immediately by the scale of them, they seemed immense, armoured, their boots and leathers exaggerating their shapes. Scarred, battered, ravaged.

They watched me as I approached, their eyes lidded, like great basking lizards. They sprawled across their machines, relaxed but alert. I was abruptly frightened of them, of their differentness, their connection to each other, and of whatever it was that had brought them to Teacher in the first place. For the first time, I realized that they could truly be dangerous.

And I realized too that I had neglected to get my story straight. I had been so busy looking for them that I hadn't sorted out what I was going to say when I found them.

'Hi. I need to see Teacher.'

They regarded me, their hooded eyes heavy with indifference.

'No, I really do. I've been looking for him for days. How can I get to see him?'

There didn't seem to be any clear chain of command, but there was one who looked more alert than the others so I addressed myself to him. He watched me with clear, slow eyes.

'What is it you have to see him about?' he asked, at the end of a long, difficult pause.

'I just – ' I really didn't have anything worked out. What was the right approach? It was too late for any fine-tuning, and in any case, the battered specimens on the bikes in front of me didn't look as if they would appreciate any of my usual lines.

'Look fellas, I really just have to see him. What do you want me to say?'

'Well, you could say why.'

I cast around for some reason, and while I was doing so the following came out of my mouth:

'Because I'm desperate, that's why.'

They watched me. I felt as if I was watching myself. I was aware of grinning, a nervous affectation around the mouth. I wiped my lips with the back of my hand.

No-one spoke for a good few seconds. I wondered if Sylvia was watching from her window.

The one I was addressing myself to sat back and looked at me. From a distance these people had seemed almost comical, idiotic cultists who would swallow anything. Face to face, they were extremely serious.

'OK.'

'Yeah?'

'Yeah, OK. But you're going to have to wait for a while.'

'That's no problem, I can wait.'

'You'll have to come with us, we'll take you there.'

'Now?'

'Yeah.'

'That's fantastic.'

'As long as you're prepared to wait. Can't guarantee anything quickly.'

'Sure. No problem there.'

'OK.'

He was holding eye contact for much longer than is usual, and even though the deal had apparently been struck, he showed no sign of wanting to release it.

'So we can go now?' I said, just to move things along really, though I was conscious also of wanting to get his eyes off my face.

'Yeah. You want to get up on the back?'

'OK.' I climbed, uncertainly, onto the great machine, and he revved up. He spoke a few words to one of the others, and we were away.

There is always a moment, in any undercover story, when you realize that you have gone beyond ordinary help or remedies. Suddenly you are alone with whatever it is you are investigating, you are a part of it, and there is no way of saying, 'Look, actually, I was only kidding back there, so if you wouldn't mind just dropping me off now.' Flying through the air on the back of this bike to an unknown destination, that was the moment. The air was loud in my ears, and all thought ceased temporarily, just shut down. Here we go, here we go, my mind was singing, here we go. I was exhilarated. I was buzzing.

He stopped to blindfold me. 'Sorry 'bout this, but you know how it is.' We rode on for fourteen or fifteen minutes more, then were abruptly decelerating, pulling to a stop. He helped me off the bike, and we walked for a few paces. He opened a door, and said a few words to someone who answered, yes, number ten. 'Are we there?' I asked, and he said, 'Yep, just down the passage here.'

He took off the blindfold and I saw a hotel corridor, scruffy, in need of decoration, badly lit. We came to a room, and he pushed the door open, and indicated that I should enter.

'Wait a minute, wait a minute, what do I need a room for? He will be able to see me today won't he?'

My man looked hard at me. 'I didn't say anything about today.'

'So if not today, when?'

'Listen, do you want this or not? I seem to remember the word "desperate" somewhere back there. I mean, if you're too busy to wait, you know . . .' He indicated the way out of the hotel.

'No no no, I want it. But can't you give me some idea . . .'

'No I can't give you some idea.'

'I'd be very grateful if it could be today. I'd appreciate it.'

'Would you. Would you really.'

We were clearly at the end of the talking. It was go into this grubby, anonymous room, or abandon the whole project.

'OK.'

I shrugged, hesitated.

I'd said I was desperate. How desperate did I have to be to walk over the threshold into this room, surrender myself to these people? Desperate enough, apparently. I went in, and the door was pulled shut behind me. I heard the key turn in the lock.

'Hey!'

Of course it was too late to do anything about it. I was locked in. I understood immediately that I had made the most basic mistake, which is to underestimate your enemy. I banged and shouted for a while. There was no response. I was where I had wanted to be all this time, only now I was here I wanted to get out again. The irony was not lost on me. I fell asleep eventually. There was nothing else to do.

8

They showed me a picture of him.

He was outside a Burger King on an out-of-town shopping centre, somewhere near Derby. The photograph showed him, in sleeveless biker jacket and chained cap, standing beside the illuminated sign, looking straight to camera. His bike wasn't in the shot.

The article that accompanied the picture was brief and completely uncritical, approving even, and was quite unable to convey the raw, screaming, torn atmosphere of the radio shows, the crackle of desperate hope running through them, the pain of them.

But the picture had an astonishing power. He stood in his leather cap and torn jacket, by the glowing pink and orange sign as the sun set in gaudy stripes behind the brick sheds of the shopping centre. His look was a composite of all sorts of things, but mostly it was strong. He looked strong enough to make all the talk about redemption less unbelievable, if not exactly plausible. He looked strong enough to see all the sickness and violence and ghastly hopelessness around him and not be disgusted or corrupted. He looked strong enough to live in this place and remain pure.

Something like that, anyway.

Also, incidentally, a shockingly handsome man,

dark-featured, his face heavily, powerfully moulded, something in his eyes.

People always say that, don't they? There was something in his eyes. 'His eyes held a balance between sensuality and violence.' 'The cruel, dark, exquisite cold heat of his eyes.' I've probably said things like that myself. I am a journalist by trade, so you'll have to forgive me. Was, rather.

He had eyes. You'd have to have seen them to know what exquisite balances and delicate, feral sensualities and primal yearnings and so on they had. I couldn't look away from this picture, those eyes, for minutes, kept coming back to it, studied it many times. It held onto me. It became, I suppose you'd have to say, an obsession.

I convinced myself that I could write the real story about it, about this healer in this place forsaken by God and man. It would be a story shot through with splendid ironies and images of malformed flowers blooming in wildernesses and so on. The gang would be dupes, Teacher would be a self-deluding crackpot zealot, and the good, sensible people of Derby would, of course, have no truck with any of it.

And this would be no interview, no PR job. No, this would be a *feature*. I would pose as a seeker after all that lovely redemption he had on offer, a supplicant. I would experience this self-deluding small-town messiah close up, warts 'n' all. At the back of my mind was the possibility that he would make damaging revelations, would make comments that would show him up for what I took him to be.

And of course, it was by having such a good scheme

and being so extraordinarily *clever* and all that I found I had become detained in a room, in a hotel that the gang used as a pen for supplicants like myself. The manager of this hotel was related to one of the gang, and had no objections to this. He was no doubt glad of the business, since trade and commerce had fled this part of the world, seemingly for good, during the cataclysm of the Eighties, and he had rooms to fill. The gang had funds: the radio show generated income, and they seemed to have ways of making more. They had good contacts in low places.

Needless to say, of course, me being so damn *brilliant*, I was paying for the room myself. Mercifully it was cheap.

And the thing was, at no point had there been any physical violence, nor even the overt threat of it. I have covered any number of rape trials and the question always comes up: did you at any point offer any resistance? Was violence or the threat of violence used? Often the answer is 'no' to both questions. By 'violence' of course, the defence means violence other than the obvious violence of the rape itself. The woman would often look furious and baffled and try to say more, try to explain the atmosphere of menace, the feeling of coercion, of powerlessness, but would not be allowed to. No resistance, no violence: she was made to look either utterly stupid or completely cowardly, or worse, complicit. Bad, in any case.

I hadn't been beaten, nor threatened, nor intimidated. I had been used with no worse than efficient neutrality. I had walked in with eyes open, had said,

'Is that the trap there, what body part would you like me to put into it, hand, foot?'

It ought to be a crime, to be as clever as I am. But then I suppose most people would say, oh well, a journalist, he had it coming. Too clever by half. Correct.

9

I got the message at noon: he would not come today. They brought me food, beer, pills if I wanted them, dope if I wanted it. They said I wasn't a prisoner, but the room was kept locked. They said I was free to go, but I could only go when I was free. Only he could make me free. So I had to wait. He was aware that I was here, he had been advised of my case. He would come when he was ready, when I was ready.

They talked like that, some of them at least. Their sentences had a sort of warped clarity, an openness, a false transparency. They appeared to be complete utterances, but when you came to consider them they were nothing of the sort. The things they said made no sense at all. Everything was contradicted by everything else, so that at the end nothing was left standing. There was just a sort of dust, a thickening of the air. When I asked them questions, they answered, but the answers were constructed so as to mean precisely zero.

'If I'm free to go, why do you lock the door?'

'You can open it whenever you want.'

'No I can't, because you people keep it locked.'

'Do you want to open the door?'

'Yes.'

'Then why don't you, man?'

'Because you've locked it.'

'It's not us who keep it locked, it's you.'

And so on. Some of them were better at it than others. One of them just muttered things at me like 'Fuck you' and 'Bollocks' which was strangely refreshing, and a damn sight more enlightening than that other stuff.

The more polished ones were much more troubling. For one thing it was somewhat unsettling to have someone six foot three and built like a cowshed, dressed in filthy leathers and combats and biker boots, with scars and tattoos and a really *hefty* personal odour, say something to you like:

'You have to look inside yourself, man.' Extremely disconcerting.

Fuckyou/Bollocks was a little older than most of them, badly scarred facially, and the proud owner of a beer gut the size of a pig, but he at least made sense. He spat a great deal and stood around and said things like, 'Holy Christ, I could do with a shag.' Apropos of nothing at all. Just making conversation. Good afternoon, how are you? Oh fine, thanks, but holy *Christ* I could do with a shag. Oh really? How terribly fascinating.

There was another one, he had slicked-back hair and very heavy eyebrows, and startling blue eyes. He brought me food sometimes, and whatever I said he replied, 'Don't sweat it, man.' He must have seen it on a film or something.

There was another one, a hard-looking bastard. He stood with his hands tucked into his belt loops and his legs spread, and looked. He wouldn't speak, he just looked. He would watch me for minutes at a time. I didn't like him *at all*.

So he wasn't going to come that day, the one I was waiting for, the one who was waiting for me to be ready. Whatever. I was actually relieved. I didn't know if waiting for this thing to happen was worse than the thing itself was likely to be. Whatever the thing itself was.

They would probably have said it depended on me. Either that or Fuck you, arsehole. Either made equally good sense in my estimation. But I wasn't going to sweat it. Man.

10

Fuckyou/Bollocks told me today that the last radio show had generated record figures for the radio station. I asked him how they knew, and he became vague and emphatic, simultaneously.

'*Record* figures,' he said menacingly, daring me to argue. I didn't. He had a tape of the programme for me. I wasn't allowed a radio or television, but I was allowed a tape player, quite possibly for this specific purpose. He played me the tape, and stayed while I listened. I suppose he thought that if he didn't watch over me while I listened I'd turn it off. Actually I found it intensely fascinating. I suppose it's a journalistic thing.

'Tell me about that.'

That's almost Teacher's catch line. Tell me about that. Oh, so you've been buggering your seven-year-old. Tell me about that. You locked your dog in the back yard and ignored its howls until it died. Tell. Your husband has been burning himself with cigarettes. Tell me.

And they did. A generation nurtured on Oprah Winfrey and Donahue, they would say just about anything on air. They had no secrets, no shame. They enjoyed talking about the details.

'For how long?'

'How often?'

They cried. I found this very difficult to listen to at first. I found them painful. I began thinking about the neat semis and the detached villas, the tower blocks and the rows of four-storey maisonettes, the tracts of grey grass, the sunsets over hills punctuated by concrete and glass. I thought about the windows, the windows, black and unreflective, or flashing out gold and red and blue at sunset. But what inside. What. What *exactly*. How many times? How hard?

I reproduce here my recollection of the tape. I suppose it's inevitable that I've condensed and abbreviated. I haven't exaggerated. I don't think I have.

'Hello caller? You're through, what did you want to talk about?'

'Hello?' Female voice.

'Hello. I'm listening.' His voice. Deep, male, heavy, slow.

'I wanted to ask you about animals.'

A pause.

'Animals? What about animals?'

'You see, it's my Uncle David.'

'OK. Yes.' Nothing you say is going to surprise me. Tell. Tell me.

'And I wanted to ask you . . .'

Her voice is perfectly composed, tinged with a very faintly childlike tone, as if she is asking her teacher about the monkey in the zoo. What's he doing now Miss Parrish?

'I wanted to ask you – '

And that's partly the fun, of course. The tension.

The thrill. They always pause, they always need coaxing.

'Yes. You wanted to ask me something. Can you tell me what it is?'

The air is full of the peculiarly thick, noisy air of the live radio contact, alive, fizzing. They've got a three-second delay, so if someone says 'fuck' or 'cunt' or something they can cut it out before it's broadcast. They can get a jingle on. 'Mahogany FM.' Two notes descending: 'Mahog-any.'

'Can you tell me? I'd like you to tell me.' Not only *can* you tell me, but I'm going to be just a little bit disappointed if you don't. Not because of the ratings, not because we're live on radio. No. This is just you and me. I know all of this stuff in advance, so you can say anything, absolutely anything. Live on air, with a three-second safety gap. You can hear those three seconds ticking like a bomb.

'Well my question is, is it normal to . . .'

And then we got the story. It involved a man and a dog, and in any ordinary circumstances it would have been funny. She came back in suddenly one day, having forgotten her purse. She could hear a sound from the living-room. She stood outside for a second, then she went in. He was sitting on the sofa with the dog, he had his jeans undone, the dog had his ears back, both looked startled.

Even here, in this hotel room with Fuckyou/Bollocks standing guard, it was *almost* funny. I tried not to laugh, I stared at the floor, then I caught Fuckyou's eye and he was grinning broadly, and I laughed. It was desperate and appalling and *funny*.

We listened to the tape, to this incredible conversation.

'Can you give me your name?'

'Stella.'

'Well Stella I'm afraid I have to tell you that, no it's not normal, what your uncle is doing. It has a name, it's called bestiality.'

'He told me people do it all the time.'

'No Stella, they don't. He lied to you, I'm sorry to say. Did he say that you shouldn't ever tell anyone? That it was a secret?'

'Uhuh.'

'Did he say that he'd get hurt if you told someone? That if you loved him you wouldn't say anything?'

'Uhuh.'

'He's doing wrong Stella, I'm sorry to say.'

Fuckyou laughed, a surprisingly genial sound. He imitated these last words, 'I'm sorry to say,' but couldn't reproduce the tone, calm, sorrowful, business-like. Stella went quiet, and Teacher allowed the silence to stretch out, allowed tension to crackle and flash down the live link.

'Stella? Are you still there?' he said finally, and the presenter added her own line to this phoney little drama.

'Are you still there caller?'

'Yes.' She sounded puzzled, as if she didn't quite know what to say next.

'What your uncle is doing is very serious. It's a crime, and it is also a sin. Do you understand?'

'Yes.'

'So what we're going to do now, we're going to pray

49

for your Uncle David. Just you and me together. We're going to pray for him, and we're going to pray for you as well, so that you'll be given the strength to deal with this situation. Is that all right?'

A pause, then:

'What about the dog?'

Fuckyou laughed noisily and gestured at me.

'What about the fucking dog,' he said, 'she wants to pray for the fucking *dog*. Holy Christ.'

'The welfare of the dog is going to be best met by the statutory agencies,' he said, and then paraphrased quickly, 'That's going to be a matter for the RSPCA.' His lapse into the social-worker-speak of 'statutory agencies' was an interesting slip, I thought. Up to then he'd been a simple man-next-door type, but that little phrase immediately betrayed him as something else. I wasn't sure, but I sensed that it was a slip-up, and that he regretted it. It was a glimpse of something he was trying to keep hidden.

The prayer followed, good, down-home, basic stuff. Stella began to sniffle about halfway in, and the moment took on a strangely intimate quality. He really was an excellent performer. I could almost believe the record ratings. By the time he'd finished she was sobbing openly, and the presenter did her spiel about how she should stay on the line and speak to the 'counsellor' who would talk to her more.

There were other calls, but nothing of any great interest. Fuckyou fidgeted and bit his nails.

'Unreal,' he said, 'totally fucking unreal.' This was his other line. It meant just about anything, from isn't that good to isn't that terrible and all sorts of things in

50

between. You had to guess from his face what shade of meaning was intended.

He waited till the show had ended and the news had come on, then took the tape out and pocketed it. I tried to detain him by saying, 'So when am I going to see him?' and he growled and said, 'Hey. Whenever. You know?' and that seemed to be the end of that.

He ducked his head back round the door just before he locked it.

'Woof!' he said, and winked.

Unreal.

11

The one I thought of as Biceps came to visit. He always knocked and waited to be asked in, not like most of them, and usually brought me a can of Coke or suchlike.

There was a settled drizzle outside, a phenomenon I generally find soothing. I was glad of the company though. He smiled very nicely and wasn't quite as thick as some of them. I called him Biceps because he wore short sleeves and had very noticeably developed upper arms, the veins thick and protuberant, like well-fed earthworms.

He'd brought two cans of beer. The sound of the ring pull was comfortingly familiar and ordinary. Not unreal.

We exchanged small talk, which he was capable of doing, again unlike most of them. A pleasant, amiable, quite intelligent young man. We chatted for a while, and I finally got my nerve up and asked him the question that was hanging in the air, somewhere just out of sight.

'So why are you here?'

I had spoken to him probably three or four times, and I hadn't dared to ask him this yet. It seemed such a vast question, somehow, monumental and monstrously intrusive. It felt as if I was calling on him to defend himself and his life to me, and it wasn't, strictly speaking, any of my business. I could have understood perfectly if he'd told me to fuck off and in fact I was braced for just such a reaction. But he smiled happily, and said, did I really want to know? and I said yes.

'I'm twenty-six years old. I've been a Son for four years. I met Teacher and we had a conversation and that was it. I was married, had a little girl, Holly. She's seven now. I never see her.' He was still smiling, and he didn't appear to be pretending or forcing it, though it did look somewhat practised and habitual.

'Must have been quite a conversation,' I said, and he said:

'Yes. It was. I'd say that I now measure my life in two periods, before that conversation and after it. Before it, I was a different person, I had a different life and a different – a different *head*. It's hard to explain.' He shook his head.

'I've always been a biker. I love bikes. I've got an old Norton, it's a collector's bike really, but it goes, I can tell you.' He was like a bank manager putting an anxious small-trader at ease by talking about golf before he got onto the figurework. A bank manager with superb upper-body development and sleeveless denim jacket.

'I ran into the Sons at the Appleby Magna services, you know, just before the M42 stops. I wasn't a member of a club at the time, I just rode about whenever I could. It was my way of pretending that I was still free, that I didn't have responsibilities, a mortgage, a little girl. A wife. I camped out a lot, I'd meet up with other bikers, other clubs. You might call them gangs.' He invited me to laugh. 'But I wasn't a member, that would have been another responsibility. I just ran with them for a while, then drifted away. I've always liked being alone. It's my nature. I was supposed to be doing a degree at the time, Combined Studies at Crewe and Alsager. Philosophy, sociology, history and cognitive studies. But I couldn't have called myself a full-time student. Not by any means.'

He lit a cigarette and offered me one, which I accepted. The drizzle outside fell steadily, almost a mist. There was a sound of an engine revving somewhere nearby, and occasional shouts: 'OK, let it go now, let it go.'

'I got talking to a few of the Sons. They seemed like decent enough blokes. Nothing too much going on up here, you know,' he tapped his forehead, 'but basically sound. And the thing about them was that they were completely dedicated to Teacher. To him personally, not to the gang, not to each other. It was all about him. They'd all had some kind of experience with him, and that experience had changed them. That was the word they used. Change. You may have noticed they're not the most articulate people in the world. Yes?' I nodded, thinking of Fuckyou/Bollocks. 'And so they couldn't tell me what it was about, they just said that they'd had this thing, this change. One or two of them used the word freedom. I got my freedom.'

The light was fading as the misty overcast sky gave way to thicker cloud and the threat of more rain.

'I asked to see him, and they said they'd relay the

message and get back in touch with me. They told me when and where to find them again.

'That was in June. I carried on doing what I was doing. It seems incredible to me now that that's what my life consisted of. I don't think of it as my life, as *me*, at all. I think of it as my pre-life, my period of waiting, of preparation. Ritual purification maybe. Or just reading *What Car* in the dentist's waiting room. I tinkered with the bike and rode around. I was reading Kierkegaard and Nietzsche, which is never a very good idea. Also I was doing a little dealing then, so I could always get any drug I wanted. I was mostly a speed freak. Speed and powerful bikes, it's a lethal combination. A bit like Kierkegaard and Nietzsche, come to think of it. Speed and *speed*. I had some near misses. I think I was waiting for the connection, for the transformation of bike against car or truck or wall or tree. Anything solid. I didn't want to die, I wanted to ride my bike at lethal speed at things and watch the world try to get out of my way. I had some freaky idea that if I did crash I'd be bringing righteous retribution onto the poor bastard I crashed into. I guess a lot of bikers think that way, though they probably couldn't tell you.'

I laughed. I couldn't imagine Fuckyou coming up with an idea like that. Biceps laughed too.

'Or maybe it was just me, at that time. I was reading too much, doing too much speed, I was mad with it all. *Thanatos*, man, you know that I'm saying?'

I let it pass. My familiarity with biker philosophy was strictly limited, and I intended to keep it that way.

'Anyway. I met up with the Sons a few times at

various places, I'd ask to meet Teacher, and they'd say not yet, wait a bit longer. I ran with them a few times but somehow I never got near. I started riding all night, alone, off my face. I have this image of myself then, black leathers, black helmet, black Norton. Angel of Death. I have a suspicion that I may have been self-dramatizing just a fraction.' He grinned conspiratorially.

'And of course I did come off. Not a glorious transfiguration so much as a misjudged corner by an off-licence on the outskirts of Rugeley. Came off, bashed up my wrist and knee on one side, knocked the front fork all askew, broke off my pillion peg, *buggered* a manifold. Slightly damaged a low brick wall and a concrete post.

'I wasn't knocked out or anything, but I lay there just the same, and waited for someone to come. I was waiting to be rescued. And the truth is I wanted it to be Teacher that rescued me. I almost expected him.

'He didn't come, of course, and neither did anyone else, it being a quarter to four in the morning and the middle of nowhere. I lay for about ten minutes, then I stood up and pulled the bike out of the road and into the kerb. It wouldn't stand up, I'd buggered the stand, so I let it lie.

'I was bleeding somewhere, my visor was all smeared with blood from my nose and face. My leg kept buckling under me. This was late July, and I was sweating heavily inside the leathers, I felt like I was swimming. It was an incredibly beautiful night, just before dawn, clear high sky. I stumbled about, bleeding, sweating.' He paused. 'And crying. I found a phone

56

box and called out an ambulance. I felt like I was dying. Shock reaction, I suppose. I collapsed in the phone box, I was curled up like a baby when they found me.

'Over-reacting again. Amazingly, in the circumstances, I hadn't broken anything. I just had some sprains and grazes, and I'd knocked my head. I was kept in for two days, because I'd lost consciousness. And because when I woke up I seemed to have a touch of amnesia. I had cunningly forgotten where I lived, my marital status, occupation, my date of birth. I'd blacked out my entire past life. I was carrying no form of identification except my dental work.

'It all came back, of course. Sandra and Holly came to collect me and everyone cried and we all said we'd try again, a fresh start. I went home. A local garage took the bike away, I was supposed to get them to do it up for me and sell it.

'Well a Honda maybe. Or a Yamaha. But a '58 Norton? Not in a million years. We got home and I sneaked out while Sandra and Holly were in the back garden and went to a phone box. The garage said they hadn't started on the bike yet. I told them to leave it as it was, I was coming to get it. A friend of mine had a trailer, and I got him to drive me up to the garage. I walked in and there it was, bruised, and scarred and an absolutely inescapable part of my life. We wheeled it up a plank into the trailer, and it was a hell of a job, what with my wrist and knee still bothering me. It took two of us to do it. He drove me back to his house, and I went home. I left a note for Sandra – 'Won't be long, just gone for a mooch round.' I grabbed my tool box and helmet and went back to my friend's house. I told

57

him that if Sandra rang he was to say he hadn't seen me, he didn't know where I was.

'I did everything I could to that bike. I'm no expert but if you *feel* something strongly enough you find ways. My friend knows a bit, so he helped out. Most of the damage was cosmetic, apart from the manifold. I stayed for eight days, ringing people up for advice, hunting down spares. I got oil worked into the grazes on my elbow. See?'

He showed me, twisting his meaty arm round so that I could look at the cross-hatching, like a tattoo executed by Dürer.

'And in eight days I had it finished. Took a day longer than God, but then God didn't have to ring round for spares.

'I rang Sandra on the first night and told her I was going away for a few days, I needed time to think. I needed to be on my own. I think she knew what I was up to, she just said she needed me at home, she couldn't cope with Holly on her own. What *you* need, what *I* need. I hung up.

'I'd been doing a lot of speed while I was working on the bike, it meant I could carry on for twelve, fourteen hours at a time. I did a little bit of spot-welding for the pillion pin, and the sparks looked amazing, all shot through with traces of liquid gold and silver. I finished the job at three thirty in the morning, and crashed out in the kitchen. My friends woke me in the morning and I went upstairs to their bed and slept all day.'

He flicked his ash, just anywhere, on the floor. Outside the rain had let up. Someone shouted, 'OK.

58

One more,' and the engine revved again. The smell of petrol filtered in, faint and exciting.

'I knew that if I got back on the bike again I was going to kill myself, sooner or later, probably sooner. I also knew I was going to get back on the bike again. I delayed it for a while. I outstayed my welcome at my friend's house by about ten days, then I had to go, and I had to take the bike with me, get it out of his back yard. I wheeled it onto the road. I stood looking at it for a few minutes. It's an extremely beautiful machine, I'm sure I don't have to tell you that.

'I got on top and rode off. I went to one of the places where the Sons had said they went sometimes, the Appleby Magna services. They weren't there, so I waited for four days. I slept in a derelict hay barn in a field nearby, and there were rats. It was warm and hazy. I tried to steal food from the forecourt shop, but they caught me. After that they'd give me food, sandwiches past their sell-by date, things like that. They were very nice to me.

'I woke up one morning and I could hear this throbbing, roaring sound coming from the service station. It was the sound of about a dozen bikes, big bikes by the sound of them, well-tuned.

'I went over to have a look, and it was the Sons. I said I had to see Teacher, right away, today, now.

'So they went and got him.

'And that, as they say, was that.'

Biceps stretched backward in his chair, pulling his gorgeous arms back behind his head, making the fat worms wriggle about under the flesh.

'I'll tell you the rest of it some other time. If you want to hear it.'

I said I did, and he ran the tap in the sink and extinguished his cigarette, then pushed the end down the grating of the plughole, frowning in concentration as he did it.

'I'll bet I know what you're thinking,' he said. 'I bet you think I'm one of those no-personality types that needs bogus spiritual experiences all the time. I bet you're thinking, hm, typical profile of a cult member. Insecure, arrested emotional development. But I'm not. Nor are the others. I know you don't believe it yet. But you will and you'll look back to this time and think: was that really me? That shadow?'

12

I lay awake till about two. Everything seemed quiet. There was still a faint smell of petrol, like a colour in the air, a pale lilac perhaps.

I was thinking about Biceps, and how strange it was that someone so clear and reasonable could be so patently self-deluding. I have encountered obsessives before and they all share one thing, the desire to convince you that their world view is correct. There's never any room for debate, and they rarely agree to differ. They have to convince you. It's as if it's not enough for them simply to hold their outlandish views, but everyone they meet has to as well. Missionary zeal seems to come as standard.

But what was stranger about Biceps was that he seemed, at least partially, conscious of the obsessive character of his thoughts. He knew he was obsessive, and it didn't make the smallest difference.

And I was thinking about what one of the others had said a few days ago. He's one of the smoother ones, but he's inclined towards cliché and the stock response. He really is a little bit like a caricature of a cult member.

He was going on and on, about life and destiny and joy, and he said:

'I'll tell you something about bikes. They haven't

got a reverse gear. You can't go backward, only forward.' He didn't just say it, he said it with *meaning*. It seemed to be serving him as a metaphor for life, destiny, joy, the whole thing. His point in this case was that I, having, as it were, got *on*, could only now *go* on, until the process was complete. I couldn't go back to what I was before.

I couldn't begin to imagine what Fiona was thinking. I had never been away for so long without getting a message to her. I couldn't have chosen a worse time to be absent without leave. She was pregnant, she needed me there with her. What she didn't need was me vanished into thin air and no phone call. I had to get out, or at the very least find a way to tell her what was happening to me.

The only drawback was that they had me stuck in my room, and they had the door key. I was just going to have to apply myself to the problem, that was all. I would get out and get to a phone, then I would think about things. I might still be able to do the story somehow. At least I knew where they were based now. I could always come back.

I got up and went to the window. The hotel is on the ground floor only, a zigzagging line of little rooms. It's set in a sort of field, there's a low hedge, and then there's a forecourt. The main road is just out of sight.

The windows are a clever piece of work, they only open to a distance of six inches or so. This is presumably a safety feature – ground-floor rooms would be unacceptably vulnerable to burglars getting in otherwise. But it's extremely handy from their point of view, since you can't climb *out* either.

Like other cheap hotels I've stayed in, however, the quality of the fittings is lamentable. The struts that attach the window-frame to the surround are flimsy, and they're simply screwed in. They hadn't even been painted over.

I tried bashing them in but this was noisy and I didn't have anything heavy enough to do much damage. Leverage also was a problem. I tried various other boy-scout-type solutions: I folded the beer can in half and twisted it backward and forward until it tore, then attempted to wedge parts of it underneath the struts, but they were screwed tight. I spent half an hour or so fiddling with the ring pull, trying to form it into a shape that would fit into the cross-thread screw heads.

Then I had a truly elegant and ingenious notion and smashed the window with my fist and climbed out, lacerating myself quite badly under the arm, as I knew I inevitably would. I cursed and fell onto the flower-bed under the window. I realized I'd left my wallet in my room, my cash and credit cards, my house keys.

I stood up, conscious of blood trickling over my hand, and headed for the forecourt, which was lit by a single lamp near the front door of the hotel.

'Evening.'

I stopped dead and looked around me. Someone was sitting on the steps quite serenely, smoking something aromatic.

'Beautiful night,' he said, and I agreed, nonplussed. He sighed and stood up. He was enormous.

'Better see about getting you a new room,' he said, and politely ushered me back into the hotel. He took a key from a hook. He took me to the room and opened the door.

'There you go.'

I couldn't think of anything to say, so I said 'Thank you', and he smiled and wished me goodnight. He locked the door after me.

The room was identical to the last one, except that the bed hadn't been made up and the window was unbroken. Also there were no used beer cans and beefburger boxes.

I wrapped a grubby-looking towel round my arm and lay down and slept.

13

Someone came in to look at my arm. I suppose it would be perverse not to call him Doc. Perhaps in recognition of his role as first-aid expert, he eschewed the dirty jeans and rank leather look in favour of a bulging white teeshirt and clean jeans. He wore trainers instead of the usual boots.

He washed his hands gratifyingly thoroughly, and came to sit on the bed. I had decided to just lie there, which was either a protest or mere sulking, I wasn't sure which. He sat down and smiled and patted my knee.

'Let's take a look then.'

Close up he seemed near forty, though all the Sons' faces I'd seen up to now had been so ravaged and scarred and pitted that it was never easy to estimate an age. His hair was neatly cropped, and he didn't have any facial hair. The others nearly all seemed to favour curious, unorthodox arrangements with moustaches and goatees and sideboards, and many of them had a haircut which was a composite of cropped and spiky on top and long and lank on the back and sides. I felt sure that there must be names for all these styles, though I hadn't yet been able to find out. Doc, in comparison, would have passed muster in any emergency field hospital. He didn't even seem to have much oil under his fingernails, though he was quite generously tattooed.

'Would you take off your shirt please?' he said when I showed him my arm, gaudily swaddled in blood-stained towel. He took a pair of plastic gloves out of their packet and snapped them on as I unwound the towel, horrified at the amount of blood. The towel had become thick and sticky with it, and the raw, hospital smell of it made me suddenly weak.

'Are you OK?' he asked gently and I nodded. I took the towel away and saw the shirt stuck like skin to my arm. I felt terribly wobbly again. Doc patted my leg.

'You seem to have lost quite a lot of blood. You may be feeling dizzy.'

I was indeed. I unbuttoned my shirt and peeled the sleeve away as best I could, but it seemed to have become a part of me. It tugged at the ragged, whitened lips of the wound.

Doc produced a pair of beautifully slim, shiny, long scissors from his bag and cut the material away.

'Looks like we'll have to get you another shirt,' he said, and smiled. 'Unless you happen to feel like running round like Tarzan of the Apes.' Another winning smile.

'I don't think I've really got the build for it,' I said, the brave patient. His manner was quite excellent, I have to say. It was bringing out the best in me. He was breathing steadily through his nose, a reassuringly calm sound.

He cleared the shreds of material away, using a pair of tweezers.

'It's not too bad,' he said. 'I've seen worse. It's fairly clean anyway.' He produced swabs and disinfectant and worked away at the crusted blood, while I stiffened and grimaced when he got close to the gash itself. He was strong and exact and competent.

'Not too bad,' he said again when the area was clearer. 'It's quite deep in places, but all the glass is out and it's clean. You've managed to miss any major blood vessels. I don't think you're going to need stitches.' He delved into his bag again and brought out a small sealed paper bag.

'Surgistrips. They'll hold it all together while it knits.' He applied the little sticky strips across the gash, manoeuvring them into place with the tweezers.

'I'll bandage you up for now, and have another look tomorrow. It may still bleed a little but not too much. If it really does start bleeding or if it starts hurting, ask them to come and get me. Really hurting, I mean. It'll sting and ache for a while I'm afraid.'

He began packing his things away again.

'Now, because you've lost so much blood I'm going to get them to bring you lots of fluids, whatever you want. Coke, tea, just water. No alcohol. You'd better stay lying down for today. Keep the arm level with your body. When you stand up keep it like this.' He demonstrated. 'Don't worry if you feel foolish.'

He went to the sink and started on his hands again. The smell of blood and surgical procedures filled the air.

'Don't do it again,' he said with his back to me. 'It's not going to get you anywhere. Being here like this, waiting to be healed, it's a painful process already, I

67

don't have to tell you that. Just for your information, I'm a fully qualified first-aider and I've trained as a paramedic. But I'm not always here. If that had got infected it could have been very nasty. If you'd hit anything major you could have spurted enough to lose consciousness, then if no-one found you you could have bled to death.'

He looked around for a towel, then pulled up his teeshirt and dried his hands.

'It was an accident,' I said, stunned by his implication. 'I'm not some desperate attention-seeker. I was trying to get out of this fucking hotel. I was trying to get away from this, this—' My voice was cracking. I stopped, closed my eyes. I felt him sitting down on the bed again, felt his hand on my knee again.

'Hey,' he said, and the gentleness in his voice brought water to my eyes, which I blinked away.

'It's really hard,' he said, 'but you're strong, you can deal with it. Some of them, they practically faint if you have to give them so much as an injection. You've met Spider?'

I shook my head; my lips were trembling. Shock. Blood loss.

'Big, ugly bastard? Scar down here?'

'I don't know,' I said, 'I may have seen him.'

'Anyway, he's six foot five, nineteen stone, used to be a wrestler. Really, he used to be on the telly. Hugely powerful man, a brick house. Not *pretty*, you understand, but strong.' Doc was smiling again, watching me closely, demanding that I listen, respond, talk to him.

'Well he came to see me one day, he had his thumb

all wrapped in something. I honestly don't know what it was, I think it was a rag he uses to polish his bike.

'So I started to take this rag off, and Spider was saying how someone had told him he should have it looked at, but it probably wasn't anything. It had started throbbing a bit though. I got down to the last turn of the rag and this smell came up, I don't know if you know it, but basically it's the smell of flesh that's started to rot. On the bone, so to speak. The beginnings of gangrene, essentially.

'I looked up at him, and he was just standing there picking his nose and looking down at his hand with great interest. I asked him how long he'd had it and he shrugged and said a week or two, couldn't remember exactly. I asked him if he wanted to look away while I took the rag off, and he said look away? what for? So I removed the rag.

'I've got an extremely strong stomach, I need to have round here, I can tell you. I see some very messy things.

'But this wasn't just messy, it was *old*. The skin was going grey and blue and purple and, basically, disintegrating. It was blackened down to the second joint. He'd gashed the meat of his thumb, under the nail, and it had got infected and swollen up. I think he'd been picking at it. I think it was one of the most disgusting things I've ever seen. Evil-smelling, very, very messy.

'So he was looking down at it and he even started to have a go at it with his other hand, the fingers of which had just been exploring his nose.

'I said for Christ's sake Spider, this has got to be three weeks old, why didn't you show it to me before now, and he said he'd been busy, he'd been doing up a bike for somebody. Usually when people say that kind of thing, what they mean is that they were too scared to go to the doctor, that they were scared of the doctor making it hurt more, or telling them it was fatal or something. But with Spider, I believe he really had just been busy and this was the first spare afternoon he'd had for a while.

'So we looked at this gangrenous, stinking thumb for a while and I did my best to clean it, but it was well beyond that. I said I'm going to have to take a little blood for a test, Spider, and he said yeah, cool, fine, whatever.

'I told him not to pick at it, to leave it alone, for Christ's sake, while I went to get my stuff. I sat him down and rolled up his sleeve, and got a syringe. I noticed that he was very tense, and I tried to get him to relax, but he'd become rigid. I thought this was from the infection, then I looked at his face, and he'd gone pale green. He had his eyes screwed up tight, like this.

'Hey, it's only a needle, Spider, I said, and that was it. He was out for the count.' Doc smiled, and I tried to laugh.

'But you, hey, you're cool. You hardly even flinched. It's not easy to be brave. I respect that.'

I couldn't help it, I was flattered. The man was a professional.

'So be brave. You're on the way now. You can't get off. None of us can. Don't be afraid of it.'

'You're not going to tell me motor bikes haven't got reverse are you?'

He laughed and stood up.

'Drink a lot of fluid. Stay flat. Try to sleep. I'll leave you some painkillers in case you need them.'

He was getting ready to leave.

'Look,' I said. 'Look. Listen. This is all a mistake. I can't stay here. I have to go. You can't keep me here. It's against the law.'

He laughed again, genial, relaxed, indulgent.

'Don't worry,' he said, 'we've got you now, you're safe. Soon you'll be free as well.'

'People will be looking for me,' I said, 'my girl-friend—'

'And they'll find you. When you're ready. When you've found yourself.'

'My family—'

'We're your family.'

'Please—'

'Don't be frightened. We won't let you go now. We won't let you down.'

He left and I drank the water he'd put by my bed. My arm was sore and stiff.

14

Someone came to bring me a six-pack of Pepsi. He was another big, hairy creature, and he had a scar down one side of his mouth.

'Are you Spider?' I said, and he said yes.

'How's your thumb?' I asked, and he said what thumb, and showed me four fingers and a stump.

15

I think they must have decided I needed cheering up. I assume that's what they thought anyway.

They came to my room, about eight of them, and blindfolded me and marched me out. I felt brilliant sunshine on my face. I could hear much clanking and revving up.

'We're going to have a run,' said a voice. He guided me to a bike and I got on. It's difficult blindfolded.

'Don't I need a helmet?' I said, and the voice said, a what?

He took hold of my hands and pushed my thumbs into what I assumed were the belt loops of his jeans.

'Hold on tight,' he said, 'but don't jerk about. Lean into the corners. Enjoy.' Again, I got the impression that the words, for him, implied all sorts of things as well as the obvious meaning. Lean into the corners, man, that's my philosophy.

He revved the engine and wheeled us round a bit. Then he yelled something at me, and we were off.

A great smooth acceleration, then a sickening belt backwards as we roared away. The wind hit my face and dragged my skin back. The air hurt my teeth, and I couldn't suck it into my lungs, they felt flattened and useless. I forced myself forward and gripped his legs.

'Slow down!' I yelled, and he took a corner.

'Oh God!' I concentrated on staying on. The road felt too close, and I tried to force myself away from it. I clamped my eyes shut under the blindfold and the road screamed under me, curving up towards me. I thought the bike was going to slip over sideways, crush me, no, *smear* me onto the road. I fought to stay upright. I thought I was going to die.

We righted ourselves and he yelled something to me, twisting his head towards me, and I screamed something back. I couldn't say for sure now what either statement was.

We slowed down, and he yelled back at me again. We pulled to a stop. He put his hands on either side of my face.

'Look man. If you can't be cool, then we're going to get into all sorts of trouble. You've got to be with me. Be cool. OK?'

'OK.' If it was be cool or die, I'd be cool. We started up again, and I relaxed my hold on his thighs and sat straighter. I concentrated on breathing. I leaned into the corners.

We rode for about half an hour, at all sorts of absolutely outrageous speeds. I have no idea what kind of machine I was riding, but I was already realizing that the more powerful the bike, the quieter it runs, and this one was *eerily* quiet. They were playing overtaking games, taking it in turns to be at the head of the line. From this I was able to tell that there were eight bikes. I still had no clear idea of how many gang members there were in total.

From time to time the bike would draw level with

another one, and there would be a great deal of shouting; the bike would wobble horribly as my driver gesticulated. At one point we accelerated so fast to such an impossible speed that I couldn't help myself and screamed.

My first fear, which was of being flung off backwards, had given way to a dread of my foot or leg getting fouled up in the wheel somehow and being torn off. It felt as if there was an awful lot of metal going round at an irresponsibly fast rate just a few inches away from my feet, and I didn't have the right footwear on. I began to understand the tendency of the gang members to wear heavily reinforced boots. What if one of my laces came undone? I tried to lift my feet up out of the way, but it wasn't possible to sit like that. I resigned myself to it and rested them back on the pillion pins.

Despite the brilliant sunshine the wind was cold and it was soon biting through my clothes. They'd given me a new shirt which was, predictably enough, much too big and very dirty. I felt something like a child dressed up in his parents' clothes, being good in the back of the car.

There were sudden accelerations, sudden jolts and sudden brakings, death-defying corners, and it all went on for so long that by the time we pulled in and wheeled round a few times and finally *stopped*, I'd almost forgotten what we were doing.

Someone pulled the blindfold off me and I climbed off the bike and my legs gave way. No-one seemed to expect me to do anything so I sat on a tree stump and watched them. There were eleven; a couple of them I recognized as having brought me food. They had a general similarity of haircut and dress. They had a strange, ferocious quality: the things they did and said they did and said energetically and without inhibition. But that wasn't it. They were together in a way that I found constantly beguiling. They were as unified as a football team in victory.

It immediately became clear that we were going to be staying overnight. They'd brought tents and sleeping bags and food and beer. An astonishing amount of beer, big plastic bullets of the stuff. The bikes were parked in a neat line; I was struck by the attention that was lavished on getting the line right. Then the ground had to be cleared, which seemed to involve a lot of kicking and swearing and throwing branches around. From time to time one of them would come up and squat by me and talk, and I was given a can of beer. I began to say, 'Actually, I'm really not supposed—' and then thought better of it.

Three of them started making a fire, which, it soon became clear, was going to be *very* big.

Of course I've been camping myself, lots of times. I go to camp sites and pitch my tent twenty feet from the next one, and I have a Calor-gas stove.

The sun was starting to set; it was going to be a cool night. A breeze was tugging at my arms where I'd rolled my sleeves up, and I rolled them down again. I wished I had my jacket. I wondered where my jacket *was*. I hadn't seen it for a while. It hadn't been taken exactly, but I'd been moved round so much that I'd lost track of it.

People sat round the fire, and I joined them. The

ground was very hard, you could feel the coldness and hardness of it.

There didn't seem to be much thought for putting up the tents. It would be dark soon and everyone was drinking. How were we going to do this?

The person on my right was sitting up very straight and watching the flames. He had a full beard and whiskers, and the spiky-on-top-long-at-the-side haircut. Two in one. He turned his head to me.

'Last time we had a big fight.'

I said oh, uhuh, and he turned back to the fire.

'Won't be a fight tonight though.'

I lay back on the hard, cold, lumpy earth and watched the fire as well. The two on my left were having a conversation which went something as follows:

'That's bollocks. That's bollocks man.'

'If you don't rebore it, if you just—'

'No that's bollocks man.'

'It's not *bollocks* man.'

'*Rebore*. Fucking Christ.'

'Listen, if you *don't* rebore—'

'Bollocks.'

'No listen—'

'Bollocks. Fuck you man.'

My driver came up and squatted beside me. He had a bullet of beer which he passed to me. It was full and heavy and I spilled quite a lot but I didn't do too badly. I hadn't had to drink like that since school. He lay beside me, cushioning his head on his arms. He said quietly:

'Butcher's got some horrible drug. He'll tell you it's Ecstasy but I can assure you that it isn't. I *really* don't recommend it. I strongly urge you not to have it. It's very horrible.'

I said OK, I'd pass on it.

'I heard you cut your arm.'

'Yes.'

'Lose much blood?'

'No, I don't think so.'

'Did you enjoy it?'

I looked at him.

'Enjoy it?'

'Yeah you know. *Enjoy* it.'

I looked away.

'No.'

'Shame.' He gave me the beer again and I took some long gulps. Lots of fluid.

'Have you got a girlfriend?'

I said yes, she was a lovely woman. I felt it strongly at that moment, though she certainly seemed a long way away.

'You get on all right?'

'Yes. We get along very well.' And I thought, that's funny, I've never really thought about that before, just how easily I got along with Fiona. We were very good friends as well as everything else. Or instead?

He spat towards the fire.

'That's nice,' he said, and I said how about you?

'Yeah,' he said. 'Yeah. I love her. She's strong, man, you know what I mean?'

The light was fading fast and the fire was going well. There were several conversations carrying on simultaneously and a lot of beer being drunk. I became aware of joints passing around me and intercepted one.

Someone had a tape player and eclectic tastes. I smoked more, lay back, sat forward. Suddenly the story was all around me, sparking and flickering round the fire, and I could see it all at once.

Later we were in the middle of a conversation when my driver said, 'Hey, stop asking so many questions man,' and I thought, how odd, I wasn't even aware I was doing it.

Later again a song came on the tape player, and I became aware of a commotion on the other side of the fire.

'He's off!'

Huge, floundering shadows rose up as a figure on the other side stood unsteadily and flailed away from the fire.

'What's the matter with him?' I whispered, appalled, and my driver said:

'He's dancing.' He paused, then added: 'He's free, man.'

The song had a lot of feedback and anxiety in it, and the dancing man floundered away across the field. Someone turned the music up and we watched him. He was a vigorous and passionate dancer, and his hair and arms thrashed around, like branches in a strong wind. He stamped and grunted. He sat down heavily suddenly, and there was applause and laughter.

We never did get the tents up.

I woke in the night, frozen, glistening with dew, with my driver's arm loosely round me. The sky was full of turbulent clouds. The fire had died down to a large pile of grey ash with faint orange lights under it, throbbing and moving. Everything seemed to be in order and I smiled broadly, at the fire, at the sky. The story had gone, though.

I went back to sleep.

16

Doc peeled the bandage away, and seemed satisfied with what he saw. The flaps of skin were pale and gluey, but there was no swelling and no sign of infection or irritation.

'Good. Fine.'

I watched him working, peaceful and contented, dressing my wound.

'Doc?'

He smiled up at me.

'Is that how you think of me?'

'Well, actually that's more or less what I was going to ask you.'

'Uhuh.' He was concentrating on pulling the Surgi-strips away, each with its little stain of blood.

'Who amputated Spider's thumb?'

He shook a strip off the tweezers into a plastic dish.

'I did.'

'I hope you don't mind me asking – '

'Speak your mind.'

' – but are you qualified to do that?'

'Yes I am.'

'I mean *medically* qualified.'

'If I hadn't amputated he would have succumbed to blood poisoning and tetanus.'

'Yes OK but what I'm asking—'

'Asking. Always asking.'

'Do you have a recognized, surgical—'

'Listen. I'm the best they've got. Without me,' he clucked and shook his head, 'oh boy!'

'So you're not *actually*—'

I jerked back and bit the inside of my cheek.

'Christ!'

Pain flared, orange and white, in my arm and up to my shoulder and neck.

'Christ! Oh Christ!'

'Shit, man, sorry, did I hurt you?'

'Yes, yes, something got caught there for a second.' Sweat broke out all over me. He'd dug something into the wound, the blunt point of the tweezers presumably.

'Shit, sorry, that must have hurt.'

'Don't worry about it.'

He carried on pulling the Surgistrips away, still shaking his head.

'Being brave again,' he said, 'that can get to be a bad habit.'

'Don't worry about it.'

'I'll be finished in a moment. I just want to swab it out a little and put some new strips on and we're finished.'

'OK.'

He worked smoothly on.

'What was it you were saying?' he asked after a minute and I said nothing, don't worry about it.

17

I asked one of them if I could write a letter to my girlfriend, so she'd know I was safe. He said he'd find out, and came back an hour later to say yes I could, but they'd have to read it before I sent it.

I sat down to write and found it surprisingly difficult to start. 'I am being held in a hotel room somewhere in the wilds of Derbyshire by a motorcycle gang, who are fruitcase Christians of some weird kind. They've kidnapped me, but I more or less offered in the first place, and I can find no way of getting out. I think they might be dangerous. Help.' Somehow, I didn't think they'd let that past.

'Dear Fi, Just a note to let you know that I'm safe and well. Sorry I haven't been in touch. I'll explain when I see you next, which will be soon, God willing. Please don't worry about me, I'm perfectly OK. Bob.'

There was enough there to ring alarms. I've disappeared before, though never for this long. The piece I did for *The Face* on the resale of drugs confiscated by the police had involved a few nights away when I couldn't contact her. They were scary people, but *simple*. This bunch were seemingly benign, or at least not violent, but very far from simple. Hopefully Fiona could get some idea of what was happening from my letter.

'Fi': I would never call her that. I would sometimes call her Fifi. I was our joke. Fifi Larue, the hooker with the heart. But not Fi. Usually Fiona.

'Safe and well': another joke. My Aunt Tess writes to me every month – 'Just a note to see iff your safe and well, your Uncle Dudley sends his best, it has bene very hot.'

'Sorry I haven't been in touch': Fiona commented often on the insincerity of many of the people she had to deal with in her work, and 'I'll be in touch' was one of her bêtes noires. 'Why can't they just say goodbye and I hope I never have to set eyes on your hideous, grinning mug again but life could never be that good? What's this "be in touch" crap?'

'Soon, God willing': this was her ex-boyfriend Aidan. He'd gone from a perfectly boring C of E to a mannered, ever-so-'umble religiosity. He had taken to qualifying more or less everything he said with God willing. I'm just taking the dog out, I'll be back in ten minutes, God willing. It had become a joke between us, then something else, no longer really a joke. Neither of us would ever use the expression. I hoped it would make her think about the kind of story I might be working on. She's very bright, and I hoped she might put two and two together.

On the other hand, she might just think that I was going over to the other side. I would have to gamble on her knowledge of me.

'Bob': Bobby, Robby, Rob, Robbo maybe. Blobby even. But *never* Bob. Bob, we'd agreed, was a dog's

84

name, not a person's. Fetch, Bob, *good* boy! She'd once known someone called Bob Grainger and he'd been, in her words, the slimiest self-abuser she'd ever met.

Maybe all I'd do was confuse her, but I was reasonably optimistic that she'd guess that something had gone wrong and perhaps even get a sense of what it was. Maybe with this letter she could go to the police and get them to start investigating. The postmark would show roughly where I was. They could surely start looking on the strength of that.

I hadn't told her what exactly I was doing. I don't like to alarm her, and, quite honestly, I enjoy the cloak and dagger aspects of it. I don't like to feel that I've taken out insurance by telling everyone where I'm going. Also, and this is something I know I share with a lot of freelances, I've developed the habit of secrecy about my work. Not that anyone would rip off my idea or anything, but I can recall at least one occasion when I've been hot on the trail of something and then seen an article bylined by someone I was talking to in the pub a few months previously, a friend. This kind of story is only hot once, then it's cold. There's a moment, and if you're not the first then you're the last.

People might already have been looking, for all I knew. If so, then my letter ought to add impetus.

And, at the very least, it would be evidence that I was still alive. In case they'd already stopped.

18

Fuckyou came in to bring me my double surfburger and garlic bread. 'Surf' means you get Thousand Island dressing on the salad. I had developed much more of an appetite since I'd been here. I suppose it was mostly boredom.

He had told me his real name, or at least the name he's known by, but I couldn't remember it. Spamhead or something.

'Double surf, frog bread,' he said and dropped the boxes onto my bed. He was eating something himself, it looked like a stick of licorice.

'Bike running OK?' I enquired. I had yet to discover any subject that he was prepared to say more than five words about, but he would usually discuss his bike, a Honda Goldwing, '82. Undistinguished perhaps but powerful.

'Yeah, yeah, good, good,' he said, but without the slightest conviction. He was leaning against the window and suddenly heaved up an enormous sigh.

'Anything wrong?' I said and he sighed again.

'I get down sometimes,' he said, his voice a ghost, lifeless. He scratched at his beard. 'Yes yes yes.'

'I thought – I mean, doesn't your spiritual life make you, you know. Happy.'

'My what?' His eyes were fixed on far horizons.

'Whatever it is you people have got. Teacher.'

'Oh yeah. Yes.'

'But you're not?'

'Not what?'

'Happy.'

He shrugged and started picking between his teeth.

'Maybe.' He shot me a strange, quick smile and licked his lips. 'Maybe not.'

'Do you mind if I ask you something?' I'd started adding this to almost all my questions. In ordinary circumstances I'd just ask, but these people could be so touchy I felt I wanted to prepare them first. It was becoming accepted that I asked a lot of questions. I got the impression that they'd been told to tell me what I wanted to know.

Fuckyou shrugged. There was, I felt, an element of pose in his desolation. Also, the licorice somehow diminished the effect he was working for.

'What are you doing here?'

'You want me to go?'

'No, I mean why are you here, in this gang?'

He twitched his lips.

'What do you want me to do, work in a bank?'

'OK, but why the Sons? Why not another gang?'

'What are you talking about, man? *This* is my gang. *This* is.' He nodded emphatically on the 'this'es.

'Tell me about Teacher.'

'Tell you what?'

'Tell me why you all like him so much?'

'I don't *like* him man, I *love* him. Do you understand me?' He turned and gave me a ferocious look, but I was having trouble taking him seriously now. He was a ham.

'So what is it about him?'

'You'll understand when you see him.'

'But you won't let me see him.'

'Bollocks.'

'No, it's *not* bollocks—' I started patiently, and ducked as something came flying towards me. It was a beer can, full, and it only narrowly missed my head. It exploded somewhere behind me, I could hear it hissing. Now we were getting somewhere.

'You think you're the only one? There's a *lot* of people, believe me, and they don't all *bitch* the whole time about having to wait.'

'A lot of people? How many?'

'Fuck you, man.'

'Six? A dozen? Twenty?'

'You don't need to know any of that stuff.'

'He seems very powerful, this Teacher. Aren't you afraid of him?'

'You think I scare easy? You want to try?'

'Would you be afraid of him if you found out he was insane?'

'It's not Teacher who's insane, man, you want to know who it is?'

'Tell me what he's done for you, you personally.'

'He's freed me. He's healed me, man.'

'No, not all that freedom and healing crap, what *exactly*—'

'I don't have to tell you anything, you're not—'

'Not what?'

He was on his way over to me, fists clenched; the

licorice was staining his hand black. He no longer looked like an actor, he looked angry. Even his beard looked angry.

'What aren't I?' I said. Then I got it.

'The police?'

'I'm telling you, man—'

'You've had trouble with the police before? Why?'

He was standing over me, blocking the bright light from the window. He was extremely solid and real.

'I'm warning you, man—'

'What's he done? Why have the police been involved?'

He reached down and grabbed me by my shirt, and lifted me up. The food cartons rolled off the bed.

'You're not the police. So who the fuck are you?' He pulled me closer to his face and took hold of my arm, twisting it round.

'Huh?' He pulled me up by my arm, bent up behind my back, until my whole weight was supported by that alone. His thumb found the wound, and pushed down, hard.

'Huh?' He was grinning. His teeth and tongue were black from the licorice. He let me fall back onto the bed again. He spat. There were bright purple and black stains on my shirt from his saliva. I held his eye as he backed away from me.

'That's quite a temper you've got there,' I said, trembling, enraged. 'Did it ever get you into trouble?'

'It's not me that's in trouble man, I'm serious.'

He walked to the door facing me and I held his eye. He stuffed the licorice into his mouth and left. I heard the key turn after him.

19

I waited till about two o'clock, then I went to the window. This time I wrapped my fist in a pillow before I smashed the glass, and made sure that I knocked out all the splinters before I climbed through. I could find no way of getting out at the back. There was a high wall, topped with security wire, and I knew I had no chance of scaling it. I would only injure myself. Attempts had been made when I was at school to make me vault over a horse or some such absurdity. I was having none of it then, and I was having none of it now. I scouted about for things to stand on, boxes or crates, but there weren't any. I would have to take my chances at the front.

I walked round and he was there again, still smoking, still perfectly serene. He might not have moved since the last time.

'You're a bugger for breaking windows, aren't you?' he said, and I came and sat beside him.

'You people leave me no option.'

'Beautiful night,' he said, and I looked up at the sky with him. He was somewhat older than average, very pock-marked face. He offered me a cigarette, which I accepted.

'Listen,' I said, 'I'm going to have to go pretty soon.'

'Uhuh,' he said.

'Yes. Sorry but I really have to get back to my life. I do have a life, you see, and I've got to go back to it. Much as I would like to stay here with all you charming people, you understand.'

He inclined his head in an old-fashioned, courteous gesture.

'So I was thinking about it this way. I'm prepared to give you people a sum of money. Any figure that you might care to think of. Within reason, obviously.'

'Uhuh.'

'In fact, what I was thinking was that you and me could go to a cash machine right now, and I could draw out some money straightaway. I mean, we wouldn't have to tell anyone. I could draw out, ooh, let's say £250, and who would ever know?'

'Uhuh.'

'And then I could leave you my card, and if you got into any trouble because of me, you could draw out more money. Do you understand me?'

'Oh yeah.'

'I mean, you could use the money for anything you wanted. You could use it for the gang. There must be things you need money for. For, you know, healing and so on.'

'Oh, right, absolutely.' He exhaled smoke into the black sky. I leaned in closer, and lowered my voice further.

'Or it could be just between you and me. We could sort it out just between us. It could be that maybe you fell asleep for a minute and I sneaked right past you. Or I could maybe hit you or something.'

'Oh yeah.' He nodded and blew out more smoke.

'I mean I could *really* hit you – '

'No, man, don't do that.'

'No? OK, but you could make it look convincing couldn't you?'

'Oh yes, I could certainly do that.'

We sat on for a few minutes. Then he said:

'Well, better see about getting you a new room I suppose. You certainly are a bastard for breaking windows,' and laughed.

20

Someone brought me back my letter.

'He doesn't like it,' he said, and there was no question as to who 'he' was.

'He thinks it's too cold. He thinks you should say how you feel.'

'*Does* he.'

'Yeah. Say how you feel about her. Tell her how you feel.'

'Really. He thinks that.'

'Yes.' He dropped the letter into my lap.

'Anything else he'd like?'

'Yes. He says tell her you're sorry.'

'For what?'

'He says you'll know for what.'

21

I woke up in the middle of the night. There was someone in the room. I could smell alcohol on his breath. I sat up suddenly, feeling blurred and caked round the eyes. The room swam around me.

'Don't be alarmed.'

It was a new voice. I couldn't see anything. There was a vague dark shape near the door.

'Who's there? What do you want?'

'Please. Don't be disturbed.'

I recognized the voice. I'd heard it before, on Fuckyou's tapes, and before that, in my car. Teacher. His voice was low and dark and dry.

'I just wanted to come and have a look at you.'

'While I was asleep?' I wasn't angry, I was just puzzled. Why sneak up on people while they were asleep?

'Yes.'

'Why?'

'I didn't want you to know I'd come.'

'Why?'

He laughed, a gentle sound.

'I just thought it'd be better that way. You wouldn't get upset.'

'I'm not upset.'

'Yes you are.'

'Well yes I am actually.'

He laughed again, and it was such a small, human sound that I couldn't help but laugh with him.

'Well don't be. Go back to sleep.'

'What, and miss all the fun?'

'I just wanted to have a look at you. I'm going now. I'll come back soon and we'll talk.'

'When?'

'Soon.'

'Can't we talk now?'

'No. Go back to sleep now. Dream dreams.' I heard him moving for the door, then heard the door shut and lock.

I went back to sleep and dreamed of fields and children and sunlight.

22

Someone came to talk to me. Actually, he said he'd come to listen to me, but what he did most of was talk. My understanding was that he was some kind of deputy for Teacher. He was supposed to be making a preliminary diagnosis of my condition, and then he would tell Teacher. Something like that.

He gave me beer and cigarettes, but he did it, somehow, very exactly, as if these were measured amounts of prescribed medicine. You smoke *twenty* of these every twenty-four hours and you drink no more than *four* of these before retiring. He didn't have a notepad to write down my responses, but I could hear him ticking off his little boxes as we talked.

'We're interested in why you came to see us,' he said, and sat matily on the bed. I noticed that he didn't have any tattoos, at least none visible, and he didn't have any facial hair. You almost *could* imagine him working in a bank, or if not a bank then certainly the better kind of garden centre.

'I came to talk to Teacher. But you don't seem to want me to, and I can't really hang around here any more. So I'd like to go.'

'I see. I see. Uhuh,' he said and nodded his understanding. He was watching me rather closely.

'Let me just tell you a bit about us, OK?' I shrugged my eyebrows. 'We're affiliated to no church, or charity, or other organization. We are a self-supporting unit, and our members give their services freely and without payment. All members are full-time members, by which we mean that no member shall have obligations outside the Sons, which will prevent him from carrying out his work for the Sons, however that work shall be defined.'

An irritating, officious little voice, scratchy and pedantic. I'd heard it many times when I was (briefly) active in the Labour Party.

'The work of the Sons comes under three headings. First there is the running of the group itself. Members do work and the reward for that work, whatever the reward may be, is channelled back into the unit. Again, members do not take any personal profit.'

'This work, it wouldn't involve drug-dealing or anything like that, I take it?'

He ignored me, with a tight little smile. He would be happy to take points of order at the appropriate time, the smile said.

'Secondly, there is the management and care of guests, such as yourself. Quite a tricky area, I'm sure I don't have to tell you.'

'Would it interest you to know that one of your managers and carers committed an assault on me yesterday?'

'And *thirdly*, of course, is what I call the ministry itself, though that's not a popular word, for some reason.'

'Perhaps they find it pompous.'

'Perhaps.' Another brief, humourless smile.

'So. That's us. But what I really want to hear about is you.'

'I've already told you. You're holding me against my will. That's an offence in law. False imprisonment. Kidnap.'

'Yes. Uhuh. So you're, you're angry about that.'

'Angry. Yes.'

'Yes. I see.'

'And I want to know what you're going to do about it.'

'You'd like me to do something.'

'I think that's what I said, yes.'

'And can you tell me what it is you'd like me to do?'

'Yes I think I can. I'd like you to let me go.'

'And that would make everything all right, you think?'

'Well it would certainly help the false imprisonment/kidnap problem no end, I'd say.'

'I see.'

'You don't seem to.'

'I'm just wondering – I mean, that wouldn't help you with whatever it was you came to see us with, would it?'

It occurred to me that I could probably take him. *Probably*. He wasn't as enormous as most of them. He couldn't have been much over six foot, and he looked less wide, less hefty, less tattooed. I could smash him in the face and just run. Or I could be elegant about it and tie him up and lock him in. I didn't wish him any harm, although, actually, now I came to think of it, it

would be a pleasure to knock out a few of his teeth.
So I suppose I did wish him harm really.

'Look pal.' I smiled brilliantly at him, and lowered
my voice. 'You either let me go or I hurt you, one or
the other, now are you understanding me?'

'You want to hurt me?'

'Right now? Oh yes.'

'Do you enjoy hurting people? Is that it?'

'I could make an exception in your case.'

'I see. OK.'

'OK what?'

'You want to hurt me? Then hurt me.'

'This is ridiculous.'

'It's your idea.'

'Look, I have no wish to hurt you, I just
want – '

'You don't seem to be very clear about what you *do*
want.'

I stood up and took a step towards the door. He
hadn't locked us in, I was certain. I waited for him to
stop me. He didn't. I opened the door.

'Howdy. I thought you preferred climbing out of
windows.' The big, affable smile, the big affable man.
Very big, very stoned, hugely immobile. I said hello,
and shut the door.

'You know,' said the assistant healer, whom I was
now thinking of as Deputy Dawg, 'you can't escape
through doors or windows.'

'I won't listen to any of your pseudo-metaphysical
bollocks, I really won't,' I said, feeling exhausted and
miserable, and came back to the bed. There was
nowhere else to sit. I turned away from him.

'You think this is bollocks?'

' 'Fraid so, Joe.'

'You think we're fools?'

'Your word.'

'And what do you think about Teacher?'

I paused. Then:

'I haven't met him.'

'I believe you have.'

'Oh sorry, yes I have. We shared meaningful moments the other night.'

'Yes. Actually, that isn't the first time he's visited you.'

My skin crawled.

'What do you mean?'

'He's been in to look at you a few times, while you were asleep.'

'That's – that's pretty creepy.'

'He does that. It means he can observe you without being observed.'

'He's creepier than I thought.'

'It makes sense. It's his method. Don't be alarmed.'

'That's what he kept saying. I'm not alarmed, I'm disgusted. What is he, a Peeping Tom?'

'You don't want people to look at you?'

'While I'm asleep? What do you think?'

'Does it make you feel vulnerable?'

'Oooh, I think I've said all I'm saying to you.'

'Really?'

'Really. Yes. In the words of one of your more polished spokesmen, fuck you man.'

He smiled again and left. I threw a can of beer at

the door. I was getting into bad habits. I picked it up a few minutes later and opened it. The spray drenched me, made my clothes and hair sticky. I drank it in four long pulls.

23

I tried banging on the walls. I was thinking about Fuckyou's remark about there being a lot of people who were waiting to see Teacher. Presumably some of them, at least, must have been here in the hotel, like me.

I went into the little bathroom cubicle. Shower, wash basin, toilet. Very compact. I pulled the shower curtain aside and stood on the tiles. I knocked, politely at first, on the tiled wall. Then I thought, for Christ's sake, and banged with both fists.

'Hello?'

I put my ear to the wall, but I couldn't hear anything. I banged again. My hands started to hurt, immediately. It's amazing, I thought, how ill-equipped the human body is for any sort of vigorous activity. Well, *my* human body anyway.

'Hello?'

I banged both arms against the wall, the whole length of my forearm, and listened again. I thought I could hear something.

'Can you hear me?'

A sound of some sort. I put my ear to the cold white tiles. It was faint and muffled, but unmistakably human in origin. I banged rhythmically, dum dum-da dum

dum, dum *dum*, then held my ear to the wall again.

It came again, and as I realized what it was I moved my head away from the wall and stepped out of the shower. It was the sound of someone howling, at first quietly, then louder, each howl the length of a breath, getting louder and stronger each time. Desolate, hopeless wailing. I wanted to knock again to say it's OK, my mistake, wrong room.

I backed away out of the bathroom as the appalling sound continued, shut the door very quietly, got back to my bed, put the pillow over my head. It continued for nearly an hour.

24

They let me go to watch him doing his thing, his act. They drove me there in their van: I had to sit inside and watch discreetly out of the back window in case I was recognized. So it was more than likely that I was being searched for. Maybe they'd already been questioned by the police about me. I was asked not to shout or bang or try to escape from the van. They left someone to watch me, he smoked continuously and had a moustache that was almost insane in its grandeur and scope. He had a face that you could imagine looking out from a Goya. And, like many of the Sons, he had a peculiar light inside the eyes, though this was dulled somewhat by the amount he was smoking. He had a slightly crafty look about him, and he spoke in a throaty whisper.

I sat on the wheel housing and peered out of the murky square of glass. It was the kind of van that someone writes 'clean me' on with a finger in the dirt, and the window was grey and fogged.

We were parked in the car park of the Burger King. There was a steady stream of people, car doors slamming, engines starting up. He hadn't yet arrived. I understood from Moustache that he usually brought three or four Sons with him. They would arrive, cruise around the site a few times, make a lot of noise, then they'd park (in formation, naturally), and just sit on their bikes. He'd attract attention to himself without any difficulty, there would be shouted exchanges, and eventually someone would come over and he'd talk to them. Sometimes a small group would form and the conversation would turn into a kind of open debate. The management seemed to regard him as an attraction rather than a nuisance.

And that was it? I asked Moustache, and he said yep, that was about the size of it. Doesn't sound like much, I said, and he said well, that was it.

What about the healing? I wanted to know.

'That comes later,' he said, 'sometimes the talking does it. Sometimes not. It all depends.'

I became aware that here I was, waiting for him again, more interested than I wanted to be.

'Was talking enough for you?'

He shrugged.

'No. Er not in my case no.'

'What else was needed?'

'I think that's rather a personal question, don't you?'

'But you have been healed?'

'Oh yes. I've got my freedom.'

'What are you free from?'

'Eh?'

'I mean, what was the matter with you?'

He dragged deeply and gave me crafty looks. He winked broadly.

'You like to know things don't you? I heard that.'

'Is it a secret?'

'Least said eh?' he said, and the conversation lapsed. 'Yup. Least said,' he repeated a minute or two later.

The light was fading, and the sodium overheads flickered on. There was a certain amount of activity in and out of the Burger King, and cars came and went. The clientele was mainly solitary men, though there were some cars full of kids and a few tense-looking young couples out on the kind of date that ends up in a Burger King car park.

Then he arrived, and the place was transformed. The noise alone was quite extraordinary. The four bikes circled and crossed and revved and roared, ending up in a tight circle in the middle of the car park. They were in full regalia, caps and jackets and boots. The jackets had the insignia on the back, The Sons of the New Bethlehem, in a circle round a crucifix. There were many other motifs and signs, badges, tattoos, decorations, scars. They were wearing their identities unmistakably, on their clothes and skins. It was impossible to misidentify them, or to doubt their sincerity. They weren't kidding.

They lounged elegantly on the bikes. Unsurprisingly he was on a Harley, though it was comparatively restrained, at least by Harley standards. He looked bigger than I'd remembered. His jacket was cut at the sleeves, his arms were thickly muscled and richly decorated. There was a tattoo I recognized from one of the other members, a skull, a death's head, but with a thick black diagonal cross over it. I had had it explained to me as 'We cancel the death of the self'. On him it looked both casual and studied.

Dazzlingly handsome, dark, deeply-lined face. A

rock face. I didn't know what I meant by that, but that was what he had. And the eyes. I found I had to make myself look away, also that I was blushing. Moustache winked again.

'Eh?'

He smiled, a crack-toothed grin.

'Enjoying the show?'

He managed to put the same slightly leering significance into 'enjoying' that I had heard others of them use.

I looked back.

Teacher was standing now, listening intently. He cupped a hand to his ear. Someone was shouting something, out of my field of vision.

'Huh?' He was frowning, grinning. He took a step away from his bike. The person he was talking to yelled again, and I could hear someone else laugh.

Teacher smiled, folded his arms across his chest. He shook his head, then turned back to the others and said something, and they laughed. He put his hands into his back pockets. Someone gave him a cigarette. They all smoked more or less continually.

My legs were getting stiff, and I wriggled round to get into a better position. The van was filthy. I was filthy. A young girl came towards him, followed by two others. Teacher swaggered up to them and hugged them, one after another. The other Sons hugged them as well. They chatted for a few minutes, and Teacher grabbed hold of one of them and danced a few steps round the car park. They kissed, not particularly casually, and he stroked her backside and drew her in to him. She pulled away and giggled, and called to her friends. There was a great deal of shouting and waving and laughing as they parted.

Teacher returned to the group again, and hands and backs were slapped. One of the Sons flicked his cigarette away, and fiery particles streaked over the concrete, carried on a small wind.

I turned back to Moustache, who was in exactly the same position as before, and who had his eyes seemingly locked onto the back of my head.

'I don't get it,' I said, and he shrugged. 'Nothing's happening. What's supposed to be happening?'

'You wouldn't say nothing was happening if you was out there.' I turned back to the window.

One of the Sons with big, fleshy, protuberant ears was staring off into the gathering darkness and I followed his gaze. I could see a shape, a young man by the look of it, standing by the side entrance of the Burger King, hiding in a shadow. Big Ears kicked Teacher in the leg, and Teacher turned and looked where Big Ears indicated. He screwed up his face, and for a moment I thought I could *see* his look, a searchlight, two parallel beams of intelligence and intent.

The young man in the shadows came forward a step, and Teacher turned away, switching off the search-lights. I assumed this was so that the young man would not be intimidated as he made his shy, faltering approach. He was eating a beefburger. He was effort-fully, painfully casual. He finished the beefburger and screwed up the wrapper, chucking it in the direction of a bin: it bounced off the rim. He lurched forward to retrieve it and pushed it in. He glanced up to see if he was observed. The Sons were studiously looking away, and he rubbed his hands and peered about him stealthily. I couldn't make out his features at all clearly, but he looked a few inches shorter than me, scrawny of build, and there was something adolescent, childlike even, in his demeanour.

Big Ears huddled for a moment with Teacher, said something into his ear. Teacher glanced over at the kid in the doorway and whispered something back.

Big Ears nodded and stood up straight, hitched up his jeans, stroked his sideboards in a quick, nervous gesture, and slowly, ponderously made his way over the car park to where the youth was standing. The youth had produced a cigarette packet and was in the process of lighting one up, clearly feeling the need for some kind of pretext to be just standing there, in the darkening, windy entrance.

Big Ears sauntered over, leaned up against him, and nodded a greeting. The youth nodded back, and smoked hungrily. Big Ears seemed to be saying something out of the corner of his mouth, not looking at him. The youth smoked and nodded. They stood for a moment longer, then the youth nodded again, and they came out of the shadows, towards the bikes, towards Teacher. They didn't speak as they approached.

Teacher turned round as they grew nearer, and smiled, and the youth smiled back. Teacher spoke, the youth nodded, hi, how ya doing, and then before you could blink, he stumbled forward and Teacher caught him, held him, clasped him. They stood swaying, locked together, and as they shifted round I could see

109

both their faces. The youth was anguished, screwed up tight, Teacher was clear-eyed and sober, and his lips were moving. The other three moved back a few steps, and Teacher and the youth swayed, embracing like tired boxers. Teacher pulled away and took the youth's face in both hands, and then the two walked into the shadows, Teacher's arm round his shoulders.

I looked round at Moustache and met his eye.

'Anything cooking?' he asked, and I said I didn't know, maybe. I thought of that tattoo, the crossed-out skull, and the claim, about cancelling the death of the self, that went with it. Would this shy, embarrassed, anguished young man end up with the same tattoo? Would he be freed?

How. How *exactly*.

I was abruptly gripped with a need to *know* that was almost painful. I had to know what was going on. I became aware that I needed to know this at least as much as I needed to be allowed to go home to Fiona.

Moustache blew smoke, a long thin stream.

'Want to see any more?'

'Why, is anything likely to happen?'

'Not in the way you mean, nothing you can see.'

'Then no, I don't.' I had a sudden wish to be away from this car park and these odd, serious people. I wanted to lie down and think.

Moustache shrugged and climbed back into the driving seat. I watched as we drove away. I couldn't see Teacher or the youth.

But I was going to find out what they were up to. Before I left here, I was going to know. Whatever it was that led these people here, kept them here, I was going to find it out, one way or another. And *then* I would go home to Fiona and the imminent patter of tiny feet. Not before.

25

I sat on the front step and smoked for a while with my enormous guard, whose name, I had discovered, was Loverman. I had learned not to enquire where the names came from: they referred to 'past lives', and were apparently intended as jokes about whatever it was that had brought the person to the point where they needed the tender ministrations of Teacher.

He asked me if I'd enjoyed the show, and I said not particularly, nothing much seemed to happen.

'Those shopping-centre things, they're really just to make contacts.'

'What happens after?'

'Depends. There'll be other meetings. Eventually there'll be a diagnostic. Then there'll be a healing, maybe. Not always though. Then there might be some follow-up. Not always.'

'So not everyone gets in?'

'Gets in?' He laughed. 'No-one gets in the gang any more. Last new member was Pygmy, that was more than two years ago. No, new members are not encouraged.'

'Why?'

'Think about it. If we took in everyone who came along we'd have thousands.'

'And you don't want that?'

'I think you're misunderstanding us. We're not one of those big ambitious firms. They're all about money. They're all about expanding, getting more members, getting more – ' He rubbed his fingers together.

'But you're not like that?'

'Can you see any money around here? Take a look at us, for God's sake. My bike needs everything doing to it, transmission, gearbox, and it's not going to get it either. I spend just about every Sunday trying to keep the bloody heap on the road. We cover costs, just about.'

'If you don't want new members, why do you do it?'

'What you seem to be having trouble understanding is that Teacher has got a power, and he's got a responsibility that goes with it. He can *heal*, man, and so he therefore *must* heal. That's it, that's all of it, and there isn't any more.'

'How does he know what's wrong with people?'

'He's got a power. There've always been people with power, it goes right back. He can see.'

'Does it come from God?'

'From wherever, man, but it works, that's all I can tell you about it. You'll see it.'

'I certainly hope so. When?'

He laughed and slapped me on the shoulder.

'When you're ready.'

'I'm ready now.'

'Yeah? Come on, let's get you back to your room.'

26

Biceps was back, smiling, telling me his life story. If
the Sons had wanted a PR man, then he would have
been the obvious candidate. I think Fiona would have
liked him. If I'd been doing a television programme,
I'd have used him a lot, he'd have been perfect.
Good-looking, fairly clean, and with a huge amount of
charm, putting aside for a moment the muscles. He was
animated and very, very personable. While he
was talking, I found myself thinking about the radio
shows I'd heard, the awful confessions of degradation
and cruelty and vileness. I thought about the shy young
man in the Burger King car park, his urgency and need.
And I was wondering: what can possibly have gone so
wrong with this cheerful, intelligent, likeable man
sitting beside me, luxuriating in his strength and vigour
and *sanity*, that could have driven him to seek some
kind of desperate remedy from the hands of Teacher?

What, I was wondering, have you got inside you? Is
it still there?

'I first met Teacher in August '88. We had our first
conversation in the kids' playground at the service
station. Giant fibreglass toadstool, you know, and
see-saw and everything. Early evening, there wasn't
anyone else about.

'And we talked about bikes. I told him about the problem I was having with the crankshaft since the accident. I called it the accident, though of course really it was no such thing. He told me it sounded like I should strip it all down again and take off the piston and check the ring-to-groove clearance, you know – you don't. Sorry, I forgot. You drive a car.' He managed to make it sound like an understandable, though still regrettable, personal lapse of some kind.

'Anyway I told him how much I loved my bike, how important it was to me. He understood perfectly. I referred a couple of times to my accident, I expected him to pick up on it. But he didn't. Whenever we came to the end of a subject he'd say something like is it chain-driven or shaft, and we'd be off again. It was almost as if he was trying to stop me talking about what I really wanted to talk about. We had all the time in the world. Once or twice I even found my mind wandering. I forgot who I was talking to. I caught him looking at me a few times, I mean *looking*, you know?'

I thought about the searchlights I'd seen in the Burger King car park. I nodded.

'Yeah? But that was really all. After about an hour he stood up and shook my hand and said he'd have to go, and could we talk again soon? I said of course, yes, and we set a time. He said did I want them to put me up, did I have somewhere nearby to stay, and I said I was fine. I'd got used to sleeping rough. It was a beautiful summer, and it was no hardship. Living in Derby. Now *that's* hardship.

'We had our second meeting a few days later. We were back in the playground again. He asked about the

115

crankshaft and so on, and I said it really wasn't any better. He said let's have a look at it, and so we did. He rode the bike round a bit, and he told me what he thought was wrong with it.

'And then I said what do you think's wrong with me? He said, oh that. That's OK. We can sort that out OK. Did I want to do it right now? Or did I want to have a go at that crankshaft? I said right now and he looked at me and said hold on, maybe not, he didn't think I was quite ready. I said I'm *ready*, for Christ's sake, *fuck* the crankshaft, help me, I'm *dying* . . .'

Biceps stopped for a second, and then smiled hugely.

'*Very* serious. Life or death. It was, as well. I was dying. Truly. Inside. Here.' He grabbed hold of a meaty pectoral and squeezed it. 'And here.' He banged his fist against his skull, then again, harder. 'And here.' He grabbed his crotch and tugged, hard, and again. 'There was something inside me and it was dying, and while it was dying it was killing me, rotting inside me.'

He stood up and paced away to the window, then back again. He was still smiling, but he was also blinking rapidly.

'Help me, I'm dying, here, here. Here. So he said OK. We'll do it tonight. Don't worry, he said, it's nothing, and then do you know what you'll have? You'll have your freedom, do you know what that means? I said does it mean I'll stop dying, and he said yes.

'So we did it. And I got my freedom. I asked him afterwards if I could join the Sons, and he said, well why not? So I did.'

116

'I don't understand,' I said, 'I don't understand what he did. What's the drill?'

He looked startled. 'What's the – oh I see. Well he let the thing that was wrong inside me *out*, and—'

'No. No I mean *what*, exactly *what*?'

'Oh you mean the mechanics of it? Oh that's nothing. It's a little death, and then hey! You're doing hundred and thirty-five on an open stretch, you've got the wind behind you, and your crankshaft is *perfect*.'

'I want to know *what*—'

'No you don't. What you want to know is, does it hurt? Is there pain? And whatever it is, is it worth a little bit of pain? You want to do that old calculation, is this worth that, the calculation that's kept you the way you are all this time. You've got your paw in the trap and you're scared to bite it off to get free, because there'll be pain.'

'Does it hurt?'

'What if I said yes, there is pain, a lot of pain. What then? Would that mean you didn't want it?'

'I don't know what it is.'

'Yes you do. But you won't let yourself believe it.'

'Believe what exactly? I'm sorry, I'm getting a bit confused – '

'No, what you've got isn't called confusion, what you've got is called fear.'

I noticed that he'd stopped smiling, and he apparently noticed as well, and smiled.

'Sorry, it's not my place to tell you about yourself. No-one can really tell you anything. Only you can say. When you're ready, you'll know.'

'How will I know when I'm ready?'

'You'll know because you'll *be* ready. One is the other.'

I smiled and shrugged.

'All a bit over my head, I'm afraid. I never quite seem to know what you people are talking about.'

'Talking isn't important.'

'Unless it's about crankshafts?'

He laughed.

'So what happened about your wife and daughter, I've forgotten their names?'

'Holly and Sandra. Well, what happened is that I left them for good.'

'Had they been part of what was wrong with you?'

'No. Except that they'd only happened because of what was wrong.'

'You're not in contact with them?'

'No.'

'Is that a rule here?'

'There you go again. What if I said yes, it's a rule. What then? Would you want it less?'

'I don't want it at all, I keep telling you.'

'You wanted it enough to come here.'

'It was a mistake.'

'No. Not going through with it, that would be a mistake.'

'My girlfriend, Fiona, she doesn't know where I am. She must be worried sick.'

'Well actually, no she isn't.'

I blinked.

'We've been in touch. We've told her that you're fine, and that you'll write to her soon.'

'You mean – how did you know where she lives?'

'If you recall, you gave us a letter addressed to her.'

'She would only believe it if I told her.'

'Well – ' He scratched his armpit and frowned. 'I'm sorry to say that we've subsequently sent her a letter, with your signature, in your handwriting. Loverman has some expertise with these things.'

'I don't believe you.'

'We only do that when we have to. You see, we'd had a visit from the police, and that's something we generally try to avoid.'

'What did you say in the letter?' My body felt a degree or two colder.

'Something like: I love you, but I have to stay here for a little while, to sort myself out. Please don't worry about me. Something along those lines. When we can be sure that she's cool, we can give her a box number to write to you.'

'She'll never believe any of that,' I said, 'she knows me, she knows I would never get involved with this kind of garbage.'

'Really?'

I was about to say too much, like the word 'journalist'.

'I mean, she knows the kind of person I am.'

'She *knew* the kind of person you *were*.' He said this sadly, regretfully. 'Would she know you now?'

'Of course she would, what are you talking about?'

'Don't you know you've changed?'

'I haven't changed.'

'And you'll change more. Soon you'll get free, and what that means is that you'll have changed so much

119

that you'll no longer be the same person. Quite often, people change their names.'

I grabbed hold of his arm. I *gripped* his arm, ferociously. My fingers dug into his gristly, solid flesh, my nails were breaking the skin.

'Let me go,' I said, 'or you people are in real trouble. I'm not fooling around any more.' The words came hissing out of my mouth like hail, my face was contorted. At that moment I no longer saw the likeable, plausible PR man, I saw the jaws of the trap. 'I'm going to do whatever I have to do to get out of here. People may get hurt. If you let me go now, we'll just leave it there. But if you don't, I'm going to see you people hurt, I mean *really hurt*.'

He covered my hand with his hand, and squeezed harder. There was blood.

'Go on,' he said, 'let it out, all of it.'

27

They took me out of the hotel, and put me in a room in a house. Someone else was with me all the time. They took it in shifts. Someone was with me even when I slept. If I woke up in the night I could see him, whoever it was, sitting, smoking or drinking or whatever. One of them did drawings, mostly obscene.

They moved me out of the hotel because I set fire to my room. I dragged all the bedding onto the floor, and dropped a match on it. The room was full of smoke within seconds and I smashed the window to get out. I thought that Loverman would have to deal with the fire and so would be too busy to restrain me, but I was wrong there.

He wrestled me to the ground, and dragged me to the office. I regret to report that I was screaming and howling. Possibly even biting, I couldn't say for sure just now. It wouldn't surprise me terribly, actually.

He locked me in the office and got to my room with a fire extinguisher. The hotel doors are very good, half-hour doors as the environmental-health people say, which means that they're designed to contain a fire for half an hour. I watched him through the little windows in the office door. There was smoke in the corridor and a strong smell. He opened the door and a big lazy plume of smoke came out, and he squirted the foam in from the doorway. He had to duck out for a second, then he charged back in. I have to say I was impressed with his agility and determination, I really didn't expect it in him. Loverman the fireman.

So after that I think they decided I needed a change of scene. I was half expecting some kind of punishment, but none was forthcoming. That would have been one of their questions: is that what you want, for us to punish you? Punish you for what?

Biceps came to visit, to smile sorrowfully, but I told him to bugger off. I think my liking for him was waning somewhat. He said, you don't have to do this kind of thing, we love you. Doc came also to check me over: it seemed that I was fine. He said I should smoke some cannabis, that it was good for the relief of stress and anxiety. Beer also, he said, can be good, in moderation. If I wanted stress relief of a more esoteric kind, Bennys or Temazzys or suchlike, he could prescribe that also. I said he could go and prescribe himself a sharp stick up the arse, or something equally clever and sophisticated, I forget exactly what. He said don't worry man, we're not going to let you go, we won't let you down, and I said why do you people insist on adding 'man' to the ends of your phrases, you're not Americans are you, and this is not the 1960s is it?

He stood up to leave and I said that the BMA would no doubt be very interested in his prescribing practices, and I would be sure to make a full report when I got out. He came back to say something else ending in 'man', and I regret to say that I spat at him, full in the face. My sophistication truly seemed to know no bounds.

They even sent in Fuckyou, and it was almost like seeing an old friend. He ended up twisting my arm behind my back in the way beloved of police at riots and demonstrations, and shouting do you want me to break it? Cos I can you know. I can break it in two places. Do you want me to? Eh? Do you?

Endless amusements.

One good thing about having someone with you twenty-four hours a day is that you can't fall prey to self-abuse. Unless you're an exhibitionist of course. Or from one of the older-established public schools.

28

I tried to write to Fiona again.

I was thinking about what Teacher had apparently said about my first letter, that I should say what I felt, that I should say I was sorry. That I would know what for.

'Dear Fiona,

I can't tell you why I've been away for so long. I'm perfectly OK, so please don't worry about me.

I also can't tell you how much I love and miss you. I hope we'll be together soon, and then I'll be able to show you what you mean to me. You're the most precious thing in the world to me, doubly so now of course.

All my love, etc.'

My companion of the moment was a lad called Stroker, a pleasant enough kid. He'd told me that he used to be in the Terrys but that that didn't give him what he wanted. I've always found something oddly touching about men who've been in the Terrys. There's something irresistibly poignant about it somehow.

I looked up and there he was, playing with the cat. There was a cat in the house, a young male, very playful. He seemed to be called Puss. And I thought, was Stroker getting what he needed here, with me, in this house? Did Teacher give him what he needed? Apparently. I read my letter to Fiona again and it seemed utterly ludicrous. I read it to Stroker, and he looked thoughtful and said, 'Nice girl is she?'

'Yeah,' I said, 'yeah she's a nice girl.'

'There was a bloke in the Terrys, and he could write these amazing letters. You should have read them, honest to God. I remember one thing he wrote to this girl, it went: when I am between your legs I feel the waves of the Atlantic Ocean surging beneath me.'

'Do you think I should use that?'

'It used to work for him.'

'Dear Fiona,

I am safe and well. Am missing you. Will see you soon. All my love etc. Incidentally, did I ever mention that when I am between your legs . . .'

And then I thought: look, just tell her how you feel. Be yourself, that's all you have to do. Nothing to it.

'Dear Fiona,

'We have been going out for more than four years now. In that time we have had a lot of sex, more sex than I have ever had before and of an immeasurably higher quality. I have always enjoyed talking to you, because you are well-educated, articulate and funny. You are very good at analytical thinking, and I have always admired your problem-solving capacities. I like the fact that you don't pretend to be interested in things when you aren't. We have never, for instance, had to go to Kurasawa movies.

'We appear to be very well suited in most important respects. I enjoy living with you because you are clean

125

and tidy but not *too* clean and tidy, and you have your own friends, but get on well with mine. If I have a criticism it would be that you sometimes take rather too long in the bathroom, and I have to piss out of the back window. This is a minor point, however, and in a certain way I even enjoy it.

'I think you are very pretty if, perhaps, not exactly beautiful, and you always dress stylishly and appropriately. You are good at finding bargains, and you have no embarrassment about taking things back to shops.

'And now, of course, you are pregnant, which is marvellous. I can't wait to be a father, it is something I have always wanted.

'I have very much enjoyed living with you, and would be very unhappy if you were ever to leave. I hope we can continue living together for a long, long time.

'All my love etc.'

I read it to Stroker, and he put his head on one side and said 'yeah, yeah . . .' thoughtfully, but with judgement reserved. The Atlantic clearly wasn't surging for him.

It was an hour or two later when I remembered Teacher's comment about saying sorry.

'PS. I'm very sorry that I can't think of anything truly passionate to say to you.

'I wish I could express properly what I feel. I do love you, though. And I love the baby too, even if it is the size of a kidney bean and has limb buds and no ears.'

I passed the letter on to Stroker. Writing it made me

realize how far away I was from Fiona, from London, from my life. It was as if I was suspended in the air. Just hanging, turning and twisting like a suicide on the end of a rope.

29

I was back in the hotel a few days later. Not in the same room, obviously, but one very much like it. Different pattern on the bedding. Someone looked in intermittently, but I'd promised not to start any more fires. I was surprised that my word seemed to be all that was needed to convince them.

I realized that no-one outside, by which I meant outside in the world, was looking for me. Not Fiona, not the police, no-one. Fiona had presumably been persuaded by Loverman's forged letter that I was not a missing person in the police sense but rather a voluntary seeker after wisdom in the bullshit sense. She was apparently prepared to believe, on the strength of a forged signature, that the person she had been living with for four years, and whose baby she was going to have, had been replaced by some kind of saddo cultist. From (fairly) successful freelance journalist to shit-for-brains, no-life, swallow-anything fuckwit in a few effortless strokes of Loverman's stoned pen.

Which was, in itself, almost as incredible as anything these people were trying to tell me. I had been, apparently, miraculously transformed, at least as far as Fiona was concerned.

How she could have believed that was, to me,

incomprehensible. Had I ever given her *any indication* that I harboured secret urges to abandon reason and embrace credulity? Had I ever worn purple or orange clothes? Had I muttered arcane things? Had I tried to worship the cat, had I tried to talk to her about esoteric texts or espoused enthusiasm for charismatic leaders of any sort? *Ever?*

If anything, it was always she who was determined to keep an open mind. I remembered her telling me about Louis XIV, who apparently healed 1,500 people at his coronation by touching them. In fact it was partly her much-vaunted open mind on such things that had led me to want to investigate this bunch. I've always been sure that the only miraculous force in the world is the seemingly infinite willingness of people to believe things, anything, the more idiotic the better.

Maybe she'd thought that the fact I was interested enough to want to do a piece on the Sons meant I was *really, secretly*, wanting to swallow the whole risible rigmarole. She was probably going around telling anyone who would listen how she had never thought I had it in me to believe something like this, but how you *never could tell with people*.

I wondered how long it would be before she found someone else to make her Atlantic Ocean surge.

These were painful matters, to be sure.

The longer I was away from her, the clearer my picture of her became. I was more and more conscious of the fact that I never wanted to leave her, that I wanted her back again, I wanted the baby, I wanted the whole thing. It was increasingly obvious with every day that passed. If I had had any lingering doubts about our future together, then they were clearing like early mist.

Which raised the question: why had I run away?

Because that was what it amounted to. I had run off on some foolish, juvenile escapade, and the timing of it was surely no accident. The amateur psychologist in my head came up with fear of responsibility, fear of intimacy, fear, basically, of *baby*. Was that it? Or was this just my last cry, my final burst of freedom before the smells of baby lotion and baby sick and baby shit came over me, enveloped me, drowned me?

Fear of the changing-mat. Fear of Fiona. It was ridiculous, but there it was. I was prepared to believe that Fiona had given up on me, because I was scared, at least in part, that she hadn't, that she was still there, in Ealing, in our flat, and that I would be going back to her some day soon, and that we would, at some point, have to go round Mothercare together. Would she want to hold my hand? The idea was awful, but also lovely. The baby was terrifying because it was so important. I wanted it. I wanted her. Maybe after Mothercare we could go to the Early Learning Centre. I've always had a secret yen for brightly coloured plastic things with bells in them.

After this job.

30

People who are shipwrecked on desert islands are supposed to scan the horizon for passing ships. I would spend hours doing the same. After all there is almost nothing you can do in a hotel room except lie on the bed or look out of the window. Normally I'd watch the adult channels and phone people up and contemplate raiding the mini bar, but since all of these little comforts had been denied me, it was either lie on the bed or look out of the window.

July was turning into August and the crops were ripening, green turning to gold. I could see a field, not far away, on the other side of a hedge. It rolled slightly upward: in the morning or evening light all the little hollows and ripples showed up, deep shadows and smoothly rounded contours. I couldn't see a road, but I could hear the occasional car or bike going by. There seemed to be hardly any traffic in these parts. We had truly been left behind.

I thought about all the little corners of England, of other countries, simply left behind, left to carry on away from the tumult of cities and stock markets and newspapers, what I'd always thought of as the real world. This world wasn't real, this hotel stuck away in an abandoned corner, these demented people, with their fraudulent miracles and convoluted thought, and their Teacher.

I could stay here for ever, live and die in this room, never again use tube trains or taxis or fax machines, never again sit in pubs, no longer feel anxious about my progress through the world, my career. My career could be in this room, lying on the bed or looking out of the window. It was a strangely comforting thought sometimes.

No-one came here because no-one had any reason to, except the gang and the others like me. I could yell out of the window or drop notes or do any of the things prisoners do, but no-one would know. Someone would have to come to cut the corn or whatever it was in the field, but he'd never hear me. No-one would ever hear me.

One evening, though, I did see someone. He was standing by the hedgerow at the top of the rise, quite distant, but clear enough. He seemed to be looking in the direction of the hotel. He had some kind of a hat on, which made me think he must be a farmer. I shouted out to him but my voice vanished in the air, leaving hardly a trace, he was much too far away to hear me. I watched him, as he, seemingly, watched me. He turned away a few minutes later and disappeared over the ridge of the low hill. He must have seen a lot of comings and goings, he must have seen and heard all kinds of things. Did he not ever wonder what was going on here? Surely he did.

Not much, but something. There was someone around, we had not been completely abandoned, not completely. He would perhaps return. I might devise a way of attracting his attention, he might help get me out, or call the police. Him just being there, in fact, was a help in itself. He was outside, external to this bunch of lunatics, not part of them. He was, presumably, sane and rational and lived in the real, dull, unmiraculous world that was spread out all around this monstrous place. The world that I was going to get back into, one way or another, soon, just as soon as I found out what was going on.

31

Fuckyou's mood hadn't improved noticeably. He hadn't been threatening to break my arm quite so much, but he had found new avenues of surliness to explore.

'Look, tell me what's wrong, man,' I finally said, hoping that the 'man' suffix might aid communication, which it did. Like an open sesame.

It appeared that Fuckyou was having relationship trouble. This amazed me, not that he should be having trouble, but that he should be having a relationship. I tried to imagine him walking round Asda with some woman, hand in hand. I couldn't. A dog, perhaps, I could imagine, but not a person. I had the impression that his beer gut was on the increase, though I never saw him drunk. Perhaps he was a secret drinker? Or perhaps he just ate too much pizza.

The problem, it appeared, was that his girlfriend Chrissy complained every time she saw him that she never saw him. She complained that he spent all his time with the Sons. He was supposed to be re-doing the cork tiles on the bathroom ceiling and getting on with the concreting for the extension. Also, he'd started doing the kitchen some time ago, and there were still live wires hanging off the walls and the washing machine wasn't plumbed in right, so it leaked, and the cat licked up the soapy water and was sick everywhere.

Was any of this, he demanded, *his* fault?

'Am I supposed to be in control of the fucking cat? Fucking animal shouldn't be so stupid, it should learn, man.'

What, I asked him, about the rest of it?

'I *put* the tiles up in the bathroom. There's too much condensation, they don't stay up. You can't have cork tiles in a bathroom with that much condensation, it doesn't work.'

'Can't you sort out the condensation?'

'Do you want to know *why* there's so much condensation? I'll *tell* you *why*. It's because she has to have about six showers a day, so you get a lot of steam, so you get a lot of condensation, so the *tiles* come off. And she won't open the *window* because she thinks birds are going to fly in.'

'So what's the solution?'

'Well. I should put in one of those ventilation units—'

'No but I mean, what are you going to do about, you know, the relationship.'

'Well.' He stroked his beard. 'I think I'm going to put a bomb through the letter-box and – boom!' He gestured explosions and demolitions. 'Then I'm going to fill up the bike, man and just – ' more gestures, flying and revving, ' – you know?'

I'd noticed this kind of thing before in other of the Sons. The only options seemed to be extreme ones, extreme remedies for extreme situations. I supposed that this was to be expected from people who'd experienced miraculous healing for their

135

unusual conditions. Except that in Fuckyou's case, I had the feeling that the cure had been less than permanent, less than total.

'What would you do about the Sons?'

'Fuck 'em.'

'Yeah?'

'Oh yeah. They don't need me. I don't need them. Fuck 'em.'

'You'd leave? Really?'

'Oh yeah. In a minute.'

'You'd leave Teacher?'

'I would do that, yeah.' His eyes were flickering, daring me to disbelieve him.

'What would Teacher have to say about that?'

'I tell you, he could say just about anything that he happened to want to say, because I wouldn't be listening.'

'You told me you loved him.'

'I don't love *anybody*. Not him, nobody.'

'What about Chrissy?'

'Nah.' He was shaking his head slowly, his eyes locked on me. 'Nah.'

'If you were going to leave,' I said, 'when would you be thinking of?'

'Whenever. Whenever, man.'

I scratched a match for a cigarette. Then I said:

'Would some money be of any use to you?'

32

He was back again, at the top of the field, closer this time. The man with the hat, Farmer Giles. I called and waved but he was wholly oblivious to me, just standing and watching. He definitely seemed to be watching. I had a thought and flicked my light on and off, on and off, not Morse or anything clever like that, just patterns, on and off, something going on over here, why don't you come and have a look? He stood, not moving, so still that he appeared to be part of the landscape, an outcrop of the field and the hedgerow. I gave up on him and went back to bed. It was hopeless. It was Fuckyou or nothing.

On an impulse I got up again half an hour or so later, went to the window. It was almost dark now, but I could make him out clearly, still there, apparently not having moved since I'd looked last. Watching.

33

Negotiations with Fuckyou had reached what is usually called 'a delicate stage', meaning that actual sums of money were being discussed. I was telling him that he had to be realistic, that though by his standards I was rich, I wasn't, in worldly terms, particularly solvent. He started talking about hundreds of thousands and I laughed. He had the good grace to blush. I named a figure in thousands, single-figure thousands. He looked unimpressed.

The only way we could make it work was that I surrender my card and PIN. He could then take out £250, my weekly limit, as a kind of deposit, good faith. When we were safely out, he would accompany me to my bank where I would draw out the remainder. There was an element of trust required here, but he seemed prepared to trust me, and I trusted him, perfectly.

I was surprised that I should be able to say that with such confidence, but I was. I had thought on a few occasions that I could tell something about Fuckyou, understand something. I had, in fact, felt that I could half *see* something, just behind his head.

Whatever it was, I was confident that he'd stick to the arrangement when it was struck. Though, having said that, I found it hard to believe that I'd actually escape. Perhaps I was just getting used to being there.

Still, negotiations were proceeding. I think both of us were trying to convince ourselves that we were really serious.

34

Doc came back to check my arm, but it was fine now. He pulled the dressing off and prodded about a bit, making little satisfied sounds. Almost healed.

'I've been wondering something,' I said as he applied a new and final dressing.

'Uhuh?'

'It's about you.'

'Uhuh.'

'You are, as I understand it, by way of being medical officer for this outfit.'

'If you want to call it that.'

'And the leader of this outfit is a person who claims that he has special powers.'

'He doesn't claim that. The people he helps, they do.'

'These powers are of a healing character.'

'Uhuh.'

'So why does he need you?'

Doc sat back and regarded me.

'I mean, why couldn't he come here and just, you know, heal my arm?'

'I don't think you quite understand—'

'And Spider's thumb. Why did it have to come to amputation? Surely a spot of gangrene isn't too much of a test for someone of Teacher's reputed abilities.'

'Not "reputed".'

'And not just that, but why does everyone look so totally bloody *battered*? And why—'

'You're asking the wrong questions—'

' – why do so many of you have long hair?' This was a new thought, and one that I didn't much like. 'Are you hiding something?'

'Wait now—'

'Scars, perhaps?'

Doc laughed, started to shake his head.

'What's your job here? I mean really? Patching up Teacher's mistakes? Why is the man next door moaning like that?'

He walked to the door, and stood with his back to me for a moment. Before he left he said:

'Do you know what you're full of? You're full of cynicism and hate and fear. I can *smell* these things on you. Your blood is full of them. It may be that you're nearly ready.'

'Are you going to recommend me for treatment, Doctor?'

He shook his head and opened the door.

'No. Not yet,' he said, and left.

35

Stroker came to bring me the letter back. The second letter. Teacher hadn't liked this one either. Stroker was apologetic.

'He says you mustn't be so hard on her, on yourself, on everything. He says—'

'Look. OK. *You* write it.'

'Who me?'

'You try. I don't seem to be able to get it right, do I.'

'Well I could have a go at making it up, but I'm not much good at writing things down.' He looked me straight in the eye, as he must have had to do so many times before.

'OK, you say it, I'll write it down.'

He grinned.

'All right then.'

He sat on the bed and cracked open a can of beer.

'Darling Fiona.'

'Darling? Are you sure?'

'What's wrong with darling?' He looked defiant. I wrote it down.

'Darling Fiona, I wish you could be here with me. I don't feel complete without you. I go to sleep—'

'Wait. Here-with-me. Not-complete-without. OK.'

'I go to sleep wishing I could feel you in my arms, and I dream that by some miracle you really are here.'

'Sleep-wishing. Dream-miracle—'

'Your warm, sweet body—'

'Here-body. Hold on.'

'Your gentle arms and full, heavy—'

'Stroker.'

'Breasts, like—'

'Stroker, that'll do, I get the idea.'

He stopped in full flow.

'Are you sure?'

'Absolutely. Just one last thing, I'm supposed to say I'm sorry.'

'What for?'

'You choose.'

'OK.' He closed his eyes, frowning. 'Finally, I'm sorry for all the times I've made you cry.'

'I've *never* made her cry, she never cries—'

'And for all the times I've lied to you.'

'Right. Got it. Thanks.'

'If you want to do any more just give me a shout.'

'Thanks. I will.'

'Is that the kind of thing you wanted?'

'I'm sure it'll be perfect.'

'Yeah.' He left, looking as if he had plenty more where *that* came from. I thought about what a delightful young man he was, and, again, what had brought him here. I almost called him back to ask him, then thought better of it. I probably didn't really want to know.

36

I woke to the certainty that someone was outside my window. I jumped up, amazed, startled. There was a form retreating into the dark, heading towards the field. A dim form, a hat. Farmer Giles. He'd been right by the fence outside my window, peering in myopically, I was certain. I was at the window in two steps.

'Hello?'

Dark outside, I could hear wind blowing through high trees nearby. In the field the corn would be waving, rippling, performing complicated compensations for the force of the wind on it, bending and swaying. My room light was off and the curtains were open.

'Listen, this is going to sound a bit strange to you – ' I began, calling out to him as he retreated, smiling brilliantly at him, to disarm, put him at ease, dispel some of the sudden night strangeness and prepare him for what I was going to say. He didn't speak, just kept walking away.

'You see, the thing is that I'm – well I'm basically being kept here, against my will, do you understand me? They won't let me out. I can't get out.'

No flicker of response. No expression on the face under the hat, except perhaps mild puzzlement. The face was old and lined and papery. The eyes were watery blue, the eyebrows thick and overgrown. No response. I spoke louder. Perhaps he was deaf.

'I was wondering if you could help me. Please. You could call the police, tell them that there's a very serious situation here, that I'm being held, I've been kidnapped, I can't get out. Do you understand? Ring the police and tell them. Please. That's all I want you to do. Please?'

He marched away, flicking at stalks as he went. Perhaps he was blind as well. His eyes had the faint reflective sheen of cataracts. Deaf and blind. Mute also.

'Please! Come back. Please! Can you hear me?'

I banged on the glass. Nothing. Then he slowly moved his head, to the left, to the right. He was shaking it. No. Nothing to do with me, son.

'For God's sake—' My voice was a breath. I backed away from the glass. I reached for the curtains and pulled them, a quick movement, convulsive. I backed away to my bed, lay down, closed my eyes. I imagined him standing, all through the short night, standing with his sheeny blue eyes and expressionless face, shaking his head. Abandoned, abandoned, who would help me now?

I cried.

37

We had reached the 'critical' stage, Fuckyou and I, where things could easily have gone either way. He was not the ideal negotiating partner, for a number of reasons.

Firstly he was anxious and greedy, and had unrealistic expectations. I think this came from his image of me, which was really little more than a fantasy projection. I represented, for him, all kinds of unattainable privileges and status. For instance, I owned my flat. I didn't pay rent, I paid mortgage. I'd tried explaining such concepts as one-bed conversion, Ealing, and negative equity, but fantasy is not so easily or prosaically banished, and 'yeah, but it's *yours* man' kept popping up like a refrain at a mass. It was quite touching in a way.

And then I was self-employed, and I worked in the media. This much I had confessed, though not the precise nature of my calling. I think in Fuckyou's eyes this placed me more or less permanently in exciting European and American cities and wearing light suits and dark glasses, drinking beer from little bottles, not cans. Women, I suspect, were massively attracted to me, in Fuckyou's version. Women without unreasonable demands and ventilation units.

And then I'd had an education, not just 'O' level, not just 'A' level, but a *degree*. A fucking *degree*, man. I'd tried explaining that almost anyone, himself included, could get a degree nowadays, but he wasn't having any. Maybe he was right.

It all added up, of course, in a seductively uncomplicated way, to money. He looked sullen when I tried – I have to confess, a little sadly – to downgrade myself. He was reluctant to believe me because that would have meant letting go of the fantasy.

His other problem was that he was extremely fearful. What he feared most, from what I could tell, was not retribution from the gang but, in a sense, its opposite: rejection, expulsion. He feared that they would do exactly as he seemed to wish, which was to let him go. He feared losing his place. This was a fear I could understand very well. He was probably right to fear it. What, after all, would he do? Go home to fit the ventilation unit? Ventilation units lacked drama, nor were they extreme, he would have no truck with them. *Fuck* them, man.

But he went on.

He was also, I was surprised to discover, afraid of me. He had, I think, paranoid fantasies of grand betrayals and desertions. He thought me clever, therefore dangerous.

Perhaps I was. Perhaps he was right to fear me.

38

I appeared to be moving up the line, in terms of processing. I had the inestimable privilege of a question and answer session with the one I thought of as Deputy Dawg.

I asked him if he was aware of the penalties he would be facing when I got out.

'Get out?' He had that therapist's trick of repeating back to you what you'd just said.

'Get out, yes. Get as in "get", out as in—'

'So you still want to get out.'

'Does that seem strange to you?' I thought I'd try to break his rhythm by turning the questions back to him.

'Why should it seem strange to me, do you think?'

'Didn't your mother ever tell you that it's rude to answer a question with a question?'

'My mother?' He seemed nonplussed temporarily.

'Yes. Tell me about your mother,' I said, and gave him an authoritative, questioning look.

'I think we're wandering off the point here.'

'The point, yes. Tell me about the point.'

He smiled uncertainly, smoothed his hair back.

'You see, I think this business about getting out is a distraction from our purpose here.'

'Which is?'

'Which is to find out how best to help you with whatever it is you need help with.'

'I thought he did it all just by looking. He has X-ray eyes or something. He can see the demons inside you. Isn't that it?'

'Well not exactly—'

'So what's your purpose?'

'I'm sorry, I don't quite—'

'What are you for?'

'What am I—?'

'For. What are you for.'

He stumbled, but he recovered. He wasn't quite as stupid as he looked.

'I usually like to talk to people, just to get a sense of who they are.'

'And you report back to Teacher?'

'I give him my impressions, yes.'

'You must get some very strange people coming through here.'

'Do you think so? I wouldn't say strange.'

'You wouldn't call expecting miraculous healing strange?'

'Isn't miraculous healing what you're expecting?'

'I changed my mind.'

'Really?'

'Really.'

He lifted his eyebrows, and clucked his tongue.

'So what impression will you be passing on about me?' I asked.

'Is that of concern to you? How people see you?'

'I'm just trying to get the—'

'Story?'

'Picture. I would think it's you who's got the stories. You must hear some extraordinary tales.' I was thinking about the radio shows, the confessions. This banal man in front of me must have heard hundreds of such accounts, must be a sort of receptacle for the monstrous and cruel and depraved in people. Strange, I thought, that he should look so much like a librarian.

'Only one story.'

'Which is?'

'It usually goes along the lines of: there's something inside me, I don't know what's inside me that makes me like this.'

'And what is it, this something?'

'Teacher has a name for it. He calls it the Bad Stuff.'

'Well I can see how that must save a fair amount of psychological and theological hair-splitting—'

'Yes I heard that about you. I heard the words cynicism, fear, hate. Cynicism is probably the worst of the three.'

'Is that my bad stuff?'

He shrugged.

'I don't make those kinds of judgements.'

'So this bad stuff. What happens to it?'

'Teacher gets it out. He locates it and channels it, and then he gets it out.'

'Where does it go to?'

'It goes back to where it comes from.'

'Which is?'

He gestured.

'Just look around you. There's no shortage.'

I became aware of the hotel room, the sad, bare utility of it. I thought of all the others who'd been in it. I thought of how a hotel room can make you a stranger to yourself, like all the other strangers. I thought of the extremities of loneliness, violence, shame, guilt, fear that had been contained inside those strangers, who had themselves been contained in the hygienic little cubicle. Double-packed for extra freshness, so to speak. The walls should have been running with bad stuff, the mattress soaked in it. I thought of my next-door neighbour, lying on his bed, wracked.

'Look,' I said, 'I don't mean you people any harm, and if all this stuff makes you feel better, then I'm happy for you, truly. But it's got nothing whatever to do with me. It can't have escaped your attention that I'm not really like any of your usual clients.'

'Are you not?'

'Of course I'm not. Christ! I don't *bugger* my *dog*, I don't torture my children, I don't – I don't do any of those things.'

'No? Well, there are other ways of falling.'

'Not me, I'm afraid. You've got the wrong man.'

He smiled, a smile that could only survive on the face of someone who thinks he's got something up his sleeve.

'I heard you went to watch Teacher at work.'

'That's right.'

'And you weren't impressed.'

'Correct.'

'And I was wondering – '

'Yes?'

'Well I was wondering what it was that you'd been expecting that you didn't see?'

I thought about this for a moment.

151

'I was expecting more of a show, that's all.'

'Nothing else?'

'Nothing else.'

He stood up to leave. He was still wearing that ace-of-clubs smile. It didn't suit him.

'We'll talk again,' he said, and I shrugged, maybe.

After he'd gone I thought about sitting perched on the rear-wheel housing of that filthy white van with Moustache's eyes boring into me, peering through the grimy window. I thought about what I'd seen, what I hadn't seen, what I'd maybe expected to see. Hoped to see. I didn't like thinking about any of it.

But I was curious, more curious all the time, it was the curiosity that was winning.

I was sure, right deep down, that there was nothing in any of this. But if there was, then I wanted to know, needed to know, what it was.

39

I broke the window so I could say goodbye to Loverman. He smiled round at me as I turned the corner.

'Hey hey,' he said, and his smile was beautiful, stoned, sexy. He was bare to the waist, he stroked his belly as we talked. He reminded me of a cat we used to have when I was little, a neutered tom. He'd had the same colossal relaxation, the boneless sprawl. *After* the operation.

'Don't worry,' I said, 'I'm not trying to escape. I just thought I'd come out to say hello.'

'That's nice,' he said. Then he added, 'But it's the windows I feel sorry for,' so gently, with such genuine regret that he made himself laugh, and I laughed as well.

'Couldn't you sleep?' he asked, and I said no.

'It's a crime to sleep on a night like this,' he said, and blew fragrant smoke into the air. 'I used to have what they call insomnia. I used to lie there and toss and turn and think about things. I used to get, like, *really* depressed. I'd blame myself for things I'd done, I'd regret things I hadn't done, I'd go back over things I'd done badly. I worried about what I would have to do next day. I'd know I wouldn't be able to

153

do those things, of course, because I'd be useless from not sleeping. I'd drink too much, but that didn't make me sleepy, it made me *stupid*. Sometimes I'd cry. Doctors gave me things, I'd pass out for four hours, wake up in the darkness sweating. When I used those pills I had dreams. I'd dream I hadn't done something I was supposed to do. In the dreams I knew what it was. Then I'd wake up, four o'clock in the morning. And I'd think, what was it I hadn't done in the dream? I wouldn't be able to remember. Sometimes it was something I had done that I couldn't remember, which was worse. Then I started to remember what it was I'd done. Really done, not in a dream. I'd wake up somewhere, not know how I'd got there, something done, something bad. I'd be scratched, marked, bruised even. Those were bad times.'

He inhaled and held, passed me the joint. He closed his eyes, and then blew out a long, fine stream of smoke.

'And then.' This seemed to be, for him, a complete utterance. I let it stand for a moment.

'Then what?'

'Then I met Teacher.'

'And what happened?'

'He got it all out of me, man. He got it all out of my head. Out of my body.'

'How did he do that?' I was aware that time was running short for me to find out. It could be any day now with Fuckyou.

Loverman gave me a shrewd look. I was reminded that it was he who had forged my letter to Fiona, but it was hard to feel strongly about that.

'Do you know what your nickname is?' he asked, and I said I didn't know I had one.

'You're called Mr Nosy. You know the little cartoon people? You're Mr Nosy.'

'That seems appropriate.'

'It certainly is.' Was it a shrewd look or just a blissed-out look? Beautiful, whatever it was. His fingers traced the lines of hair on his stomach. 'Yes. It certainly is.'

We sat and smoked for a few more minutes, and I wanted to say something but was unable to. He looked over at me and clapped me on the shoulder.

'Better get you tucked up in bed eh?' he said, and we both laughed. I would miss him.

40

I had it all settled with Fuckyou. It was perhaps inevitably a rather stupid plan, but his paranoia was mounting and any modification I suggested was regarded as an attempt to confuse or deceive him. We had agreed a sum of money, single-figure thousands, a fairly low number. I had surrendered my card and PIN number, and, as I'd known he would, he returned with the card and the money, £250 'deposit'. Together we counted out the notes. It was clearly very important to him that I should know that he'd stuck to the arrangement. He had seemingly had a long history of being disbelieved, accused, suspected. This, he was insisting, wasn't extortion or blackmail or anything of that sort. This was merely a payment for a service. We agreed that he'd taken the correct amount and shook hands. For a moment I thought he was going to give me a receipt.

The plan was this.

He would come to the hotel, late. We didn't manage to specify what 'late' meant. Just *late*, man. He would tell Loverman that there was a phone call for him, or that someone wanted to see him. Something like that. Why anyone would have to talk to him *late* wasn't clear. Perhaps it could be his wife, or something, an emergency or something like that. Was Loverman married? Fuckyou blinked and said shit, probably. Anyway, whatever. Loverman would be got out of the way. Fuckyou even hinted darkly that he might use violence if that was needed. I mentally measured them against each other, and Fuckyou did not come out the winner. Perhaps if he used his whole beer gut with extreme force behind it and got Loverman off balance he might manage to knock him down. Maybe.

We toyed with the idea of overpowering Loverman somehow and locking him in the room, which had a pleasing symmetry to it, but we couldn't think of a way. I started to outline an idea which involved Fuckyou having an urgent message for *me*. He could come to my room, let me out and then we'd both tackle Loverman. Fuckyou wasn't having it. What was to stop me just doing a runner and leaving him with an irate Loverman to handle all by himself? I tried to explain that he was planning to deal with Loverman single-handed *anyway*, and so that wouldn't make any difference, but I gave up. In any case, the less contact I had of that sort with Loverman the happier I was going to be. I was feeling bad about deceiving him at all.

So. Loverman would be 'got out of the way', and Fuckyou and I would ride off into the night.

Since he wasn't prepared to face the girlfriend, whom I always pictured now as holding a ventilator unit like an emblem, he was going to stay with me in the palace I owned in Ealing. Quite what Fiona was supposed to make of this I couldn't say. Fuckyou would stay until he 'got himself sorted out', which sounded like an ominously long time. But we would deal with that when we came to it.

If I was honest about it, I suppose the reason that I wasn't worried about Fuckyou invading our flat was that I didn't believe that it would ever come to that. I found it very hard to imagine that we would ever get as far as Ealing. And as for the three of us all mucking in together, Fuckyou kipping down, presumably, on the sofa, until the ineffable process of him 'sorting himself out' got under way, it was clearly a non-starter. Fiona wouldn't stand for it for a moment, and she would be absolutely right not to. But I could quite happily agree to it, because I was increasingly sure that it would never happen, I just couldn't see it.

But then I wasn't exactly overwhelmed with other options. Fuckyou was flawed material certainly, but it was him or nothing.

He couldn't say exactly which night he was proposing. I was to stay awake and be prepared. Watch and wait. He would come when he could, when he thought the time was right. I was to trust him. I was to be cool. Man.

41

And, amazingly, it all went to plan.

I was asleep, when I heard the key rattling. I sat bolt upright, terrified. I've never been able to wake up quickly, and I felt as if I were in a dream.

Fuckyou walked in, grinning, and I remembered. Excitement gripped my bowels.

'Where's Loverman?'

'*Gone*, man.'

I assumed that he must, after all, have had a wife. I struggled out of bed. I was fully dressed, apart from shoes and the jacket that I had seemingly permanently misplaced.

I followed Fuckyou out into the corridor, and out of the front door. Loverman was nowhere to be seen. I found it hard to believe. I was still half in a dream. The air outside was cool and moist and delicate. There was no sound. I was vaguely aware of clouds flying overhead. It was very late.

He had his bike facing in the wrong direction naturally, so I stood while he wheeled it round the right way. No reverse. I thought of requesting a crash helmet, then thought better of it. This was an escape fantasy, and you didn't wear a helmet.

I climbed on behind him and got my feet securely

on the pillion pins. I reached behind me for the back rack and locked my hands onto it in the way I'd seen the others do it. New as I was to pillion etiquette I knew that gripping on for dear life to your driver's thighs and jacket was *not* cool.

'OK?' Fuckyou enquired and I said OK. He revved up, and we were away.

The acceleration was brutal again, and the wind immediately got in all over my upper body. I was instantly chilled to the marrow. He was exactly the driver I'd imagined him to be, sudden, jerky, tense. His corners were sickeningly abrupt and completely unexpected. I held on somehow. I don't know if I was leaning in or not, but I held on.

Wind whipped my face, dragging back my cheeks, scouring my nasal passages, my throat, my ears. My fingers quickly became numb, and I dug a thumbnail into my palm to try to convince myself that I really was holding onto something, that I wasn't just sitting, free and unrestrained, on this heedlessly rapid machine. My arms ached behind my shoulders.

After a few minutes he stopped, very abruptly, and I was flung onto him. He rubbed his eyes, wiping his hands on his greasy jeans.

'Are you OK?' I said, and he muttered, yeah. He coughed and spat. We started up again.

I was beginning to get comfortable, or at least managing to relax my thighs a little, when we pulled to a halt again.

He kicked down the stand and climbed off. He stumbled away, and wandered into a field of something tall and leafy and green. I thought that perhaps he needed to attend to a call of nature, but it didn't look like it. He got a few paces into the field, with his back to the bike and me, and just stood. Then he bent down from the waist, his straggly hair hanging down round his shoulders. His shoulders were shaking. I became aware of a sound coming through the damp air, a sound that I was not at first able to place.

The sound grew louder. He was crying, great, unrestrained, full-throttled bursts of it.

He carried on in this way for a good five minutes. I couldn't think of anything I could usefully do or say. It was a very awkward situation to be in. The tall green plants were shaking round him, as if in sympathy. He slapped his arms against his sides, he thumped his legs, his head. There were words but I couldn't make them out.

He came back to the bike, snuffling and grinning with embarrassment.

'I don't think I can go on.'

I started to say come on, it can't be that bad, you have to start looking ahead, it'll all seem much better in the morning, and so on.

'No, I mean I can't drive any more tonight. I've got a headache.'

'You want to stop? Here?' I gestured at the fields, the clouds, the ground.

'Get a few hours' sleep. It'll be OK, they won't think of coming this way to look. Trust me.'

Trust me. I looked hard at him, then I looked just *behind* him, to his right. I was certain I could see something, but it was the middle of the night and we were both tired and slightly desperate.

There was a good-sized tree a few hundred yards further down the road. He stood the bike behind it, gently, almost tenderly. It wasn't a cold night but it wasn't warm either. There was no way of escaping the hard ground. He roamed about a bit tearing up armfuls of the plants, and we made pillows. I tried to make a cushion to go under my hip, which was aching already. I suggested using the saddle of the bike, but he said he'd tried it a few times and it was just too high and entirely the wrong shape, it twisted your neck something brutal. You were better off on the ground.

We made our nests a few feet apart, under the tree. There was no shelter anywhere for miles. I worried briefly about rain, but the tree was wide and leafy and it would probably protect us against the worst of it. And if it didn't, then it didn't. There was nothing to be done.

We lay down to sleep. I thought of something I wanted to ask him, then I realized that I didn't actually know what his name was. I couldn't very well call out 'Hey Fuckyou?' His name in the gang, he'd told me, was something like Spamhead, but I wasn't sure I'd remembered correctly and anyway it felt too foolish to be calling out 'Hey Spamhead?' in the middle of a field in the middle of the night.

'Hey.'

He didn't hear or didn't respond.

'Hey.'

'Yeah?' I could heard the stalks adjusting to the weight of him and his beer gut. He seemed to be trying to flatten them out by rolling on them.

'If they do come to find us, will you fight them?'

'They won't come.' He sounded flat and hopeless.

'If they do though?'

'If they do? I'll kill 'em.'

'Oh. OK.' I didn't want to excite him. I said goodnight, and he murmured something.

'Hey.' This was a few minutes later. My bones were trying to drag me down into the unyielding ground, trying to dig themselves in. My hips, my shoulders, even my elbows. It was astonishingly quiet.

'Hey.'

'Yeah?'

'I don't know what your name is.'

There was no reply for a few seconds. Then:

'Leonard. Len.'

'OK. I just wanted to know.'

'Sure. Go to sleep, man. Dream dreams.'

42

I awoke to some kind of commotion happening somewhere near me. The stalks were snapping and thrashing. It was still dark. I sat up, feeling entirely disorientated. My pelvis jabbed viciously at me.

I thought at first that there was a storm going on, a small localized tornado, perhaps, the kind of storm that is sometimes used as an explanation for the appearance of crop circles. A spinning vortex or something of the sort.

I stood up. I could see the stalks dancing, falling. Then I saw Fuckyou. He appeared to be dancing as well, his hair was swinging wildly. His head bobbed up, then he disappeared from sight again.

There was an object lying in the flattened imprint where he'd been lying. A black plastic thing of curious shape, something like a D in outline. I approached it, picked it up. It was the tool kit; I looked over to the bike, the saddle had been taken off, there was a hollow underneath where it fitted.

The tool kit was open. Scattered round it were various things: I was able to identify ring spanners and a plug spanner, a feeler gauge, a grubby white cardboard NGK spark-plug box. There was a thick folded booklet, very oily, basic maintenance in English and

Spanish, with complicated little diagrams. There were notes in the margins, I couldn't read them.

Funny kind of time to be doing maintenance, I thought. Funny also to be dancing while you did it, and several yards away from the bike itself. Very funny.

I crept up to the edge of the arena where the stalks were dancing. I saw his head bob up above the plants: he was doing something with his hand and head. He moved his hand away and I could see the handle of a screwdriver sticking out from his ear, a slow trickle of blood seeping along it. He brought his hand back up, this time he was holding a small stone. He banged the stone against the handle of the screwdriver, driving it further into his *ear*. Into his brain. A terrible sound emerged from his mouth and I ran, crashing into the crops, forcing a way through.

I ran blindly for about a minute, a dreamlike feeling of time being suspended, the corn of whatever it was falling away in front of me, rising up again behind. I fell and banged my head, hard. I lay dazed. The clouds chased each other overhead.

43

I don't know how long I lay, watching the clouds. I felt incapable of moving. Or rather I was incapable of doing what I knew I had to do, which was to go back and get Fuckyou to a hospital. I told myself that I'd never be able to get him to go, that he'd fight me, that it was probably too late already, that he must have inflicted colossal brain damage on himself. I told myself that he was probably dead by now in any case.

The idea of going back to him made me feel sick and cold and exhausted. So I didn't. I lay on the hard ground and watched the clouds. One looked like a frog, another like a buffalo. I was waiting for something to happen. I didn't know what it was I was waiting for. It would be daylight soon, and I would have to do something then; so perhaps I was just waiting for the light.

They came about forty minutes later. I heard the bikes from miles away, the sound very small and clear in the damp air, growing steadily. I estimated about six bikes.

They pulled in, and I knew there was no point in trying to hide or run. I got up and walked back through the tunnel I had carved in the corn.

As I approached the tree I could see them, they were

standing round under the branches, looking upward. I recognized one of them from the Burger King car park, Big Ears. I followed the direction of their gaze and saw a dim, dark figure hanging from a branch, swaying slightly, turning in the breeze. His bike was lying underneath him, he'd kicked it away. The fuel tank was dribbling, the ground smelled strongly of petrol. He'd hanged himself with the spare throttle cable while I'd been lying on my back watching the clouds. Blood trickled from his ear and nose.

They took him down and laid him on the ground, beside his bike. They looked up at me as I came forward: I said, it's not my fault, I didn't kill him, I had nothing to do with it. I remembered how I had thought I'd seen something behind his head, and I realized that what I'd seen had been a rope. What I thought I'd seen.

Now, of course, was my moment to escape. They would have to occupy themselves with getting Fuckyou down, and I could just melt away. I had no clear idea of where I was, but that didn't matter, any direction was good. I even thought of jumping onto one of the bikes and roaring off into the distance. They might pursue me but I would outrun them, blazing into the rising sun, my exhaust emissions like a comet's tail.

I didn't though. Big Ears sent one of them back to get the van, and the others sat round Fuckyou's body, talking quietly.

One of them saw the end of the screwdriver handle protruding from his ear. He leaned forward to examine it, and I said:

'It's a screwdriver. He banged it into his head.'

They looked at me and nodded, uhuh.

'Then he hanged himself.'

Oh yeah, uhuh.

'He was helping me escape. I paid him some money to get me out. He wanted to get away as well.'

Right, right.

'He would have had to be insane to do that with his ear, wouldn't he?'

Shrugging. Maybe.

I got the strongest feeling that they were less surprised than I would have expected. They were completely unperturbed, only slightly subdued.

'So. This kind of thing happen often does it?'

No reply.

'What's going to happen to him now? Is someone going to get the police?'

Big Ears spoke up:

'We'll take care of him.'

'How do you mean exactly?' My tone had become tight and indignant.

'Just that. Us. We'll take care of him.'

'Do you mean to say that you propose to *bury* him?'

Big Ears stood up and came over to me.

'You've had a bit of a shock. It would probably be best for you to lie down somewhere. None of this really concerns you.'

'He drove a *screwdriver*—'

'I know what he did.' Big Ears was standing very close to me and speaking very quietly. 'This is an internal matter. We'll deal with it internally, understand me?'

'What will you do if I just leave now?'

'I don't think you should let this get in the way of your—'

'What will you do?'

'You mean, will we restrain you? Yes.'

The old calculation, would there be pain, was this worth that. And anyway:

'You're wrong. It does concern me.'

It has long been one of Fiona's complaints, that I don't feel anything. When she came back from the doctor's that time, blushing, smiling, oozing pleasure and delight from every pore, and finally managed to say the words 'it's positive' to me, I apparently nodded and said 'great'. She often relays this story to people, as corroboration that I am cold and passionless and generally reptilian in manner. It is another of the things that she believes to be genetic or hormonal, which are her code words for shoddy, inferior, male. And it's true, great storms of passion are not often to be found whipping up the whitecaps on my internal seas.

But to feel something so much, so strongly, that it led you to this desperate scene below this tree; to feel *so much* that the only way to manage it was physically to try to drive it from your head, and when that failed to string yourself up, beyond anyone's aid; this was something I needed to know about.

Fuckyou, coarse, seedy, disloyal as he was, had been full of a passion that was exalted and consuming and total. He had the kind of strength of feeling that I knew to be missing from myself. Insanely, I envied him. And I knew what the source of this storm was, I knew where to trace it back to: Teacher.

I had to see him. It was becoming more necessary

every day. I knew I couldn't go now until I'd seen for myself what this was all about.

And in another way I felt that I owed it to poor Fuckyou, poor Leonard, to understand what it was that had brought him here. I owed it to him because I couldn't hide from the fact that I had myself had some part to play in his undoing. I had encouraged his defection from the only real family he had, I had waved wads of money under his nose and promised him a new start, a new life, promises I knew I could never keep, had no intention, in fact, of keeping. I was involved. It concerned me.

Big Ears shrugged.

'Whatever. If you say so.'

So I went to sit with the others by Fuckyou's poor body and waited for the van.

44

I wasn't allowed to go to the interment. I understood that there was a plot of ground somewhere near by, and this was where departed Sons had their final resting place. I don't know what they did with his bike, but from the look of it it was probably good only for spares. I don't know either what happened to the money: perhaps they gave it to his girlfriend, possibly to encourage her not to make too public a fuss. She could replace the tiles in the bathroom now. That might be a comfort. Everything was smoothed over, anyway, and things went on.

The night after they buried him, I had a dream.

I was with Fiona, at the flat in Ealing. She was in the front garden, which was barely big enough for two people to stand abreast. She was saying to me, look at the hedge. I looked: there were large white flowers all over it. Privet doesn't flower I said, and she said no, this is convolvulus. You don't notice it at first, it gets in everywhere, and then it suddenly flowers like this. She started to pull at the long strands of leaves and big, ghostly, gaping white trumpets. You have to get it all out, she said, or it just comes back again. I watched her for a few minutes, then I said you'll never get all of it out, not unless you use

A screwdriver.

He'd been trying to get the bad stuff out of his head. He'd tried to puncture a hole to let it out, because it was building up inside him, driving him mad, pressing against the inside of his skull. I could feel it.

Teacher must have missed some.

Whatever Teacher's method was, it clearly went wrong sometimes. It wasn't infallible. When it worked, it was apparently capable of achieving the most extraordinary results. People were brought back from the extremities of despair and hopelessness, were blessed, released, healed.

But when it failed, then the results could be catastrophic, as with Fuckyou. And who knew how many others?

This was not the first incident of its type, not at all. In fact they had their own graveyard to bury them in. No post-mortems or awkward questions. I wondered about the police: they were conscious of a high incidence of missing persons in the area, I knew that from my ten-minute interview with the Derby Constabulary. I knew that they had a file on Teacher and the Sons, but that they had no live lines of enquiry. This was no amateur operation, and the Sons were clearly adept at covering their traces. In a way, Teacher's deliberately high profile was a canny move: anything the police did in connection with him would receive maximum publicity because of his notoriety. They couldn't just come and quietly get him out of the way, nor could they casually fit him up for drugs or some other handy violation. They would have to move very carefully, and their case would have to be very good indeed. They wouldn't want to risk the bad press that they would inevitably receive if they prosecuted without a strong case.

Of course, for all I knew, the police were putting that case together right now; they might even have their own plant inside the group. They would almost certainly have some form of surveillance operation on the go. The concern for secrecy within the gang, which at first seemed paranoid, was probably entirely justified. It was no wonder that I couldn't get a single one of them to tell me what it was that they did at their healing sessions, what exactly the nature of Teacher's gift was.

Then I thought: I wonder what you'd see if you rolled up the Chief Inspector's sleeve. Would you, perhaps, see a tattoo, a skull with a diagonal cross over it? Would he talk, privately, off the record, obviously, about how he'd been healed, how he'd been given his freedom? Mistakes *will* happen, even in the best-run organizations, but you have to set that against the successes. Put it in perspective.

Or even: strictly just between us now, but those it doesn't work for, it gets them out of the way and we're all saved the expense and trouble of trial and custody for whatever it is they're guilty of. Because they're all guilty of something. They wouldn't be there if they weren't.

Was that what had happened to me? Had I gone so far outside the system now that it no longer mattered what became of me because I was guilty anyway?

I speculated about the exact scale of this operation. I wondered: how many healed? How many dead? How many outside turning a blind eye, happy for their human detritus to be collected up in this way?

It was a bigger story than I'd imagined, and at the centre of it was Teacher. I was determined now, more than ever, to get the story, the whole story. I would do whatever was necessary.

But I really couldn't do very much stuck on my bed in my hotel room. I needed access. I needed to get to Teacher, to get to the other gang members. I wanted to see the other hotel rooms, I wanted to see the graveyard. I had to see the healing, *see* it; I needed evidence.

I wrote a letter, to Teacher. It said:

'Before he hanged himself, he gave me a message which he said I was to give to you, only to you. I'll tell you what it is, but face to face only. I won't speak to any of your intermediaries.'

I gave this to the Son who brought me my pizza and Coke.

'Will you give it to him?' I said, and he said, 'I'll pass it along.'

So again I was waiting, again chewing my nails in anticipation. But this time he didn't have it all his own way. I had something he wanted, and he'd come and get it eventually. Of that I was certain. His vanity would compel him.

So I was staying then.

The thought surprised me, but it was a fact. I wasn't going anywhere until I got what I wanted. There was nothing else that I had to do, nothing else mattered at all. Fiona had become a speck on the horizon, a little puff of smoke, getting further away all the time. I would catch up with her again, soon, just as soon as I got my story. As soon as I understood. I owed it to myself, to Fuckyou, to however many others there were who had got mangled in this mill. That's what I told myself, anyway.

45

Could it really have been that easy?

He arrived at my room very late; I was asleep. I heard the key turning and, opening my eyes, saw a flash of light from the chain on his cap. His eyes seemed to flash for a moment too, like a cat, but I think that must just have been a trick of the light.

I felt a bolt of excitement through me, in my bowels and bladder, a surge of something. He didn't turn the light on, and very little came in through the window, so again I didn't see his face fully, but I could feel him, he had an immensely powerful presence somehow. It's the quality that people usually call 'charisma', though all that usually means is that there is something serious, something sexy. I've conducted interviews with charismatic people before, and come away with the memory of a powerful occasion but nothing on the tape recorder beyond evasion and cliché and double-talk. They are charismatic only in the flesh: it is a quality of the body, like weight or smell or the animal magnetism of the old hypnotists. In a silent film it would be indicated by a strong backlight and a wild, sparkling quality in the eyes.

He moved round the darkened room, and I followed him with my eyes. I could smell oil and leather, the leather creaked a little. The light, such as it was, occasionally flickered on the peak of his cap or his belt buckle, but mostly he was simply a moving darkness against the gloom of the room.

I felt that he was smiling, though I couldn't see his face. I knew he was looking at me, very hard, I was certain. I wasn't afraid, I just felt that excitement, that thrill, in the cavities of my body.

'I heard you wanted to talk to me,' he said finally, and his voice was thick and strong and sweet, like the tea sometimes given to people who've been in an accident and had a nasty shock.

'I've been wanting to talk to you for a while now,' I said, and I heard him laugh gently.

'I know you have,' he said.

Strangely, after all the time I'd spent waiting for him, waiting for this meeting, I found that I didn't really have anything to say. It seemed oddly irrelevant somehow. I felt as if I was sunbathing in his charisma, swimming in it, breathing it.

'Something about Len?'

'Who?'

'Len. Spamhead.' Again he laughed.

'Yes. That's right.'

I expected him to say something, maybe something like what a shame it was or how shocked everyone had been. I suppose what I was expecting was the usual banality that a death brings out in people.

'What was it?' he said after a few moments of silence. His voice was gentle, patient.

I hadn't yet thought of anything.

'What did you feel about his death?' I asked, to gain some thinking time.

'A death is a death,' he said, and then, 'Don't you want to tell me what you have to tell me?'

'OK. He said, "I don't think he got it all out, it's started coming back."'

'I see.'

'He said I should tell you that. Then he – '

'Yes. Yes.'

He fell silent again.

'Was there something else you wanted to tell me?' he said, out of the blue, and I was surprised that he was still there, that I was still there. He seemed to have been with me for a considerable period of time, a month, perhaps.

'Yes, actually there was something else.'

This was completely unscripted, and I had no idea of what was going to come out of my mouth until I'd said it:

'Sometimes I see things too.'

I considered this statement with some interest. I had no idea where it had come from or where it was going to.

'I saw a rope round his neck. Before he died. Days before,' I said, and Teacher moved gently in the darkness, like the shadow of a branch in a wind. We were riding the waves of a tension, as if we were on opposite ends of a see-saw, perhaps the same one that Biceps had sat on with him in the playground of the service station. He was watching me so closely that I could feel the strength of his concentration playing over me. I began to feel unlike myself, a stranger, in this strange hotel room. I might say anything.

'I can see things. I can see something in you.'

He shifted again.

'Tell me. Tell me what you can see.'

My head felt as if it were being gently squeezed, from inside. My fluids and cavities were behaving most oddly, swelling and rolling. I looked over at the dark from where the voice had just come. Could I see anything?

And then I suppose you would have to say that I had an inspiration. I really did see something, or at least I was able to believe I did with complete certainty, at that moment, in that room. I was inspired, and I said:

'I can't tell you, but I can show you. Where it is in you.' He said, all right. Show me then, and I leaned forward, I sat up and leaned towards him, I stretched out my hand and I touched him. It was his crotch.

'There.' I said. 'There. It's there. Isn't it?'

He didn't move, didn't flinch, didn't back away. He didn't speak. I felt appallingly foolish suddenly and took my hand away.

'Sorry.'

'Don't be sorry.'

'I'm sorry.'

'Don't be.'

I'd been in this room for too long, it was starting to get to me. I heard his moving, then I heard the door opening, and a ghost of light fell in from the corridor. It caught the side of his face, part of a mouth and an ear. Then he shut the door again, and the charisma left the room with him.

I put the pillow over my head and tried to sleep.

179

46

I seemed to have hit on something. Entirely by accident, or whatever word is appropriate to a freakish mood in a half-waking condition, I became a stranger and said something, and, like a cocky novice with an unsteady hand and cheap equipment, I hit the target first time.

If I had needed any further convincing that Teacher was a genuine victim of his own delusions, his apparently meek swallowing of my absurd demonstration would have been enough. You would need to be seriously deluded not to see it for the sideshow it was. It was as if he was an Edwardian table-rapper who had not only convinced himself that the spirits really were speaking to him, but that the eerie new guest with the husky ethereal voice was also in touch with the Other Side, and could truly produce ectoplasm. He believed in his own powers so completely that he could believe them to be present in others. Not a fool, then, not a fake, but more dangerous than either, a profoundly convinced, profoundly deceived individual. I was certain of that now.

My own freakish inspiration, my lucky guess? Well, take just about anyone, or at least just about any man, and tell them that they'd done wrong sexually, and they'd grin and admit it. Oh yes. *Many* times. In fact, there was this *one* time— Only in his case there was no grin, and whatever it was was deep and dark and possibly very nasty. He had clearly healed himself of something, and it was something that he feared very greatly, something that might come back. That was the target I'd hit. His bad stuff.

Fuckyou's noose: could I be certain that the thing I *thought* I'd been seeing behind his head was a rope? It could as easily have been a hank of hair or just nothing, a persistent trick of the light. It was easy to tell yourself afterwards that you'd known all along. I always *knew* he'd do something like that, you say, in fact come to think of it I had the most peculiar dream the other night, and he was in it. And so on. Anything rather than believe the truth, that we know nothing, that we live and die and there is nothing. We stumble about blind and convince ourselves that we see the colours, the lights. We tell everyone about it, and they say, you as well?

Teacher sent word, through Big Ears, that I could come and go at will, unmolested. It was understood that I was to be accompanied at all times, and that any attempts to sneak away would not be smiled upon. But I was to be let out of the hotel room.

Big Ears, all too obviously, didn't like any of this. It was not the usual way things were done, and he was protective of his leader, more so even than the others. I think he saw himself as favourite son, even perhaps next in line. He feared being usurped, I could see it. I mean it was evident. He made no attempt to keep his feelings to himself, in fact he was commendably frank:

'No-one around here likes you too much, not after that trick with Spamhead. We're watching you. You think we're easy? You try us, man. We're hard, better believe it.'

I assured him I would be sure to keep that thought *firmly* in the forefront of my—

'Listen.' He came very close again, and I tried to keep my place but found myself backed against the wall. His body was on mine at the chest, the belly, the knees. His arms formed a cage round me. He was a good head taller, at least three stone heavier. I could smell the oil and the sweat. His smell was stronger than mine.

'Listen brother.' His voice was an angry whisper, hoarse. 'You found out something about Spamhead. You found out that he was desperate, and so you gave him money to betray himself. You gloated, because he was venal and stupid and you could buy him. Then he had to hurt himself, very badly, because of you. You know what you said? You said, not *my* fault, no dirt under *my* fingernails. Now you've got some secret message and you can see things and so now you can come out and ask a lot of stupid questions. Mr Nosy. You think you know some things. Let me tell you something now. We're not new to this. I've been with Teacher for twelve years. We've had hundreds through here, hundreds. They come, they go. We've had some freaks, I mean *freaks*, people you wouldn't want to be in a room with alone. Very bad. We've had people who have done things that you probably can't imagine. And amongst them we've had people who can do things, know things, see things. They've got secret messages, they can talk to God, they've got Satan's telephone number, they've got angels living in them, they've got the spirits of *animals* in them, they pick up demons like you pick up shit on your shoes, they've got devils in the pockets of their trousers. Serious, heavyweight people. So if you imagine that you can see or do or know anything that is going to interest *me*, then I'd like to see it, I truly would.'

He grinned, and it was not an attractive sight. His teeth looked narrower and sharper than is usual. His body was crushing me. His sweat was rolling down his sides and dripping onto me. He licked his lips.

'The world outside, that's gone now. Wave bye bye. You're with us now.' He shoved himself off me. Cold air came between us. I wiped my mouth.

47

There were twelve rooms in the hotel. Five of them were occupied, not including mine. They were all kept locked. I was allowed to go in when they had their food taken in. I wasn't allowed to ask questions.

On this first occasion it was my companion from the van, Moustache, who was doing the feeding. The food was in padded pizza delivery bags, but even so it hadn't improved in its journey to the hotel. He had a complicated, grubby and much folded list of what was for whom, but even so he didn't appear to be entirely certain. The whole undertaking seemed to defeat him. I guessed that he'd been smoking just a little bit. There seemed to be far too much food.

Room four. Moustache fumbled what he thought were the right things out of the bag and unlocked the door.

The room was empty. I looked at Moustache, who was depositing the food onto the dressing-table.

'It's OK, he's in the bathroom.'

'I see.'

'I mean *always*. He's *always* in the bathroom.'

'What's he doing?'

'How do I know? Having a crafty wank for all I know.'

'All the time?'

'Guess what we call him.'

'Give up.'

'Randy.' He laughed, a ferrety little sound.

I looked round the room. An exact copy of mine, but laid out the other way round. Like me, he didn't seem to have any personal possessions, and the room was pristine. I wondered if there was a rule against bringing things in. I wondered if he had his jacket.

Moustache gestured me out. As he locked the door I said, 'No, that's not it,' and he said, huh?

'That's not why he's in there.'

'Oh yeah?'

'It's because he feels safe.'

'Uhuh?'

'Yeah.'

'How'd you know so much about it?' he said and then remembered. 'Oh right. You can see things. Ha fucking ha.'

'You don't believe it's possible?'

He spat.

'I believe it's possible he's in there – ' he made a gesture with his fist – 'you know?'

We carried on down the corridor, Moustache worrying at his list. He couldn't remember who was in what room, who wanted what, what was in what bag; he couldn't remember what the abbreviation NMS meant.

'Why's he here?' I asked, and Moustache smiled a secret, ugly smile.

'I can't tell you things like that,' he said, 'd'you really want to know?'

I nodded.

'Well it seems that he got a taste for breaking into people's houses and you know, making a mess in there, on the carpets and that. Like a fucking dog or something. He'd do it in the gardens as well. Can you picture that? Him creeping round your garden in the middle of the night, taking a crap on your lawn? Eh? He's a bit of a messy bastard actually. He heard about Teacher and said he was possessed, the usual thing. He kept saying he had an "unclean spirit" and in his case I would say that was about right.'

'What's Teacher going to do about him?'

'He'll do what he does.' Again the nasty little smile. 'Oh yeah.'

He was rummaging in the bag. He took food packages out and opened the door of number seven.

The occupant was standing at the window. He half turned as we came in and I was shocked. His face was ashy white and drawn. He was wearing a good suit, but his shirt was filthy and the room was full of his smell.

He thanked us and turned back to the window. His voice was faint and scratchy. His face contained no trace of vitality. He looked stolidly ahead, a faint, puzzled frown on his face.

'How ya feeling, Mr Turner?'

He shrugged, almost imperceptibly.

'Don't let it get cold.'

We left the room, left him standing in ghastly immobility by the window. Moustache gestured to me to bend down, so I could look in through the keyhole. Mr Turner was motionless, his head sunk down a little. I wasn't even certain that he was breathing.

'Mr Turner,' Moustache said. 'Come round here any time, night or day, and that's where he is. He must eat but I've never seen him doing it.'

'What's the matter with him?'

'You mean to tell me you can't *see* it?' he said and gave me one of his crafty looks. I said no.

'He thinks he's dead. I mean actually, really dead. He thinks this is hell. He believes Teacher can get him out. And we're all devils or something. Or angels. Hell's Angels. Ha ha.' He cackled, a peculiar, lewd sound. 'Right,' he said, 'number ten, number ten.' He squinted at his list. 'Can't read this fucking thing.' He pulled something out and we stood outside the door.

Number ten was lying on his bed, flicking a pen at the ceiling. The curtains were drawn.

'Hello,' he said and smiled. 'My friend with the moustache and someone new. What's your name, friend?'

'Robert.'

'Robert. Greetings.' He inclined his head in a neat little bow. 'You're not in costume I see?' He gestured at my comparatively clean jeans and lack of conspicuous leather or ripped sleeves. 'Didn't they have anything in your size? Or is leather just not your thing?' He turned back to Moustache. 'Did you remember about the mushrooms? Why do I even ask? I *know* you didn't.'

Moustache shrugged.

'Oh yeah. NMS. I knew it meant something. No mushrooms.' He grinned.

'You can't help but like him can you?' said the man

on the bed, twisting the pen round his fingers, and seemingly speaking to no-one in particular. 'After all he can't help it, now can he? He probably means well. He's probably very kind to animals and children. And he's got such a likeable face, wouldn't you say?'

'Oh yeah.' Moustache was grinning all over, loving it.

'And then I suppose a lot of his *higher* powers have gone into the moustache, you see. People think you can just *grow* a moustache like this, but that is not the case. You have to *will* it into being, you have to create it, imagine it, millimetre by gruelling millimetre. Isn't that so?'

'Right right.' He nudged me, and gave me a secret wink.

'Just one word of warning: don't ever try for a beard. You'll never manage it. It'd be too much for you. You've suffered enough already. We all have.'

Moustache grinned and nodded, and we left.

I asked my question and Moustache said: 'He said he discovered that some people were carrying little devils round on their shoulders. Just little devils, about so high. He could see them grinning at him. He was on a bus, and he realized that the man sitting across from him had one of these devils on him. So he did what anyone would have done in the circumstances and tried to tear it off with his fingernails. He got about half of it off, he said, when he realized that he didn't like what was underneath, it was messy. The devil was really stuck in there, really rooted in. It was screaming at him, spitting. He did this a couple of times, and he always managed to get away somehow, but he thought he should wear a disguise now, cos they were looking for him, you know? So he started wearing some stupid mask, but it got so that he couldn't always be sure if he had it on or not. Yes?' Moustache made a gesture against his temple: nutcase. 'And then one day he tried to take it off, except that he didn't have it on. He kept trying anyway until someone interrupted him and he ran. When we got him in here Doc sort of had to stitch parts of his face back on. He doesn't look too terrific, to tell you the truth. He's said he won't do it again until he's seen Teacher. Teacher's asked him to wear gloves but he forgets. You can have a laugh with him, though, you know what I mean? He's got a real funny streak.'

'He seemed very interested in your face,' I said, and Moustache laughed.

'Funny bloke. Maybe he won't try to rip bits off me if he likes my face.'

'He might think he can improve on it.'

'Yeah well I carry a knife, you know, so he better not. OK let's see, let's see, what's next – '

He was meandering down the hall, past number twelve, the room next to the blackened doorway of my old room. The key was in place. I turned it, pushed the door open. Someone lying on the bed. 'My head aches,' he said, 'my head really aches. I need the doctor. Send the doctor. I've got a headache.' I watched him for a moment. Moustache was halfway down the hall, unlocking one of the doors.

'OK, hold on, just hold on a minute – '

I caught up with him outside number fourteen. 'OK. Last one.'

We were in and out of number fourteen fast. Moustache opened the door, looked round for a second and dropped the food onto the night table, then pulled the door to.

'What's the matter? Can't I see him?'

'Not with me around. I'll tell you the truth, I don't like him very much. He's a little bit *weird*, if you know what I mean. He says there's a little man inside him that wants to come out. He can feel him trying to scratch his way out. We took him on a trip once, and he got up in the night and started eating the fucking soil. To bury the little fellow, you know? He nearly died. I asked him once how the little fellow got in there in the first place, and he said I ate him. So I don't really feel like hanging round with him, watching him eat, if it's all the same. Why have I got all this *food* left over?' he said, and I said:

'It's probably for me. Double surf burger, garlic bread?'

Moustache handed it over.

'So what are these fucking wings?'

I shrugged. 'Maybe they're your Hell's Angels wings.'

He grunted and spat. 'See things, huh? Right.'

48

I had put myself into an absurd position. If I was going to get the story I'd come for, then I was going to have to be healed. To be healed I would have to have something to be healed *of*, and not only that but I'd have to convince Teacher that it was true. Until that could happen I was stuck here, in this hotel with dead people and people with other people living inside them and so on.

The problem of course was that there was nothing whatsoever wrong with me, no demons, no delusions, nothing. When I looked in the mirror I saw nothing untoward, no noose round my neck, no sinister signs or ominous portents or any of that black magic crap, I just saw my face, same as always, and not a bad-looking lad if I did say so myself.

Could I invent something? I enjoy torturing animals, I eat dead babies, I worship the devil naked in disused churches? More like: I sometimes exaggerate the amount I'm paid for a story and I'm occasionally somewhat brusque with people I think stupid. Was that so terrible? Surely not. I tried saying aloud: 'I am possessed by Satan,' and found that I couldn't actually *say* it without putting on a foolish Boris Karloff accent or my Milton Keynes accountant voice. There was no way I could convince Teacher of any such disorder.

So how was I going to get my story?

All the gang members I'd spoken to so far about their healings had refused absolutely to say anything specific about what they'd had done to them. It just wasn't spoken of. If I could have found an ex-member, perhaps someone who'd become dissatisfied – someone, in fact, like Fuckyou – then they might have opened up. Fuckyou might have told me, had he lived, poor sod.

There just didn't seem to be any dissenting voices anywhere. The Sons were apparently solid in their loyalty to Teacher. The ones I'd seen waiting were in no condition to tell me anything, even if they'd known what I wanted to know. And if there were any living failures I didn't have access to them.

There was only one way forward, and that was for me to see someone else being healed, and I very much doubted that anyone particularly wanted me to. So I would have to do it by stealth. I would need to find out when and where, and without arousing too much suspicion. The fact that I already had quite a reputation for asking questions would help there. It would just be me being Mr Nosy again. Then I would have to hide out and try to see what was going on. I wondered if these things were done indoors or out, daytime or nighttime, in private or with an audience.

The first thing to do was to get more information. I ran the possible candidates through my head, and came up with the one I thought to be the weakest link. Stroker.

49

Stroker and I went for a ride. His cornering was decisive but considered, his accelerations were smooth and his road sense exemplary. To most of the others, road sense meant flashing your lights a great deal and swerving abruptly round unexpected obstacles. Shouting and hand signals of a wide and varied kind were optional, a refinement.

We rode out for miles, past fields and barns and hedges. Bleak, open countryside. It was a warm, still, overcast day; the light faded and then faded again, threatening rain. Even with Stroker at the wheel I didn't much relish riding on wet roads. *Cornering* on wet roads.

Stroker knew where he was heading for and we arrived in the early afternoon. We walked through a small wood of ash and sycamore. The light crept in, mottling the ground with patches of purple.

'Through here,' he said, and pushed through what looked like a solid wall of bramble and ivy. I followed him through and almost fell down a steep bank.

'Watch yourself,' he called out from the bottom, 'it's steep.'

I scrambled down beside him. We were in a long sunken avenue, with the banks veering up on either side covered in bramble and ground elder. The floor of the avenue was too shaded for anything much to grow apart from low creeping things, and there was a shallow carpet of leaves and twigs. It was clearly a disused branch line of some kind. The whole area was scarred with rail and tram lines, sidings, cuttings, all abandoned, overgrown, hopeless, given up.

'I used to come here a lot,' said Stroker, and then fell silent. We walked on and an odd shyness sprang up between us.

'Yeah, I used to come here with Lynn,' he said after a few minutes. 'My girlfriend. Used to be anyway. We split up though.'

'Because of the Sons?'

'No, this was before all that.' Another silence. 'We used to come out here of a weekend. I hadn't known her long, she was the sister of one of the ones I used to kick round with. Wasn't a gang or anything or a club, we just used to ride round together a bit. Had a bit of a laugh, you know. Then I met up with Lynn and I rode round with her instead. Pillion, you know. She was an interesting girl. She used to like it round here.'

'So what happened to her?' I wasn't really listening, I was just prompting him to keep him talking, then it wouldn't seem so odd when I asked about the next healing.

He went into a long story about Lynn and how she'd had to have an abortion and about how they hadn't felt the same about each other after that. The railway line stretched ahead, curving gently to the right.

'Then after that I'd come down here on my own.

Sometimes I'd spend the whole day here.'

I could make out something a couple of hundred yards ahead, some large structure. Stroker was droning on peacefully beside me, telling his tale of woe and desolation. It was a sweet, mournful sound, like the call of a forest creature.

'I used to go in there,' he was saying, and I realized what it was we were approaching. A railway tunnel. What were we doing here? I tuned back in to what he was saying.

'This is where he found me. I'd been here for days.' We were close to the tunnel opening now, a great brick section of a circle, and the cutting widened out into a flat arena, like the stage of an amphitheatre. I stopped.

'What were you doing down here?'

Stroker shrugged.

'Nothing.'

'Nothing?'

He stood on the rim of the tunnel, a simple shape against the yawning black hole.

'For how long?'

'When he found me I'd been in there for about four days.'

'How did he find you? How did he know where you were?' Again he shrugged, and it seemed a perilously small movement against that gaping mouth.

'He saw me.'

Stroker smiled at me over his shoulder for a moment, then walked into the tunnel. The tunnel at the end of the light. He took a few paces in and I couldn't see him, at all. I followed him.

The air changed dramatically, from big to small.

Suddenly there was no space and sound bounced about proving it. The walls were damp and crusty and pitted.

'I don't understand,' I said, and my voice was dreadfully small and localized, pitifully frail. 'I don't understand. What were you doing down here?'

'I can't remember,' he said, his voice a pale echo of my own, emphasizing the confinement. The darkness seemed to crush it down, extinguishing it like a flame. 'I know I was here, but I can't remember why. I think I was talking to someone, someone from inside the tunnel, but I don't see how that can be.' His voice sounded more distant.

Cold also. The tunnel was full of cold black air, and I had no idea how far it went.

'Stroker?' I couldn't see him. I couldn't see anything. Blind.

'Stroker?' I felt a little tug of cold air from further down the tunnel. I groped forward. 'Stroker? Hold on.'

'Do you want to know what he says I was doing, when he found me?'

I wasn't sure I did. 'Stroker? I can't see you.'

'He says I was standing in front of the wall. Touching it, trying to dig my way out. That's how I got my name. My fingers were all messed up. Bleeding.'

'How much further you going to go in, Stroker?'

No reply.

'Stroker?'

I didn't like the sound of my voice. I was in this tunnel trying to talk to someone, someone from further inside the tunnel. Feeling my way, not daring to turn my back, I edged out backward until the bricks fell away and the sky and the air returned.

'Stroker?' I shouted in, but there was nothing.

I sat on a ledge of low brick and waited. He was in there for, I estimated, about half an hour, perhaps a little more. He grinned as he emerged into the daylight.

'What kept you?' I said, and he smiled and would say nothing until we were walking back along the track, towards the bike.

'He came and found me, I don't know how; one minute I was in the tunnel, the next minute there he was. He took my hand away from the wall and said something like, "Are you ready to go?" and I said yes, and we left. He brought me back and I met the Sons. A while later he gave me my freedom and when I come here now it's all right and I don't need to stay.' His voice was still faint and faraway.

'How did he give you your freedom?'

Stroker shrugged.

'By seeing what was wrong and putting it right. Letting it out.'

'Yes OK but how.'

'I could probably have died in there. No-one knew where I was, they'd never have found me.'

'*Yes* but—'

'And he found me.'

'I've got to know, Stroker.'

'You will.'

'I need to know now.'

'No, I don't think you need to know quite yet. Not quite yet. Soon though.' His voice was all wrong, thick and laboured. I grabbed hold of him by the beefy shoulders, and shook him.

'Stroker, look at me.'

197

His eyes were fuzzy, and a small stupid smile played with his features.

'Did you take something while you were in there just now?'

'Uhuh.' He grinned and giggled. I got him to sit down.

'You're not going to be able to drive us back are you?'

He shook his head, blinking, licking his lips.

'OK.'

We sat with our backs to the bank. He was dreamy and unfocused, but entirely conscious. I decided to risk it.

'Stroker?'

'Uhuh?'

'Who's next for healing?'

'Who's next?'

'Yes.'

'Man in number fourteen.'

'The man with someone living inside him?'

'Uhuh.'

'When?'

'Huh?'

'When, Stroker?' He was with me, but not entirely with me. I felt certain that he wouldn't remember this conversation when he was himself again. At any rate he wouldn't be sure. I could probably convince him that he'd been talking to himself in the tunnel. He thought he'd left all that behind, he thought that Teacher had cured him of it. But I doubted that he was *certain*. I could probably plant a doubt, undermine his confidence, confuse him.

'Thursday night.'

'Where?'

'Field at the back of the old tyre place. Usual place, you know.'

'OK.' He was frowning now and shaking his head. I'd got all I needed, and he was starting to look confused and worried.

'OK. Go to sleep, Stroker.'

'Uhuh.'

'Dream dreams.' His eyes closed and his head fell against my shoulder. His breathing was deep and regular.

50

Stroker and I had had to spend the whole night outdoors. I'd considered getting him back to the tunnel mouth so we'd be protected overnight, but I didn't much care for the idea. So we stayed where we were. There was no rain, and the overhanging vegetation kept the wind off. Stroker slept peacefully, making hardly a sound. I couldn't sleep at first, and found myself again staring at the clouds. They were slower-moving this time, bigger, fluffier, more statuesque. Stroker woke up in the dark at some point, waking me as well, and wandered away to relieve himself, then returned and laid his head back against my shoulder. He woke up again, cross and confused in the early morning, and we rode back to the hotel in silence. He was clearly unsure of what had happened: this was all too obviously not the first time in his life that he'd woken up in circumstances that puzzled him, with a worrying gap in his memory. I wondered if he remembered taking me into the tunnel. I was fairly sure that he wouldn't remember our conversation afterwards. He certainly didn't refer to it. He did seem reluctant to meet my eye, however.

I felt I needed to be ready to get cleanly away after the session on Thursday, so anything I wanted to find out I'd have to find out soon. I'd decided that it would be useful to have before and after comparisons from the man in number fourteen, and so I had to get to talk to him. My idea was crude but, as crude ideas so often are, effective.

I was talking to Biceps in the corridor when I saw Doc coming out of number seven, where he'd been checking on Mr Turner.

'Doc? I think you'd better come quickly. There's something wrong with number fourteen.'

'Him? What do you mean?'

'I was outside his door earlier on and I heard him shouting.'

'Shouting? He doesn't shout.'

'Yeah he was. I heard him, something about getting out.'

'Are you certain it was him?'

'Well it was his room. Number fourteen.'

'OK. I'll have a look.'

He locked the door of number seven and went down the corridor, with Biceps and me following.

We stood outside number fourteen. Silent. 'He's quietened down not, but he was making a hell of a racket earlier on.'

Doc looked at me, then shrugged and unlocked the door. We entered the room. He was motionless on the bed, seemingly asleep. Not shouting. No sound.

'Mr Sellars?' Doc spoke firmly, demanding attention. The eyes of the figure on the bed flicked open.

'Mr Sellars? Are you feeling all right?'

There was nothing for a second or two, and I got

the impression of him gathering himself together, assembling himself.

'I'm perfectly all right, Steven.' His voice was deep, very steady.

'Are you sure? I understand you weren't feeling well earlier on?'

'Nothing to complain about. The condition is stable, as you medical people say. There is no change. We must watch and pray.'

'Would you mind if I made a quick examination?'

'I wouldn't mind in the slightest. Be my guest.'

Doc approached the bed, and I noticed that Biceps, consciously or not, took up a vigilant posture close by. Doc performed routine checks, pulse, temperature.

'No pain anywhere?'

'I have no pain, dear doctor, no pain.'

'And the little fellow?'

'Quiet today. Growing though. Will we get him out, do you think?'

'We'll get him out, Mr Sellars. He can't stay in there.'

'So I tell him. Perhaps he'll listen to your marvel man, your Teacher.'

'I know he will.'

'What'll happen to him then?'

All faces in the room turned to me; it was my voice.

Mr Sellars smiled, and sat up on one elbow. His face was disfigured by a tattoo across his forehead, it said LOVE OR DIE, and he seemed to have no teeth. His eyes glittered.

'Then,' he said, grinning fiercely, 'I'll eat the bugger!'

Outside the room, Doc pinned me against the wall.

'It would be better,' he whispered, 'if you didn't ask them any questions.'

'Is there something inside him? Has anyone done an X-ray?'

'Nothing shows up on any X-ray.'

'Then maybe I can see something.'

Doc unhanded me, slowly. There was clearly a conflict here. He didn't believe my 'sight' any more than any of the rest of them did, any more than *I* did. Teacher was the only one who did. But he was the only one who mattered.

'I'll give you two minutes with him. I'll be watching you. Don't give me any trouble. Don't do anything stupid. And don't try to be *clever*. He's not safe.'

I assented, and he unlocked the door and we went in. The eyes on the bed flicked open, the figure assembling itself again, from whatever pieces it had shattered into.

The light wasn't good and the man on the bed was indistinct, a slight, rumpled form. Doc went in first, then stepped aside.

'Did you forget something?' said the man on the bed, and I saw his flesh falling away, revealing a slighter, smoother, more pallid shape, naked, with limbs, a body, a face, a mouth. Teeth. It turned its pale, smooth head towards me. I backed away as the mouth opened and a sound came out, and Biceps caught me as I fell.

Doc came after me, and wanted to know what I'd seen. Nothing, I said, I'd seen nothing, there was nothing to see. Nothing.

51

Stroker came to see me. He still wouldn't look me in the eye. He asked me if I'd enjoyed the ride, and I told him I had. Then he asked what did I think of the tunnel? and I realized what he was up to. He was trying to find out the extent of the gap in his memory. Probably a well-rehearsed routine for him, I imagined. Whatever it was he'd taken in the tunnel, it had had a pre- as well as a post-amnesic effect. I gave him a puzzled look.

'The tunnel? Well what can I say? It's a fine tunnel.'

'Sometimes it has quite an effect on me.'

'It certainly does!' I said, and he laughed with me, but nervously. 'Where did you get to? You were in there for hours. I couldn't find you. I went in part of the way but I'd lost you, you were too far ahead.'

'Yes. Yes I went in first.'

'That's right. I followed you, then I thought I heard you talking to someone.'

'Talking – ?'

'But you couldn't have been, could you? So I suppose you must have been talking to yourself.'

'That's right. Yeah, I used to do that sometimes.' Another laugh: we're all a bit crazy round here!

'I couldn't hear what you were saying though. Then

you finally came out, and you didn't want to ride back cos you thought it looked like rain. So we camped out.'

'That's it.' He nodded a few times. 'Yeah, I was talking to myself in the tunnel.'

He didn't like that idea much. That was the sort of thing Teacher was supposed to have cured him of.

'Well I thought that was what it was anyway. Could have been an animal or something. Could have been a fox or a bird that got in there maybe.'

'Yeah. Cos the sound in there, it's really hard to know *what* you're hearing.'

'Unusual acoustics.'

'Acoustics.' He seized on the word, as a drowning man seizes a piece of driftwood. '*Weird* acoustics in there.'

'That'd be it. It probably wasn't you at all.'

'No because you see I don't really *do* that kind of thing any more.'

'Must have been the acoustics then.' I began to regret this conversation. All I'd meant to do was cast some doubt on his recollection. I hadn't meant to bring back his old demons.

'But we had a nice talk though. Before we went in the tunnel.'

'We did indeed. You told me all about your girlfriend and so on.'

'That's it.'

'And then, later on –'

'Yeah?'

'Well you seemed a bit *tired* when you came out of the tunnel, so we didn't talk much.'

'No. We probably just lay down and went to sleep.'

'We did.'

'Yeah.' He smiled and shrugged. Then he leaned forward and whispered, with a hint of a blush, 'You see, sometimes I forget things.'

'Really?'

'Sometimes. I have this medication, and it makes me forget things sometimes.'

'Oh?'

He sat back, then leaned forward again.

'But I'm sure I don't talk to myself any more.'

'I must have mistaken what I heard.'

'Because of the –'

'Acoustics.'

'Yeah.'

There was a shadow on his arm, just below the elbow. It shifted as he moved and I couldn't see it clearly, but it could have been a syringe, the needle still stuck in the vein, hanging from his arm. A needle full of heroin, too much heroin. I was suddenly terribly worried for him.

'Yeah OK.' He sat back again and the shadow slipped away out of sight. 'You see, I used to get scared in that tunnel. I used to talk to people, except there wasn't anyone there, only me. You know? Sometimes they'd talk back to me, tell me things. They'd say come in further, come in a bit further. It was as if I forgot who I was. Then I would suddenly, you know, remember. I'd come to, and I'd be standing in the tunnel. In the dark. No-one there. Each time it happened, I'd be a bit further in. The time Teacher found me, I'd got so far in that I couldn't remember how to get out again. I couldn't see anything, and I got scared, so I tried to dig myself out. My hands were all bleeding.' He smiled, a quick, embarrassed grimace. 'Stupid isn't it? But I nearly died in there. That's what the voices were trying to do, to pull me in, so far that I would never get out and die in there. Sometimes I got so scared that I would just stand there, for hours, not daring to move. Worst of all,' another twitch of a smile, 'was that I was starting to like it, while it was happening, I wanted to go in further, I wanted to stay. I thought I would turn into one of the voices. I wouldn't be so, you know, so bloody *lonely* all the time.' 'Lonely' came out hard, through ground teeth. Again the smile. 'I was really sick.'

He met my eye, and I was certain that he was going to die soon. He was too vulnerable, too damaged, to last. 'So that's why I asked you, about the talking to myself. You see, if I was talking to myself, that would mean I was going back to what I used to be. Before Teacher. Do you see?' He was pleading with me.

'I'm sure it wasn't that,' I said, 'in fact the more I think about it the more sure I am.'

'Really?'

'Yeah.'

He seemed to be disintegrating under my hands, like a rotten board.

'Maybe I was talking to you, after I came out of the tunnel,' he said. 'Maybe that was it.'

'Could be. Yes.'

'But you can't remember what we were talking about? You see, when I've had my medication I say things I shouldn't. Sometimes. I've got into trouble with that before. I didn't say anything I shouldn't have done, did I?'

'No Stroker, you didn't.'

'Oh God I did didn't I. Oh God – '

'Stroker, just calm down now – '

'Oh God oh God – ' He was turned away, so I couldn't see his face. I leaned forward, gripped him by the arm, tried to twist him round.

'Everything's OK.'

'I wasn't talking to anyone in no tunnel, I was talking to you, I shouldn't have talked to you. Why did you want me to talk to you? I didn't want to talk to you, you kept asking me questions, I didn't want—'

'Please, Stroker,' I was shaking him, trying to make him listen to me. 'Stroker everything will be fine, believe me,' I said, though I knew it would not. He pulled away from me. He wouldn't meet my eye any more. I didn't blame him.

I dreamed about him that night. He was in the tunnel, standing unsteadily, his head wobbling, holding his syringe. I heard voices, all around me. 'Don't listen to them, listen to me,' I was saying, but I couldn't make myself heard over the sound, he couldn't hear me. He disappeared into the whispering blackness. I went in after him.

52

Wednesday night, the night before the healing was scheduled, I had another nocturnal visit from Teacher. I didn't know if nighttime sessions were usual or if he was trying to visit me in secret. I realized I'd never actually seen his face in full light.

As before he didn't, at first, have much to say for himself. I woke up to find him watching me, and he laughed gently.

'Here we are again,' he said, and I laughed with him. He really was irresistibly charming, apart from anything else.

'I was just passing,' he said, 'so I thought I'd look in on you.'

'Don't you ever sleep?'

'I've got a lot to do.'

'You should get yourself a trainee.'

He grunted, and I could hear his clothes creaking as he moved round the room. 'Funny you should say that,' he said, and paused. 'Anyway, I was wondering – '

I kept track of where he was as best I could.

'I was wondering what you'd seen.'

'Seen?'

'I hear that you've been making the most of your liberty, asking lots of questions, visiting the guests.'

'I've always enjoyed company. I like to meet people.'

'And has anything struck you?'

I thought of Mr Sellars lying on his bed with his pallid companion, I thought of the confusion and pain in Stroker's eyes as he tried to piece together his recollection of our trip to the tunnel.

'The only thing that's struck me so far is that some of these people would surely be better off in a hospital.'

'Do you think so?'

'Well don't you? Mr Sellars, for example. He's a very sick man.'

'Is that what you saw? A sick man?'

'I'm not one for name-calling, but he's quite obviously insane. Surely he should be in a hospital.'

'I understand that he has been in many.'

'Shouldn't he go back?'

'They have released him. They can't help him any more. They think he is being cared for. In the community, apparently. We, presumably, are that community.'

'No offence, but I really don't think this is quite what they meant – '

'You doubt their wisdom? So do I. I think that the reason they have failed Mr Sellars so completely is that they have failed to recognize that his sickness is a sickness of the soul.'

His voice was conversational, with no trace of the zealotry or the tiresome fervour that would usually accompany such statements.

'So how do you treat a sick soul?'

'With love. With strength. With *insight*, God's insight.'

'And you have those things?'

'There are certain services that I am able to perform, with my maker's help. I am less interested in naming or describing them than in using them.'

'I've noticed that no-one around here is very keen to talk about what those services may be.'

'You saw Mr Sellars.'

'Yes I did.'

'What did you see?'

'Nothing.'

'Nothing?'

'That's right. I saw a seriously deranged man.'

'You also, I think, have some reluctance to discuss the things that you are capable of.'

'I'm not capable of anything.'

'I think you are, more than you realize. You must go carefully, my friend, softly. But you must use what you've had given to you. It's a covenant. It's a trust.' He was on the move again. 'You are the kind of man who likes to do deals. This for that. Shall we do a deal? Trade stories like old men on a fishing trip?' There was a delicious tang of irony in his voice.

'What kind of deal do you have in mind?'

'You are interested in methods. Nuts and bolts. You have a nuts and bolts kind of mind. So I could show you some of the nuts and the bolts. You could perhaps watch me working. In return you could tell me what you saw in room fourteen. What else you've seen.'

'I see.'

'You see some things and not others. I believe it's what is sometimes called the Human Condition.'

'I don't understand,' I said. 'I don't understand why you're so interested in my capabilities.'

' "Interested". What a dull, squat little word. I don't have "interests". I think you could be of use. You could help me. And I could help you.'

'Help me? Or heal me?'

'That will, I think, become clear.'

'Let me think about it.'

'Of course.'

He was leaving, and I realized how strong his presence was by how conscious I was of his absence. It was like a drug leaving the body. You wanted it again, more of it.

He was right, of course. We weren't talking about interests, but needs. He appeared to be offering me what I was planning to take by stealth, the details, the nitty-gritty. The story. Poor Stroker had perhaps betrayed himself for nothing. But in return I would have to pretend to become some sort of psychic X-ray machine, penetrating the inner darknesses of these crazed people, shining my bogus torch into their dripping caves. This little light of mine – Even if I could have done it I knew I didn't want to. The smooth, white head, the pale lashes flicking open, the mouth opening, and then the sound emerging— I was seeing things already. If I stayed much longer, who knew what I might start seeing next?

No. I would find a way of seeing the healing the next day, and then I would just get out of there. I had, I felt, seen just about enough. Nearly enough.

53

Late on Thursday afternoon I asked Moustache, who'd been assigned to accompany me for the day, if he'd give me a driving lesson. We rode out a few miles, and then he showed me the basics, gears, clutch, throttle, brakes front and rear. It was more intricate than I'd realized. The movements were finer than those for driving a car, and the whole machine was so light and responsive that it was easy to overcompensate.

I rode pillion as he instructed me, then I drove and he rode pillion. The next step, obviously, was for me to ride solo.

He stood by my side as I got into position, and gave me final instructions:

'Just take her easy. Take her steady, man. Be cool.'

I assured him that I was, that I would be. He slapped me on the shoulder, and I pulled away.

'Great!' he called out after me. 'You look great! Now, bring her back round.'

'Where's reverse?' I yelled, but I was fairly sure that he wouldn't be able to hear me over the engine noise. 'I can't find reverse!'

He ran a few steps towards me as I disappeared down the narrow road, the fields flat and bathed in evening sunshine.

'Turn her round!' he was yelling. 'Bring her back round!'

I put her into second and roared away, my exhaust fumes, of course, resembling a comet's tail. He disappeared in my side mirror, dancing on the spot, holding his hands up to his mouth, yelling at me to come back.

I kept going for about half an hour. By the time I stopped it was nearly dark, a sweet, warm night. The crops were wafting their wet, heavy fragrances at me. I hadn't been aware of anyone following – Moustache would have had to walk back to raise the alarm, and by that time my trail would be cold. I was probably safe.

I can't pretend that it didn't occur to me just to keep going, to escape once and for all from that deranged bunch. But something asserted itself in me, I didn't know quite what it was. I thought at the time that it was professional pride. I still didn't have my story, and I wouldn't be satisfied until I did. I've always believed in seeing things through. I've always fancied that the stuff of which I'm made is stern stuff. Was, rather.

I was far enough away from them to be safe from pursuit. But my next move had to be to go back, to take myself back to their madhouse, secretly. If my information was correct they would be too busy with their healing session to be able to keep much of a look-out for me. And then of course they would hardly be expecting me. All they knew was that I had got away. I wondered if they might become nervous and postpone the healing, but I felt somehow that they wouldn't. I was certain that Teacher would find it impossible to believe that I would betray him, go to the police with my stories of false imprisonment, suicide, secret burials. I knew that he regarded me almost as a kindred soul to himself, a brother. Maybe even an apprentice. His daily trade was delusion, and he was himself its worst victim. I almost felt sorry for him.

There was also the little detail that I had been with Fuckyou when he died. Alone. I had been there and I had failed to report the death. Was I going to go to the police in the role of sole witness to a suspicious death? They might find it very difficult indeed to believe that someone would drive a screwdriver into his own head, unaided, just like that. What had I been doing while all this was going on? Sleeping? While he mutilated and then hanged himself? Some sleep, that. And why hadn't I got help before the others arrived? I had to admit, my actions were unclear, even to myself. I really didn't want to have to try and explain them to anyone else.

And then there was the matter of the money: could I prove that I hadn't killed him to get it back? I was less than anxious to be questioned about the incident. Could I prove that I had previously been held against my will? As far as anyone knew, I was just another devotee who had become embittered and decided to make trouble. I could hardly claim to be there unwillingly now, could I? It was only my own stubbornness, my greed for the story, that was holding me there, and whose fault was that? Teacher's? If anything, my continued presence amongst them looked suspicious, complicit even.

No, all in all, I wasn't going to go to the police, I knew it and Teacher knew it. So the healing would certainly go ahead as scheduled.

The old tyre place, Stroker had said. I thought I knew where he meant: there was a scrapyard about a mile from the hotel, on the A52, the Ashbourne road, right out in the middle of nowhere, and the far end of it was marked by a high wall of used tyres. There was a chain-link fence round the perimeter, and the night guards were all ex-clients of Teacher. I had ascertained that the yard was owned by someone who was related to whoever it was that owned the hotel. They really were quite a scruffy little Mafia. It would all come out in my piece.

I rode back to within a few hundred yards of the scrapyard. I dismounted and pushed the bike the rest of the way, which was no easy task. I was beginning to understand why the bikers all seemed to have such overdeveloped physiques: it took quite a lot of simple physical strength just to manoeuvre one of these things around. Not for the first time I reflected with great tenderness on the discreet charm of my Saab, its elegant lines, its refinement and power.

I parked the bike, pointing the *right* way, as close as I dared, and crawled towards the perimeter fence. No-one seemed to be around. I edged round the fence until I was screened by the wall of tyres. I climbed up and made myself a comfortable seat, a nest, so I could lie still, see clearly but not be seen. This was all assuming, of course, that I was in the right place, but I was sure I was. I was feeling superhumanly confident, as I got myself ready. It was a mood that had been growing in me for some time. I couldn't fail.

I made myself comfortable in my nest, and surveyed the scene. It was a very suitable location. The wall of tyres was an effective screen from one side, the north side, then there was a clear arena in front, and then a small building, a brick shed of some sort. I guessed this was where the night-watchmen would sit out their uneventful hours. It was hidden from the road, set back behind a long two-storey corrugated-iron structure with barred windows. From the road all you could see was the top of the wall of tyres and part of the fence. It was as good as private.

No-one was about. I dared to leave my nest and scale down the wall of tyres and drop into the yard. I stood by the brick shed and looked up. I could see the place where I had settled, but I was sure I wouldn't be spotted through the tyres. Even if someone had been looking for me, it would be next to impossible to make me out. I would be thoroughly hidden. I jumped back up and hauled myself to the top again, then dragged over to the other side and settled myself once more. I had no idea how long I would have to wait. I wished I'd brought something to drink. The night drew in around me.

54

They arrived about an hour later. I counted twenty bikes, which must have been just about the whole complement. They parked in a wide semicircle, and again enormous care was taken to dress the line. In so far as there was a formal uniform they were wearing it, caps with chains and badges, leather jackets with the chapter logo on the back, sleeveless denim jackets, engineer boots. The leather and chrome glittered in the accumulated glare of the twenty headlights. There was some effort to focus the beams on the wall of the brick shed, but this was only partly accomplished, to the accompaniment of a colossal growling and roaring. I spotted Deputy Dawg, who seemed to be having some difficulty directing his beam onto the right place. People sat and stood in the warm air, and there was a murmur of conversation and occasional laughter.

After a while Teacher came out into the crisscrossed beams of light and stood near the focus, against the wall of the shed, and I saw his face, clearly, for the first time. A cock-eyed, asymmetrical thing, broken nose with a flat bridge, slightly twisted. The eyes, of course, sorrowful, menacing, sexual. The mouth luscious and orificial under the heavy, drooping moustache.

He stood in the crossed headlights and there was

scattered applause and catcalls. He acknowledged a comment off to his right, and for a moment it was Bruce Forsyth introducing *Play Your Cards Right*.

'OK.' His voice was clear and loud, but also relaxed, conversational. 'O-K. We all know why we're here. In a few moments we're going to try to do whatever we can for one of our brothers. But before we do that I'd like to say a few words – '

Good-natured heckling, as at a wedding when the bride's father says he'll try to keep it brief.

' – well maybe more than just a few – '

laughter

' – about why I'm here.'

The fragrance of cannabis floated up to me. The gang were in pairs and threes, sitting astride their bikes or standing nearby, their attention intermittent between Teacher and themselves. From my grandstand view they looked almost artificially posed, film extras.

'As one or two of you may know, I haven't always been the clean and sober pillar of the community that you see before you now. I used to take a drink, I used to smoke. I used to fuck. I used to do all these things an *awful* lot. And I was happy, because I knew no better, God help me, than a pig in shit. I had quite a time, I won't try to deny it, anything I wanted I had it. Even when I didn't want it all that much, I had it anyway. This went on for years. Years.

'And then a strange and terrible thing happened. I was riding, drunk, high, along a long, dark stretch of road, when I was flung to the ground. I could say there was a great light, but there was no light, or I could say I heard a voice on high, but there was no voice. But I was flung down, and I was *filled*, and I was *changed*. I saw my maker and he was beautiful.' His voice was lower now, and as his voice dropped the attention of the group focused more closely on him, as if riding on the intersecting beams of light. He had made this confession many times before, I was sure. He was waiting for something, building himself up, circling round something. His hand was at his crotch, stroking, teasing.

'And then after that I could see things. I could see the pain and the sorrow and the despair. I could see the poisons and the impurities in the flesh, and in the blood. I was able to see the bad stuff. And that wasn't all. Because I said, why are you showing me these things? Why are you letting me see all this?'

He paused and turned round slightly. He had everyone's full attention now. He turned back.

'Why?'

He looked round the circle of watching figures, his handsome face puzzled, pained, troubled.

'Why are you showing me this? Do you think it's pretty? It isn't. I look and I see veins and arteries and cavities full of poison and hate and vileness. I see bodies full of bitterness, I see brains rotted away with desperation and hopelessness. I see lives blighted and blistered with emptiness and casual cruelty, delusion, terror. I see the *seed*, the *seed* inside these men, and it's blackened and rotted and tainted. Dear God.'

He looked down again.

'Dear God.' He was silent for a moment.

'Do you think it's easy to look at these things? To

be shown those things that normally go concealed? Do you?'

He paused again.

'It's like looking at the night in the daylight. It's like seeing under all the stones in all the pits. The death of the self.'

He was standing bathed in the light of twenty headlights; his skin, damp with sweat, was glistening under the ferocious light. The hollows of his face were ink black and hard-edged. He was working himself up, waiting for something.

'But that wasn't all. You showed me these things, but you also showed me what to do about them. You gave me the power to draw out the bad, to suck it out, to release it, to relieve the body from its baleful influence. You taught me how to *free* the body. With your guidance and help.

'And that is what we have to do now, with our brother, Mr Sellars. He is sick. He needs our insight, your insight. He needs our force. Your force, Lord.'

I noticed for the first time a figure sitting astride one of the bikes. His head was bowed. He wasn't in leather or cap, he had no visible Sons insignia. One of the Sons, one I didn't recognize, was behind him: I realized that the hand on the shoulder wasn't merely resting but was actually holding him up. It was the man from number fourteen, Love or Die, Mr Sellars. The one who had someone living inside him. He looked like he was dying. I suddenly felt very uneasy on his behalf. I felt again, very acutely, the absence of any recognized authority; no doctors, no police. This was the Wild West, and Mr Sellars was completely at its mercy. I feared for him. I even entertained a short-lived fantasy about swooping down from my eyrie amongst the tyres and rescuing him, fighting my way through the massed ranks of leathery bikers, carrying him out to a place of safety somewhere. A very short-lived fantasy.

Teacher was still speaking. His delivery was altering subtly: the conversational unaccustomed-as-I-am-to-public-drinking jocularity was gone now, and a low, whispering, husky tone was replacing it. His words were changing also, becoming somewhat more convolute, technical even, as he searched for whatever it was that he needed. This, I felt, was more like himself. This was the language of the 'statutory agencies' slip I'd heard on the radio show. He seemed to need a certain formality, or perhaps just a clarity of tone, to get where he had to get to. The precise terms of his contract with whatever he felt was out there helping him. His maker. He needed to set it all out, define it exactly. I heard words like 'intercession' and 'covenant'. I was watching Mr Sellars: I noticed that Doc was standing just a few feet away from him and was also watching him, intently. I felt that he too was waiting for something, for some sign. I wondered what had been done to Mr Sellars already to get him this far.

Teacher's voice rang out again.

'We have been made and we have grown. Somewhere along the way we start to take in the bad stuff, from all around us. Sometimes it finds us, sometimes we find it. It gets in, it finds a way in, and it starts to grow.

'I first got drunk when I was twelve years old; I

223

drank so much I was sick. After that I didn't drink anything for three years. Then at fifteen I met a girl and we used to get drunk together and fuck. This became an obsession. When her parents said I couldn't see her any more I got drunk and waited outside her house for her father. I had a knife. I slashed his face and stomach and he collapsed. Then I called an ambulance for him. I was put under psychiatric care, and I attended a rehabilitation centre for young offenders. The varieties of evil I saw there were so many and so sophisticated that I fell, I freely confess it, I fell many times. I committed uncleanness with men, which is an abomination, and when I got out of that place I continued to practise my abomination, for money. For money. Except it wasn't really for money.' He scanned his audience. Some of them looked sheepish, embarrassed. They glanced away, at the floor: they had heard all this before, but still it had the power to unsettle them. They didn't like this uncleanness with men thing, they looked as if they would have preferred just to skip over it and get on with the next part.

'Not really for the money. I did it because I knew it was forbidden, and because I was starving for love of any kind. I was introduced to the less expensive recreational narcotics, the lighter fluid, the glue, the solvents. Once I nearly died, suffocating on a plastic bag full of glue. I was seventeen, alone in a shop doorway, shivering. I wanted to die. Every breath I took, it fed the bad which was by then lodged securely inside me. I fell further, more often. Then one night I was with a man, he gave me something, I don't know what it was, but when I found myself coming to, his head was smashed in against the side of the bathroom sink. I took his money, his cheque-book, his cards. He had a great deal of cash, also a not insignificant amount of cocaine, which was a new drug for me. My hands were sticky with his blood, the money was covered with blood. I was shaking, terrified, exhilarated. Something inside me was saying: do it again. Do it again.

'I bought a second-hand Yamaha, for cash. I thought I was free. But it wasn't me, it was the bad stuff that had got free. The balance had shifted and it was now bigger than me. It was starting to get so that it was on the outside and I was living inside it. I was getting smaller and weaker as it grew stronger and taller and more powerful. It was even beautiful, more beautiful than I was. Attractive. Seductive even. I fell, I pulled others with me, I planted bad stuff in them. The ground was soft and fertile, sweetly scented.

'I was shrivelling away, to nothing. I found myself driving down dark roads, roads I didn't want to travel down. Roads that led to terrible places. And I found I couldn't go back. No reverse.'

He smiled, and there were a few murmurs from the gang. I thought I heard someone say Amen, but I couldn't be sure.

'No reverse. The bad thing that I had almost become straddled the bike, strong, hard, swollen with blood and sex, irresistible. It loved the power and the violence. It needed more. Always more.

'So that when someone now says to me, I did this or I did that, I am not disgusted, but I recognize it, I see it for what it is. There is nothing that any of you have done, nothing that anyone has told me, that I have not myself done, haven't myself thought.'

Doc was leaning over Mr Sellars's shoulder, and I saw him lift an eyelid, then pull the skin below the eye down. He took his pulse. He looked over to where Teacher was speaking, and some kind of signal passed between them. Teacher went over to him and they whispered together for a moment, Teacher's hand on Doc's neck.

Together they took hold of Mr Sellars and hauled him to his feet. He was walking, but only just. He stirred and seemed to be struggling as he became fitfully aware of what was happening to him. Big Ears emerged into the light and took Mr Sellars from Teacher's hands. He and Doc held the swaying, groggy figure, standing behind him, holding his arms rigid. His eyes opened and closed and he licked his lips frequently.

'OK.'

Teacher was pacing in front of him, shaking his hands, tossing his head. You could see him working himself up, like a boxer sparring on the way to the ring. The muscles worked across his shoulders and down through his arms, over his back.

'OK Lord.'

His voice was loud and declarative again. He paced up and down, in and out of the crossed headlights, and his movements were jerky and spasmodic.

Then he came to a standstill in front of Mr Sellars and I felt it for the first time that evening: his charisma, his power. He'd turned it on in himself. He'd found the switch.

226

He faced the gang, and held up his arms. There were calls from gang members, whistles. He was trans-figured.

'OK Lord. We're at this strange and terrible place again. I'm here again, and I'm going to ask you to come into me again. I'm going to ask you to cast me down again and fill me up. Like you did before, like you've done many times. I need you now, Lord, to come into me so that I can effect a change in this man here. He is in my hands Lord, and I am in yours.'

He turned back to Mr Sellars, who was drooling slightly. He took hold of his head and squeezed. His hands moved down over Mr Sellars's neck, then back up to his forehead. He traced the letters of the tattoo, then stroked the head, his fingers working through the hair, as if he were a chimpanzee grooming. He was murmuring, breathing hard, face tight and rigid.

Mr Sellars stirred and Doc and Big Ears held him more firmly. Teacher broke away from him and turned to the gang.

'Our brother is tormented, in pain. Our brother needs our help. Help me Lord.' More calls from the gang, shouts, murmurs. 'Help me.'

He stood silent for a moment, then he seemed to deflate. His chest fell and his head slumped. He walked quickly away, out of the glare, and I saw him approach one of the Sons, I didn't recognize him, he had long hair, it was forming into locks in places, matting together. Teacher spoke to him, and then I saw them embrace, a long swaying hug.

Doc whispered something to Mr Sellars, who swayed his head in response. Doc reached into the back pocket of his jeans and produced a small bottle, which he held to Mr Sellars's lips. Liquid spilled out round his mouth and down his chin, and Doc wiped his mouth with the back of his hand. Mr Sellars coughed, and Doc said something to Big Ears, who spoke quickly back.

Teacher, meanwhile, was talking to the boy with dreadlocks and laughing, as if they were just standing around somewhere with nothing particular to do. The rest of the Sons stood and sat, talking quietly and uneasily. Tense.

Teacher started back into the light, then ducked back and said something else to Dreads, who nodded and dropped down. He started to fiddle about with his bike, I couldn't see exactly what he was doing. Teacher ambled back to where Mr Sellars was being held upright. An abstracted smile was flickering over Mr Sellars's face, and I got the opposite impression of the 'assembling' I'd thought I'd seen as he lay on the hotel-room bed. He looked as if he could come to pieces at any moment.

Teacher again took hold of his face, then opened his shirt. He ran his hands down to the neck and shoulders, over the chest, down to the bare belly, bone white in the fierce light. His fingers were working, probing, what a doctor would call palpating. This changed to a gentle stroking motion over the belly.

'OK.'

He turned to the gang. He was back, and the gang coalesced around him, focused on him, on him alone. He raised his arms, and the gang swelled and murmured. His voice now was confident, loud, declarative again.

'Our brother here has a sickness. He has been subjected to treatments and cures of all kinds. Therapeutic procedures such as applying electricity to his brain, powerful chemicals which have reduced him to the state of an idiot, talking cures which have confused and enraged and humiliated him. And then, after all their ill-conceived meddling with him, when they'd finally finished fucking him over in this barbaric and appalling manner, they decided that he should be *released*. They *released* him. They promised him freedom, and instead they gave him misery and loneliness and neglect. His condition worsened, and that is what we have to grapple with tonight.

'When he came to me he was as sick and weary and desperate a man as I have seen. He told me his story, and I feel compelled to admit that I cried. We sat together in his room, and we cried. I spoke to the Lord and asked him to give me his wisdom and power to help him. Power to *see* him, truly to *see* him. He has told me that he believes there is another man, who lives inside him. The other man is growing stronger. He fears that he will escape. He fears also that he will never come out, or that he will destroy him as he emerges.

'Brothers. What drugs, what procedures, what regimen will cure this? I think I know his condition, because I have felt the same thing. During my period of degradation, before I was flung down and changed and filled, I too felt another inside me, a part of me that had rebelled, gone sour, gone bad, I felt it grow. I had no remedy, and in the end it took me over and nearly extinguished me. But there is great mercy and great power, and it came to me before it was too late, before I went out, like a match in a damp and draughty room.

'So Lord. Send me down your power.'

He was hot, glowing, I could see the passion flowing through his flesh. I noticed a movement beside him. Dreads was holding out a small rectangular tin. I thought of how Dreads had immediately started tinkering with his bike after Teacher's final comment to him. And I wondered: what was in that little tin?

'With your blessing, Lord, I will purge him, so that when you send me your spirit I will have his body whole and ready for you.' He held the tin up to Mr Sellars's mouth. Teacher murmured something and tipped the tin against his lips. I saw an expression come over Mr Sellars that filled me with shuddering disgust: it was an expression of evil, malicious and grinning and gleeful. A kind of smile. Then he opened his mouth, and Teacher poured in the liquid.

He drank it all, several mouthfuls. It dribbled down his chin again and dripped onto the concrete of the yard, enough to make a small puddle. It was iridescent in the glare of the light. Petrol.

Teacher stroked his stomach again, then moved away. A look passed between him and Doc. We were waiting. I didn't really want to watch any more. I wanted to get away, a long way away. Mr Sellars began to tremble, then retch violently. Doc turned him to face the wall of the shed, and he vomited. His legs gave way and Doc helped him to the ground. Teacher turned back again to the gang. Calls and whistles, vibration, heat, insanity . . . building, building. I could see the anticipation, the lust for whatever was to happen. They licked their lips, they shifted and gestured.

'I'm asking you Lord to come down into me now and take me over. Come into me and fill me and use me, Lord, for your purpose. Our poor brother here is ready for you now to deliver him out of the sickness that is in him. I give myself to you Lord – '

He gripped himself with both hands, at the nipples.

' – I turn myself over to you – I can feel you now – I can feel you now – '

His eyes were closed, his face held up to the sky, his legs spread wide.

' – come into me now, I'm ready for you now, come into me now, I can feel you coming now—'

He went rigid and jerked, and then his eyes flicked open, and now they were floodlights, flashing and scanning the darkness. I felt his eyes burning through the darkness and through the tyres, and I felt him looking at me, *seeing* me. He held the look for a second, then he turned back to Mr Sellars. Love or Die.

'Hold him up.'

Doc and Big Ears picked up the sagging figure and supported him, bracing his body against themselves. He appeared to have no real motive force of his own, except for the ghastly glimmer of a smile that seemed unable to leave his face.

Teacher paced in front of him a few times, eyes flashing, flexing his great arms, balling and relaxing his fists, surfing on the noise and heat and lust of the gang, nearly ready now, nearly ready now –

He stood in front of him and, taking careful aim, drove his fist into Mr Sellars's stomach, pulled back, hit again. The smile slipped, returned, flickered. Teacher was making a sound, grunting. He hit again, again. Mr Sellars slumped further. The sounds kept coming, the sound of flesh being pounded, the grunting. At one point blood and saliva flew out over Teacher's face, and he wiped it away, smeared it over his face. And then at another, later point I thought I saw his fist enter his stomach, grip, fasten on something, pull on something. Mr Sellars opened his eyes wide and the smile changed as his mouth stretched into a wide O.

A terrible sound emerged from the toothless hole of his mouth. I saw Teacher push his fingers into the hole, I saw him pull. I stopped looking before I could see what it was he was pulling. I scrambled down the wall of tyres, half-falling, stumbling, catching my elbows and knees and feet inside the tyres. The gang yelled and whistled at my back.

I hit the ground and ran for the bike.

55

I was aware of pursuit behind me, I didn't know how many or how close. The noise of my descent down the wall of tyres had alerted them. I had a few seconds' advantage, while they scaled the chain-link fence, and got down the other side. Others, I was sure, would start up their bikes and follow. As I scrambled and pounded through the scrubby growth underfoot, it would have been possible to persuade myself that I was doing Mr Sellars a service by distracting Teacher's attention from him, and so saving him the dubious benefits of any more of Teacher's ministrations. Whatever it was that came next.

But the blood pounding in my ears and chest and the air rasping its way from throat to lungs and back again was not interested in doing favours for Mr Sellars, nor even saving his life. It was interested in getting me away from that scene. That alone.

I reached the bike and kicked the stand away. I got it started and in seconds the night air was driving water from my eyes and interfering with my breathing. The engine was screaming as I went up through the gears. I was going much too fast, far beyond my ability to control the bike, and I forced myself to slow a little. Bends came, and junctions, and I took them, slower but still at an appalling and reckless speed. The air was jamming itself into me, the road flinging itself under my wheels, snaking crazily as my hands trembled on the fork.

Lights appeared in my wing mirrors. They gained on me quickly. My own noise drowned out the noise of my pursuers, then one of them loomed up behind me and I could hear his exhaust. I couldn't make out his face. He drew level, then overtook. He sailed past at an unbelievable speed and the roar and smoke of his wake was hot in my face. Within seconds he was vanishing ahead of me. There was a long slow bend and he was soon out of sight. I couldn't imagine what the tactic was. The others behind me began to fall further back, and I was suddenly alone again on the road. Fields stretched away on either side, and I could see the lights of a refinery far off to my left, out near Hilton. The wind was sweet and cool. There were no stars.

A light appeared ahead, suddenly close ahead, coming towards me, in the wrong lane, coming for me. I swerved out into the right-hand lane, the light ahead swerved also. He was aiming for me. The light and air and noise coalesced as he screamed onto me. I flung the fork round and felt him whistle by, heard the scream of tyres. I mounted the bank, roared into the field, swayed insanely, stalled, crashed. He was right behind me. I disentangled myself from the bike, something had gone wrong with my foot, my knee, but I kept on thrashing through the field, through the air. I felt his hands on my shoulder, round my neck. I fell, he fell with me, onto me. He straddled me, forced my arms apart. He was sitting astride me, sitting on my back. I had my eyes closed, but I could smell him, the oil and leather, the sweat. Petrol. And I could feel him. The weight and muscle. And I could *sense* him. I could sense that strange physicality, that authority, that power. Teacher.

'Quite a little bundle of fun, aren't you?' he said, half whisper, half hiss, as he consolidated his grip on me. He seemed to know a great deal about restraint; I was sure he wouldn't leave a single identifiable mark. He was an expert. I struggled with whatever strength I could muster, which wasn't much. I shouted, I don't know what exactly.

He wrenched my arm up and I gasped. My cheek was stuck, hard, into the soil, the smell was strong in my nostrils.

'Guess who died?' he said, his voice a barely controlled wind, hissing, hot on my neck.

'Guess. Guess who.'

He wrenched my arm again.

'He was found earlier today. He left a note. He was *sorry*, he thought he'd let me down, he couldn't live with himself. Guess where he was found? In the tunnel. He had the needle hanging out of his arm, he had his eyes open, he was facing the wall. His fingertips were *bleeding* – '

Another twist on my arm. With his other hand on the back of my neck he shoved my face further into the soil. His breath was hot and ferocious, prickling the hairs on my neck.

' – he was back stroking the walls again, trying to dig a way out. Guess why he was sorry. He was *sorry* because he talked to *you*, man. You were with him all day and all night on Tuesday. Weren't you? And now, he's sorry and he's dead. You've been here five weeks, there's two dead now, three if Mr Sellars doesn't make it.' Another wrench on the arm. 'What is it about you? Huh? You seem to have this effect on people don't you?' His breath was an angry wind on my neck. He was so close I thought he was going to bite through my neck, sever the tendons. 'I don't like your smell. There's something in you, I thought it was a gift, now I think it's a sickness. I don't want it round here. I don't want you round here. You come back here like this, you come round my brothers again like this, I'll kill you, I swear to God.'

Another jerk on my arm, I was sure it was going to snap at any moment. His breath retreated from my neck, and I felt his weight lifting from me. He stood over me. I knew something bad was about to happen, then something whistled into my back, my kidneys: his boot, like a lump hammer flung from a tall building. I curled round the flaming, orange emergency in my side, I attended closely to the grunts that were coming from my mouth; something inside had torn, some essential thread had been twisted, snapped. I knew there was another kick coming, I could see it. It landed perfectly. Then a kick to my head, ringing, unbelievable, obliterating. Something black crawled away from my writhing body, it was my self. It crept away into the field, and my body moved softly, carefully, surrounded the pulpy, tender, agonized mess, became still.

56

I woke up several times that night. The pain in my side flared and subsided, glowing from white to a dull orange throb. I was content to lie and smell the soil and the crop. There was a sliver of a moon, fantastically delicate, I charted its progress across the sky as I woke and slept and woke again. From far away I heard the periodic rumble of traffic, a slow, muffled roar moving across the fields.

I thought: when it gets light I'll head over there, to where the traffic noise is coming from. The road I was lying beside was a backwater, going nowhere. If I was going to get away I was going to need a bigger, more major, more serious sort of road altogether. But, mercifully, I didn't need to do anything until it got light, and meanwhile I could lie still and nurse the pain in my side and not move my head. I wondered idly, on and off, if the bike I'd been on was still there, and if so, still usable. It hadn't been much of a crash, I couldn't believe much harm could have come to it. They might have come and taken it away while I was asleep. I didn't much care, I was happy for Moustache to have it back again. I was a poor excuse for a biker, I didn't really have the stomach for it. Or the kidneys, come to think of it. I felt certain that my medical advisor would have advised against riding in my present condition.

So when the daylight came, lo! I would arise and walk, across tall fields hung with glistening spiders' webs, to the road, where some bleary truck driver would stop and give me a ride somewhere. I could stop at a service station and phone Fiona. Reverse charges, a procedure I had never used before. Could you still do it? I had no idea. Maybe the trucker would stand me a cup of coffee in Sarah's Pantry. Or maybe he'd have a Thermos under the front seat. I hadn't hitched anywhere since the Falklands war. I remembered a news bulletin coming over the radio as we drove towards Oxford, and the driver had whooped and clapped me on the leg. A few miles later he'd said, 'Little bastards. We showed 'em.' I remember grunting in acknowledgement, not daring to say a word.

I would ring Fiona. She too would be bleary, since it would be exceedingly early. She wouldn't understand who it was at first, then she'd say things like where are you? are you all right? I can't believe it's you. She'd probably cry. I'd say, I'm OK, I'm on my way home. I might even say I love you. I certainly wasn't ruling it out. I love you. Sorry.

57

We were in someone's spare room, guitars and chests of drawers and cardboard boxes full of board games and old bank statements. Our coats were on the bed, the spare bed, and we were trying to find them, preparatory to leaving. The two Friends of Fiona were leaving with us: we were going to share a taxi as far as Acton, then Fiona and I would go on to Ealing. Fiona's friends had found their coats already, and so had Fiona. She had also by this time found mine, and was holding it.

I had them in the palm of my hand. Fiona was playing with her glass with that look on, but the others were right in the palm of my hand. I couldn't remember their names, they were some of Fiona's people, whom I had come to regard as a single complex entity. I called them the Friends of Fiona. Witty, that.

The look that Fiona had on her was distracting me a little though. I had been playing a bit with my glass too, filling it up and then making it empty again. It was a good game. You were off on your thing again, she'd say tomorrow, do you remember that? She would probably ring them from work and say something about it. Apologize. I know she did that. She didn't always agree that people really *had* been in the palm of my hand. She doubted. She may well have been right.

You were on your thing again. Do you remember that? We were all waiting to go and you were standing in the doorway, holding forth. That's what she was planning to say, that was the meaning of that face. My voice rolled on, mellifluous, well-modulated, well-stocked with description and explanation and embellishment. Fiona would remind me the next day of the new variations on the story, of how my role in it had grown in importance and drama. She seemed to be keeping some sort of record; I wondered if she didn't have it all written down somewhere.

But this was, of course, my story. It had been written already, and had even appeared, in much abbreviated form, as a couple of columns in *New Statesman and Society*, with all the Midlands Mafia and drug-dealing and kidnap parts removed, on the grounds that we would have a little difficulty in substantiating any of it. Now it just read as a human-interest piece about a bike gang with a charismatic leader. Gone were the unlawful imprisonments, the unrecorded deaths and illegal interments, the savage, uncontrolled beatings administered as healings, the obsessive secrecy and the near-worship of Teacher as some kind of superhuman figure, the—

Off on your thing again.

Fiona pushed past me, and stood by the stairs to phone a taxi.

'Ten minutes. OK.' I knew she wanted to ask them for one to come sooner. Ten minutes was an awfully long time. She sat down carefully on the stairs, cradling my coat, hugging it over her swollen belly. Downstairs people were surging about and finishing off the leavings. I had cleverly secreted a bottle in the coat room, and thus was not reduced to scavenging from abandoned cups and bottles, half of which would have cigarette ends in. There were a few glassfuls left. Ten minutes. I knew she wouldn't let me take the bottle in the taxi. I drank faster.

One of the friends was drinking too, I think she was called Yolanda. The other friend was just waiting. She slipped past me and sat by Fiona on the stairs. Yolanda started to talk about something or other, and I listened intently, drinking, waiting for my cue to carry on. I poured wine into her cup, and we sat together on the bed, with the coats thick and uncomfortable underneath us. She finished speaking and my voice came on again, authoritative, wise, swollen like a great rolling river in spring. Yolanda looked very drunk, her head was moving oddly on her shoulders. I heard Fiona sigh on the stairs, and her friend said something, and they laughed. Ten minutes was nowhere near long enough: I was right in the middle of a complex piece of explaining when Fiona came to stand behind me saying, 'Taxi's here.' We rolled downstairs, the four of us, and people shouted goodbye.

Yolanda and the other one got out, outside a kebab shop in Acton, and Fiona and I spread ourselves more comfortably on the back seat. It was a further ten minutes or so to Ealing. A long time. She held my hand, though, after a few minutes.

58

I couldn't really get on with anything. I moped about and cleaned things. Fiona was concerned. We hugged a great deal and I remembered how much I liked her. She hadn't had any letters from me, as it turned out, she'd had no idea where I was. After twenty-four hours with no word she'd rung the police, who'd told her that you can't be a missing person until after three days. After that they'd told her that my picture would be circulated round the country, and had I had anything on my mind before I'd disappeared? Had it happened before? She'd come clean and told them about my absurd pretensions to undercover journalism, my testosterone-driven compulsion to get myself into trouble. Yes OK it had happened before, but this time was different, I'd always managed to ring her up to now.

They'd said there was really very little they could do. It's a big country. People go missing all the time. Was she conscious of any other friends I might have? The word 'friend' had been inflected slightly. What do you mean, friend, she'd demanded, if he was with a friend he'd ring, wouldn't he? He's in *trouble*, I *know*. They'd said was it possible that I wasn't missing so much as just gone away? She'd hung up. They'd come round to question her the next day. Just in case she'd done me in and buried me under the floorboards.

A policewoman had rung up that afternoon and given her the number of an organization who help people who have had loved ones disappear. Not help with *finding*, of course not, help with *coping*.

Day had followed day, she said, and it had come to seem strangely unreal. After a week the police had circulated posters round Ealing with my picture on, not a very flattering picture. She'd kept the poster. She'd told them, she said, that I wasn't *in* bloody Ealing, so what was the point of the bloody *poster*. She said the whole thing had been like that. Everything they did was wrong, too little, and she wanted to tell them, but also they were the only chance she had of finding me so she couldn't risk antagonizing them. And in truth, she thought, what could they do really? You couldn't knock on every door in every street in every town and say excuse me, you don't happen to have this man hidden in your spare room do you? They were waiting, they said, for a lead.

And it had become increasingly unreal. She went to work as usual, and she couldn't go in every day and say, well, he hasn't turned up yet. People stopped asking, out of embarrassment or incomprehension. She couldn't cry in the toilets every day. She went in one day and there was a crisis to do with faxes that hadn't gone out. It was eleven thirty before she remembered that I was still missing. She had moments of panic that she wasn't responding right, that she was doing too little, that she ought to be doing something.

Someone she talked to at the self-help group told

her that this was quite normal. This woman's husband had literally gone out for ten Marlboro and never returned. Twelve years ago. Fiona said the woman began to feel completely detached about it. She would wonder sometimes, was he ever here at all? Was he ever really here? She had wedding photographs, holiday photographs, *children* for God's sake, yet she would lie awake thinking: did I just imagine him? Imagine it all? Sometimes, she'd said, that seemed easier to believe than that someone could just vanish, for ever. And it was impossible for anyone else to understand it. Her mother had said that he must have gone off with another woman, what other explanation could there be? Friends, workmates – well, six months on, what could they possibly say? She'd remarried, and as she'd stood in the registry office she'd been sure he would burst in and punch the man beside her to the floor, pick her up and carry her out. She would look at her new husband sometimes and wonder: are you just going to disappear as well? Maybe it's something about me. He'd go off to work, and she'd say: if he's not back by midnight . . .

Fiona and I were very close at this point, edgily close. Something had been added. We were both bigger, we'd both been enlarged, me by my experience with Teacher, her with her sudden drama of desertion and abandonment. And she was bigger in another way now, astonishingly so, big with our baby. Our child. She wore different clothes and her skin had changed, become more oily. She tasted different, exciting. We'd both had our adventures alone, now we could enjoy sharing them. We felt bigger, bolder, braver. She hated

244

it when I started talking about it to other people because she was sure they didn't want to hear it all again, but in private we went over and over it. We'd meet each other's eye, on the tube or in the pub, and laugh: we were so much more exciting than our drab, secure setting, like precious stones set in tin. Each saw a reflection of our own excitement in the other. Sex, which had been largely a matter of affectionate routine, had taken on an edge, a delicious little twist.

59

Or that's what it was at first, anyway. Soon though the little twist got bigger. One night I found myself on top of her, she was motionless and clenched, her eyes clamped shut. She rolled away from me.

'You're going too hard,' she said, 'you're hurting me.' We tried again later and she pushed me off her and said, 'I don't know what's got into you,' and I demanded to know exactly what she meant by *that*, and it all got nasty. Not violent, but definitely nasty. I wasn't quite certain that it wouldn't become violent at some stage, though. By 'it', I mean, of course, 'I'. We put all this down to readjustment and stress.

Being separated from me had been hard for her, but that's not to say that it was entirely bad either. She said she'd had all sorts of thoughts, about men and relationships and life. And she said that after a few weeks she couldn't imagine any actual time of day when I would turn up or when the phone would ring. It had come to seem utterly unlikely. It would happen one day, of course, but today? When she came in from work and pulled off her shoes and skirt? While she was in the bath? Not very likely, somehow. She said that she'd even come to like the idea of this thing that would surely happen one day, but not just yet. She had started to enjoy waiting for me.

She'd also, incidentally, started to like having the flat to herself. She could sit in the bathroom with the door open, not doing anything. She could keep the curtains open at night. On Sunday she could lounge about undressed and pick her toenails. Or she could pull the curtains and stay in bed all day if she felt like it. Have the telly on. She could try on different clothes and make-up, without feeling embarrassed or defiant. She didn't feel criticized. She could be herself. Living with someone in a one-bedroom flat, she'd almost forgotten how good it was to have long, uninterrupted stretches of time to herself. And of course she could go out with whoever she pleased, and not have to worry about whether I liked them or not, or what time it was. There were other times too, times when she imagined me dead, laid out, peaceful. She hated herself for it, but this vision of me comforted her. At least she'd *know*.

So when I did finally show up, in the middle of the afternoon actually, so that I was there when she turned her key in the door, she couldn't help feeling invaded by me. I was suddenly very big and *there* and in the way. She was worried about how this sounded, but I understood exactly what she meant. And not only was I back suddenly, but I had all these things I wanted to talk about, and I wasn't quite, exactly, the same person any more.

I've never met anyone psychic, but if anyone is Fiona is. She tries to be solid and straight and speak-your-mind, but she has a curious capacity for putting her finger on things. So when she rolled away from me, I knew she'd seen or felt something about me, some new element that had been added. And when she said, 'What's got into you?' I knew that she was seeing something different about me.

She claimed that it was just a figure of speech for God's sake and why did I have to try to read meanings into everything she said? I never used to.

You could have said all sorts of things, I said. Like what's the matter with you? or you seem different somehow or are you feeling all right? But you didn't, you said—

'I know what I said. What I mean is, you're behaving rather strangely, are you aware of that?'

'Really.'

'Yes. Including this close bloody textual scrutiny of every bloody word I say.'

'Really.'

'Really. Yes.'

Never one to let matters alone for a minute, she carried on.

'The other night. When you stopped because I said you were hurting me—'

'I'm sorry. I *said* I was—'

'What were you thinking about?'

'What do you mean?'

'You know what I mean.'

'I wasn't thinking about anything.'

'Are you sure?'

'Yes I'm sure. What do you *think* I was thinking about?'

She hesitated. It's actually quite hard for her not to

say exactly what she thinks. I have in the past seen this as both a strength and a weakness. It gets her into all sorts of trouble, which she could easily avoid with just a few degrees of evasion or imprecision. But she can't, she can't help herself. You can see her trying to control it sometimes: it looks like she's got indigestion.

She was trying now. She shrugged her eyebrows, she bit her lip, she smiled and twitched her nose.

'I'm not saying,' she said finally. 'You'll just get upset and start shouting.'

'No I won't.'

'Huh.'

'OK don't tell me.' This was all part of the procedure, except that I'd cut out some of the preliminary phases.

'You were thinking about him.'

I stood up and went into the kitchen to make a cup of tea. There was no milk so I went out to get some. I did *not* throw things around and then storm out, making next door's dog start barking.

Nor was I gone for hours. I just had difficulty finding a shop open at that time of night. And when I came back I could hardly help waking her up.

'Why did you go to bed?' I asked her. 'Didn't you think I was coming back?'

I brought her a cup of tea.

'You're wrong actually. I wasn't thinking about him.' This was minutes later.

'Fine.'

'I'm not going to carry on saying I'm sorry for the rest of my life.'

'No-one expects you to.'

'What do you mean anyway? Do you mean that I was pretending that you were him?'

'Forget it.'

'Or that I was him? What?'

'Forget it. I'm sorry I said it.'

We were quiet for a moment. Next door's dog still seemed to be upset. He's extremely sensitive to any kind of domestic tension, even if it is next door. He can't stand an atmosphere. I sometimes think he's psychic too.

'Just another throwaway comment eh?' I couldn't let it drop. She was quiet, which wasn't like her. She was as much a devotee of the protracted disagreement as I was, usually. I wanted to ask her, what's got into you?

We made up, of course, if only to quieten him down next door, and did our usual, courtly, well-mannered thing together. I didn't think about anything. We weren't ourselves. We just weren't right. I could see it.

60

And afterwards, of course, I dreamed about him. Always. We would be wandering round a large house. Sometimes it was a ship or a warehouse. He was ahead of me so I couldn't see his face. We would be on our way to a particular room, where he wanted to show me something.

'Wait,' I would say, 'I think I know what it is,' but he wouldn't wait.

'I know what it is,' I'd say, 'you don't have to show me.'

'You haven't seen it all yet. I want you to see it all,' he'd say, and I would have no choice. Sometimes, during the day, I'd stop, certain that I could remember what it was. But it wouldn't come. A tree. It had to do with a tree. Not Fuckyou hanging, something else. Sometimes it would be the front room in the flat, there would be something I had to see. Something I didn't want to see.

Sometimes we'd be on his bike. He was solid and heavy in front of me. The wind rushing past us was scented and carried sounds from far away. Shouts, cries, bursts of music, moans. We were on our way to them.

I was awake at night a lot at this time. I would find

myself standing by the wall, my head twisted, listening for sounds from next door. Taps dripping, the dog scuffling about, an occasional raised voice. Opera. Bursts of television laughter. I tried to piece it all together, as if it were a story, as if it meant something. On a few occasions I left the house and walked round the Broadway Centre, the shops redundant and meaningless in the middle of the night. I would look at the displays in the windows. I stood in front of a DIY shop, staring at vices and chisels and drills. It all meant something.

Fiona wanted me to Talk to Somebody. I was holding out. And after a while that was all I did. I held out.

61

We went camping, four of us, in my beautiful Saab. It was something we'd arranged months ago. The two with us were Graham and Sue. Sue was someone Fiona used to live with, and I knew Gray from Labour Party activist days. We used to sit at the back at meetings and snigger. Funny how those patterns stay with you. School: snigger at the back. Grow up, go to university, snigger at the back in lectures. Develop a political consciousness: go to Labour Party meetings: snigger at the fat bloke who said 'Fabian' with a long 'a', 'Farbian'. On the way to the New Forest Gray and I sat in the back of the car and convulsed ourselves about Fiona's hair, as seen from behind. She glared into the rear-view mirror and exchanged businesslike conversation with Sue about mutual friends and their idiotic men.

It was September, late in the year for camping, but we'd been lucky in the past. This would be the third time Fiona and I had shared a tent. It had become a fixed event, despite our increased affluence and ability to have undreamed-of foreign trips, in aeroplanes and hotels. We had these separately – she to somewhere hot, Cuba, Mexico, Egypt, me usually to the fleshpots of Austria and France, skiing with two or three others.

We would bring each other back silly presents and decide to go away together next year. Water-skiing down the Nile perhaps.

Fiona was driving because she enjoyed it. I love driving, but I detest having passengers. They slow you down, clip your wings. Fiona seemed to like it, though. She was an excellent driver. I always felt my beautiful Saab safe in her hands.

We arrived mid-afternoon and the sun came out. There were surprisingly few people around. Our usual, favourite spot was occupied by an immense trailer with canvas marquee at the front and washing line. We found somewhere even better, though, with nearby trees and a clear sightline to the shower block. This has always mattered, since Fiona has an unusually poor sense of direction, and can spend hours wandering around optimistically.

Fiona and I had a splendid dome tent that took about ten seconds to put up. Gray and Sue had borrowed something, a monster that looked no longer used and ad hoc and foul-tempered. It came in a battered cardboard box instead of a neat shiny nylon bag. When they'd put it up it looked like a dull green precaution against some kind of unspeakable calamity. We all zipped ourselves up in our respective tents to lie down for an hour, and Fiona and I tried to make as little sound as possible. So did Gray and Sue, though they were, I think, less successful than we were. We were giggling more than they were, though.

Later Gray and I succumbed to gender stereotyping and went off to explore, get supplies, check out the neighbours. Gray was an odd young man, an actor who hadn't actually acted in anything for over a year: he was perpetually attending auditions for adverts where he would be ritually humiliated and sent home. At Christmas he dressed up as Santa and spent his days in grottos lying to avaricious children. He enjoyed every minute of it. It was a joke that he was 'kept' by Sue, and had to perform unusual sexual acts in payment. He would become morose when drunk and berate, belittle and traduce his less talented (more successful) contemporaries.

The camp-site shop was shut. Its opening times were eccentric; a card in the door told of a van that came round at some insanely early hour. We peered inside: we could see bread and tins of soup and boxes of cornflakes. We told each other how incredibly stupid we'd been not to bring anything with us. I didn't say that I'd been expecting Sue to bring things. She's such a sensible woman, I'd been certain she'd have all sorts of goodies.

There was nothing for it. Instead of crouching over a dangerously hissing Calor-gas burner for twenty minutes in a light drizzle waiting for beans 'n' bangers to heat up, we'd have to go back, climb in the Saab and cravenly seek out townie food. Naturally, we were disappointed.

We found a fried-chicken take-away in the graceful, well-kept-up little town a mile or two from the site. The bored children of the local dentists and antique dealers stood around in small groups, being decorously rebellious. They looked like they might discover punk at any minute. Gray and I got carried away by a particularly good offer and emerged with a great gaudy

255

bucket of hard-to-identify chicken pieces in soggy batter, and several dozen sachets of salt and paper napkins, all of which would come in handy. It was hard to see how the pieces could ever have fitted together to form real live chickens.

We drove back at high speed, and I got grease all over the steering wheel. When we arrived at the tents, Sue was crouching on the grass with a bright red plastic thing with a handle, which she was turning vigorously. She glanced up pityingly at us and our bucket of carrion.

'Sue? What's that?' Gray asked and she looked at him very directly and said:

'It's a salad spinner.'

Gray snorted and turned away and I saw a wicked little look and tried not to laugh.

We all squatted on the damp grass and ate fried chicken and Sue's strenuously spun salad. Fiona congratulated Sue on her foresight and good planning. I wasn't *completely* sure that Fiona didn't also have a wicked little look.

'I mean, who'd have thought of it,' Gray said, 'bringing a salad spinner away with us.' Sue ignored him and talked to Fiona about feta cheese. There are different kinds apparently.

'Watch out for the olives,' she said, 'they've still got the stones in.'

'What, you mean you didn't bring the—'

'Gray.' Fiona caught his eye and gave him a quelling look. Sue bristled slightly and Gray and I tried hard not to make each other laugh.

It was a warm, soft evening. The trees above us

stirred fluidly, humming and twitching, as if they were full of bees. The people with the marquee and the washing line had dogs too. There always seem to be dogs next door to wherever I am. These were tough, hard animals. They were barking gently, like an old man coughing. The woman had big, meaty arms and a pink sundress. The man had baggy floral shorts and a muscle vest (but no muscle). There was a girl, fat, ill-favoured, resentful, nagged at.

I turned my face away so I could murmur to Gray:

'I bet *they* haven't got a salad spinner,' and he choked slightly and sprayed chicken and started me laughing again.

Sue gave him a hard look, and I patted him on the back; he was alternately laughing and coughing. He didn't seem to be able to catch his breath, which fact seemed to be making him laugh harder. The dogs were barking louder. He stood up and moved a few steps away, but was still coughing and heaving. I went after him. I could hear Sue and Fiona picking up the conversation. Olives. There are, it seems, many different kinds of olive too.

'Gray?'

He turned to look at me. His face was running with tears, his eyes were bloodshot. He tried to say 'I'm OK,' and was immediately gagging again, choking, panting. His breathing wasn't working properly. I caught his eye and he looked panicky. I looked over to Fiona and Sue, and met Fiona's steady gaze. She picked up a trace of my fear. Gray coughed, heavily, and tried to take a deep breath, but was immediately choking again.

'Gray? You OK?'

He leaned on my shoulder and coughed, a great series of deep hacking coughs, pulling him down to the ground. He had his head between his knees. He took a breath and was racked with spasms. He couldn't breathe. I banged his back harder. He tried to stand straight, couldn't, fell down, his body curling into the foetal position. His face had gone from red to white.

'Jesus Christ.'

I tried to pull him upright – he was twisting and dragging away from me. I saw Fiona stand, followed by Sue. They were looking over, unsure of what was happening. Sue was used to Gray carrying on in annoying and exaggerated ways.

Gray was now crawling away from me. Fiona was at my shoulder.

'Is he OK?'

'I don't think so.'

Very quick, quiet exchange. I went after him, grabbed him under the armpits, tried to force him upright. It seemed essential that he be standing. I managed to get him up on his knees. His chest was heaving. A fragmentary memory came to me: you lock your hands together, you get behind the person with your hands under the rib cage, the solar plexus, and you *drive* upwards with all the force you can manage. You don't worry about fracturing ribs.

I bent over him and tried to get my hands into the right position. His lips were turning blue. He dragged in a great agonizing heave of air and I jabbed upward, his body doubling under my hands. Not hard enough. I jabbed again, a short stilted movement. I didn't have the confidence to really follow through. He grunted, uuugh, and I jabbed again.

Sue was behind me now, unable either to believe in the seriousness of the situation or quite not to. I imagined us all inside the ugly green tent, surrounded by flapping walls of musty canvas.

'Is he all right?'

She lived with this actor who didn't act every day. She wasn't going to fall for it just like *that*.

'No. I'm trying to do the Heimlich manoeuvre.'

'The what?'

I jabbed again. Uuuugh. He was limp under me now, at the end of his breath. He inhaled, a rasping, desperate sound. His eyes were bulging.

'Do you know how to do it?'

'No.'

'Is there anything I can do?'

'I don't think so. I've just got to try to get the obstruction out.'

'Try again.'

We spoke calmly, in low voices: it was simply a matter of technique, applying the correct procedures. Gray had become a technical problem. The fact that he was turning blue before our eyes served merely to illustrate this.

I hauled him to his feet. I wriggled myself into position, like a golfer lining up his stroke.

'OK,' and I

heaved,

desperately hard, again, and then drove my balled fists into him. I don't think I got the right place. He was moaning, a thin, weak sound. I became exasperated. Sue was saying 'Try turning him upside down,' and Fiona was crouching in front of him repeating 'Gray? Gray? Can you hear me?' We were all insane, but in a very orderly way. I became aware that Gray could *die*, actually *die* here under my hands.

'Bastard.'

I jerked him up, again, he was limp again, a floppy exhausted thing. My technique became erratic. I was flailing, beating him, pounding him, as the dogs barked and I imagined the tent collapsing softly around us.

'Bastard!'

'Robert.' Fiona was holding my arms, trying to catch my eye. 'Robert. Stop for a second—'

'Bastard!'

'You're going too hard. Robert!'

We were slipping and sliding in and out of something, it was in the trees and in the grass, in the air. It was in me. Something was in me.

'Bastard!'

I felt something give under my hands, something shifted out of position. I was cracking his ribs. His hands were at his neck, plucking feebly. He was making soft little sounds, as if he were trying to clear his throat. I twisted him round to face me, my hands under his armpits. He looked grey and exhausted, there were specks of foam round his lips. I grabbed the back of his head and kneed him in the stomach.

'Uuuugh.' Again.

Again.

'Robert, for God's sake you're—' Fiona was all but shouting, trying to pull me off him.

Something flew out, a gobbet of some slimy

substance surrounding a little piece of bone, daubed with blood. It fell onto Sue's shoulder – she knocked it away with something like horror. Gray fell gasping to the ground, spitting bloody foam, his arms wrapped round his stomach, his whole body focused upon the breathing of air. I looked down at him from a great height. Sue knelt beside him, stiffly, and Fiona walked away from me.

62

I awoke to the sound of roaring outside the house. It was a sound that had been pursuing me through dreams for weeks: now it had caught up with me. I twitched back the bedroom curtain.

Half up on the pavement, belching and spluttering to a halt, a red and black Kawasaki, and on top of it a sizeable, untidy figure, combat fatigues and battered leather, battered leather face as well, much marked, great oily hands. He lurched off the bike and stumbled, rocking back on his feet. He took off the half-face helmet, and pulled something from behind his ear, a little stub of something, and lit up. The smell drifted up to me through the clear early morning, sweet, aromatic, heady.

He peered at the number on the house and came up the path, rocking backward again. He flicked his head, as if twitching a fly away. There were no flies. He dropped the roach and rang the bell.

Fiona stirred: it was half an hour or so before her alarm clock would go off. I slipped out of the room and padded down to the door. I found that I wasn't surprised that he should be here. I had been expecting somebody, waiting. Holding out, even.

He was leaning against the door jamb, huge and

shabby beside the neat paintwork and garden. He looked utterly inappropriate in this decorous suburban setting. He looked like a sea monster in a paddling pool.

'Hi.' His face lit up as I opened the door, a big beaming smile. 'How ya doing?' He was still leaning, and showed no immediate sign of moving.

'What are you doing here?' Not the most gracious of welcomes, but the best I could manage.

'Just thought I'd look you up, man.'

'What, you were in the area and you just thought you'd drop by?'

'Yeah.' No let-up in the smiling. His eyes were blunted by the dope, but there was something else going on in his face as well, the beginning of a disorder or the end of one, I couldn't see which. But I thought I could see a mark, a fresh-looking mark, behind his ear. The hair was scrubby and uneven round it. I glanced up and down the street. No-one about yet. I stood looking at him, and annoyance welled up. What was I supposed to do about him? He couldn't just stand there, leaning and smiling, with that process going on behind his face all day, could he? What would Fiona say when she left for work? Er, Robert, there's some kind of blissed-out weirdo leaning against the door, friend of yours?

'You can't stay here,' I said quickly, glancing past him nervously. 'It's not possible.'

'Can't go anywhere else, man.' He was not so much leaning, I noticed, as *propped*. Still smiling, still that occasional flick of the head. 'I've been driving all night. I've got to stop. I'm not feeling too good, if you want

263

to know the truth. Little bit wobbly.' Just chatting, passing the time of day. Going nowhere. Smiling.

'OK. You'd better come in. Just for a minute.'

He stumbled in and I sat him down on the couch. It looked too small for him. I worried about oil stains. His face was slipping about all over the place. He really didn't look well. His eyes slid shut, open, shut again. He started saying something about an oil change, and in the middle of a word he was asleep, his head falling awkwardly against the side of the couch. He mumbled and licked his lips. I sat watching him for a few moments. I couldn't think of a single thing to do with him.

I knew his face, but I couldn't at first put his name to it. Their names were all so stupid that it could be almost anything. I was still sitting there when Fiona came out of the bedroom. I started to say something to her, not to be alarmed, he was perfectly safe, but she just stared at him and said I don't believe it, I just don't believe it. Go to work, I said, and I'll get rid of him when he wakes up. What does he want? she asked. I can't believe— Leave him to me, I said, just go to work. She came out of the bathroom fifteen minutes later and started to make her coffee.

'Why did you let him in?' she demanded from the kitchen. 'Huh?'

'I couldn't just leave him on the step, could I?'

'Why don't you call the police?'

'Why?' She was starting to annoy me. I wished she'd just go to work and leave me alone, so I could think of what to do. His name popped into my head, unannounced: Loverman. Obviously. I thought of explaining this to Fiona, but I could imagine the looks she'd give me. I wasn't ready for them. She could be something less than sweet reason first thing in the morning. She needed about an hour and three cups of coffee.

She put her head round the door.

'*Why?*'

'He hasn't done anything wrong. He just needed somewhere to crash. I'll get rid of him when he wakes up. Don't make a big drama out of it. Go to work.'

'Right, well if he's still here when I get back, Robert, then *I'm* going to call the police, OK? Is that OK with you?'

'Fine. Whatever.'

She banged about, transforming herself as if by sheer determination and noise from grumpy woman with funny hair into cool PR professional in black maternity leggings and loose linen jacket. She looks gorgeous in her work clothes; that's how I always think of her, sleek, busy, smart. She gave me a peck on the forehead as she left and I called out after her, 'Don't worry, I'll deal with him.' She pulled the door shut and her shoes clacked down the stairs, then the front door slammed.

I heard her slam the car door, start the engine up. It doesn't always start first time. I heard her revving the engine, pulling out. The noise travelled down the quiet morning street, she turned the corner and was gone. I slumped in my chair and closed my eyes. Loverman muttered and flicked something away from his face. There was nothing there.

He woke up about eleven thirty and sat up. His

unfocused eyes found me, watching him, and he smiled.

'Hey!' He stretched and yawned, hugely. 'Do you mind if I use your bed? This thing's horrible.' The bed. Brilliant thick white sheets and pillow cases, white duvet cover, little blue and green pillows, stuffed tiger. Clean.

'You'll have to take your clothes off.'

'OK. I mean I usually do, you know?' I wanted to ask him if he'd mind having a bath first, but he was already on his way, pulling at his filthy combat trousers. I shut the door behind him and retreated to the front room. The curtains were still closed, and I felt a great reluctance to open them.

He came out to the bathroom at about one o'clock and went straight back to bed. I realized that I'd been sitting in my chair since eight o'clock. Five hours. I had no idea of what to do, none. I couldn't leave the flat, even though I found it hard to imagine him making off with the video and the stereo. How would he get them on the bike? But even so, I couldn't just leave the flat with him sprawled out on my bed. Fiona's bed. I was just waiting for him to wake up. I found myself reading an old *Empire* magazine. In a way, it was nice to be relieved of the responsibility for doing things, since I didn't really have anything to do in any case. I had no story to work on, no research, no phone calls to make. Nothing. My life had come to a halt, here on this chair with this *Empire* magazine and Loverman in the next room. The phone rang and I jumped, startled, grabbed for it.

'Hello?'

'Robert it's me. I've only got a minute. Are you OK?'

'Yes, I'm fine.'

'Sorry if I was short earlier on, but my God, Robert. Who is he anyway? One of that bunch of weirdos?'

'One of them, yes. He's called Loverman, believe it or not. Yes he's still here, yes he's still asleep, no I don't know why he's here, and no I don't know when he's leaving. All right?'

'Robert, don't you think you should call the police? He might be dangerous.'

'He isn't. I met him a few times and he's OK, he's just got a funny manner. He's completely harmless, honestly.'

'He doesn't look harmless.'

'Oh they all look like that. It doesn't mean anything.' I thought of the little flicks of the head, the brushing away of imaginary flies. I didn't remember him ever doing that before. And wasn't he slower, more sluggish, less steady? 'He probably just needs money. There's no problem, really.'

'I just don't like the thought of you getting mixed up with them again, you may think they're harmless but my God Robert they weren't exactly harmless when you were last with them, were they?'

'Look look look. I'll send him away and that'll be that. What can he do to me in *Ealing* for God's sake?'

'I'm just worried about you Robert.' Traces of a little-girlie voice. Wobert. 'I don't want you to be exposed to them, any of them, while you're – '

'While I'm what.'

'Not yourself. You know what I mean. I think they could confuse you, take advantage – '

'Fi-on-a. We've been through all this. Last time they were holding me against my will, they didn't *persuade* me of anything, they didn't convert me *to* anything and I'm not some helpless brain-dead *cultist*. I do have a mind of my own, you know? They can't do anything to me here.'

'But he's not staying, is he Robert?'

'No he's not staying.'

'I'm just worried about you.'

'I know.' I lowered my voice a notch. 'Thank you for being worried about me, I appreciate it. I really do.'

'I won't be late. See you later.'

'OK. Bye.'

I put the phone down and stood up. Some kind of action was called for. I made two cups of coffee and took them into the bedroom.

'Hey.'

No response. He was an unquiet heap on the clean white bed, bits of him sticking out at odd angles, his head buried in the pillow. From what I could see he was naked. His clothes were a limp pile by the bed.

'Hey!'

He twitched violently, lifted his head up and squinted at me, then fell back again. 'I made you a cup of coffee,' I said and put it down beside the bed. He shifted his head round away from me, and I shook him gently by the shoulder. 'Come on pal. Wakey, wakey.' My voice was resolutely tough, but I wasn't at all certain that he wouldn't lash out, was ready to get away quickly if he should turn nasty. He stirred and reached out a hand for the cup, took it, righted himself and sat up, at least partly. He looked white and tightly muscled, much-decorated skin, much-scarred, a band of little shells round his neck. He stretched luxuriously and started smiling at me.

'So. What's the plan?' I said, tough guy.

'The plan? Weeeell, I'll have to go and have a look at that bike. It wasn't sounding right last night. I need to change the oil, but I think there's something going on with the transmission. Sounds like that anyway. I'll have to get in there and have a little look.'

'No, what I mean is where are you going to stay? I have to go out in about an hour and so you'll have to go as well. You can't stay here.' I felt I needed to keep on saying it to get past that smile. I wasn't sure he was understanding me. The more I said it the less certain it seemed to be, so I had to say it more. 'You're going to have to go. OK?'

'Well, you see, thing is that I'm going to have to stay, at least until I get the bike going right. Can't go sailing off with a dodgy transmission. Not recommended.' Big, big smile. 'But I can probably sort it out today, don't worry.'

'Probably?' Immediately I was explaining it to Fiona, it's just for tonight, he can sleep on the sofa and tomorrow he'll be gone. Just one night.

He was lying back on the bed now, eyes closed. He showed no sign of being in a hurry. He didn't look like hurry was a word he knew. Hurry, man, what's that? He looked as if he was on the other side of all struggle and urgency and rush, coasting down towards some point where he would just fold up and stop. He was

269

reaching an ending. I thought I'd better feed him, see if I could get him going.

'These beans taste funny,' he said, sitting fully upright now, plate balanced on his knees.

'Sugar free,' I said, and he grinned hugely, and repeated the words back to me, 'sugar free' as if it were the punchline to some outrageously tired old joke. I laughed, surprising myself.

I left him alone to get dressed and he emerged, massive, his clothes like armour. He sat himself on the sofa and I made more coffee.

'I always wondered what London was like,' he said, gesturing to the room, the drawn curtains, the pale carpet.

'It's like this,' I said. We sat quietly for a few moments.

'Look, I don't know why you've come but – '

'You can't stay here.' Another punchline. 'Right?'

'What are you doing here?'

'I just had to get away. For a while. And I had your address so I thought I'd pay you a visit. Look you up. See how you're getting on.' So innocent, it would be a crime to speak sharply to him, impossible to throw him out.

'Why did you have to get away?'

'Oh oh oh Mr Nosy rides again, right?'

'Come on, just tell me why you're here.'

He waved the question aside, as if brushing off the flies that weren't there.

He went out to tinker with the bike and I sat and worried about getting rid of him. Or rather about telling

Fiona that I hadn't got rid of him, that he was staying, I didn't know for how long. I even thought of explaining to her that I'd been waiting for him, that he was what I'd been holding out for. But I couldn't quite imagine any one of her many moods that would allow such a conversation to take place. There was the sound of footsteps on the stairs.

'Excuse me?' He was back again. He must have left the front door open. 'Sorry. I need a rag or something. Tea towel would do.' I found him a cloth in a drawer in the kitchen and he said, cup of coffee'd be nice. If you're making one. I made one and took it out to where he was working. He was lying on the pavement, head underneath the frame, tools and odds and ends around him. He looked happy and intent. I glanced nervously up and down the street, at the houses on the other side of the road, but there seemed to be no-one about, no nets twitching, no-one tutting and thinking of calling the police. And why should there be? He had a perfect right to be there, didn't he, a perfect right to fiddle with his bike in the gutter, sprawled out on the pavement like some misplaced piece of heroic statuary.

He pulled his head out from under and said, 'I need something like a jar, empty coffee jar or a can, you wouldn't have anything like that would you?' He was diffident and apologetic for the trouble.

We were crouching together beside the bike, listening to it turning over, when I heard the sound of Fiona's car pulling up on the other side of the road. I couldn't believe it was so late. I stood up and Loverman stood as well, with some difficulty. He seemed very stiff. Fiona walked past us, smiling tightly, head down. I left

Loverman standing by the kerb and went into the house after her. I was out on the pavement again in two minutes.

'I have to talk to Fiona for a minute. Would you mind staying out here?'

Fiona was tight, livid, derisive. I couldn't remember her ever being so angry. He's not staying Robert – he hasn't got anywhere else to go – I don't *care* – I can't just abandon him, he seems to be in some kind of trouble, he doesn't know anyone in London. *Why* can't you just abandon him, do you owe him something? What? Huh? What do you owe him? Or is it that you just won't leave these people alone, that you *will not* leave them alone. Is that it? He might be able to tell me something— Robert. That story is finished and gone, you have got to forget about it and get on with something else, anything else I don't care what, but please, will you just leave it alone. He has to stay for tonight. On and on. I quite enjoyed it. I don't know if Fiona did. We'd never argued much, not like this, at any rate. This was more than who stayed and who didn't, this was Do you love me? How much? What about the baby? Can I depend on you?

I didn't tell her he'd been asleep in our bed, and there were no visible signs. Later she went to bed and Loverman and I watched television for a while. He didn't seem to have anything much on his mind, and his comments were all comments about television programmes. I asked him to try to keep the noise down, since Fiona was a very light sleeper and she had work tomorrow. He grinned assent, and I left him.

Fiona was inert beside me, breathing steadily. We

272

weren't speaking, which was the first time that had ever happened. I almost felt like saying, hey! our first real row, snugglebunny, but didn't. I couldn't just turf him out and that was that. It was only for one night. I could understand why she was so furious, and I could understand that she hated not feeling in control of who was in the flat. There wasn't, after all, exactly room to spare. Fuckyou would have been deeply disappointed, had he lived to see it. Loverman seemed happy enough though. So this is London, I always wondered what it was like.

We had talked, Fiona and I, about how we were going to move on to a bigger place, now that she was pregnant. We were going to need another room, at least. She was doing well at work, she was rising smoothly, efficiently, inexorably up. The only reason we'd stayed in Ealing so long was that she liked the flat. I had been doing well, quite well anyway, with the promise of better to come. It didn't look as if I was going to have to give up the freelancing and try to find something steadier, more dependable, not just yet anyway. Or it hadn't, six weeks ago. But in six weeks I had done no work of any kind except for that one short piece.

We had some slack, but not that much. I was drawing on an account that was not supposed to be drawn on, a fact I had yet to appraise her of. She liked things to be orderly. She didn't like me hanging round moping, doing no work, she didn't like that at all. I sometimes thought I could see her looking at me in a particular way, evaluating: is this the father of my child? Is this my husband? Is this what I want?

And into this walked Loverman, big, dirty, burnt-out

eyes and imaginary flies, slow and getting slower all the time. Disorderly in the extreme. And I let him in. He was one of the people who'd kept me hostage for weeks, five weeks, organized forged letters, brought chaos and unmanageable degrees of uncertainty into her life. Taken me away, and then allowed me back, subtly different, not myself. One of the ones that I refused to report to the police, but wouldn't stop talking about. Of course she was furious. And yes he would almost certainly leave a nasty ring round the bath and mess up the towels and break things. Would he know not to use anything metal on the non-stick pan, not to use the blue scouring-pads on the stove top, would he use the extra-virgin olive oil for chips? No, no and probably.

But I couldn't just turf him out. That was all there was to it. It was a simple humanitarian thing, and I was surprised and disappointed that Fiona couldn't see that, I really was.

63

I don't know what time it was, Fiona was awake beside me, burglars! I sat up in the dark. There was a noise coming from the front room or maybe the kitchen. Gender stereotyping: *I* had to get up, silently, and creep to the door. All I needed was an ugly statuette in my hand and it was an Ealing comedy. I opened the door a crack. Definitely from the front room. It had to be Loverman. I gestured to Fiona and shut the door behind me.

I opened the front-room door, slowly, quietly, a bit at a time. He'd evidently decided to abandon the couch and put the cushions on the floor, which was a sensible move in my opinion. He had some blankets, but he'd managed to get them tangled up all round him. He was making a low sound, and he was fighting down there on the floor, fighting something, I couldn't see what. I mean I couldn't imagine what.

I approached him, cool with dread, he seemed to be in the grip of an ecstasy or final spasm. I crouched beside him. I held his hand, which gripped mine, hard, too hard. I don't know what grand-mal epilepsy looks like, but I think this was close to it. His teeth locked together in a rictus, and he was grunting, quickly, rhythmically. There was a smell. He had lost control of his bladder. No, Fiona wasn't going to like this one bit. The whatever-it-was passed over him and he relaxed again, still asleep, or perhaps more than asleep, but peaceful now; his grip loosened and he mumbled and drooled and turned over, sleeping like a baby. He was even smiling again.

I watched him for a moment, then slipped back to bed, to Fiona. He's OK, I said, not thinking about the carpet, the cushions, the smell. Not thinking about the way he looked, the face smiling itself into oblivion. He's OK, it was nothing. She was lying, eyes open, looking away from me. What was he doing, she said, and I said nothing, he's fine, just go to sleep. Dream dreams.

64

'So what's happened to you.'

He was back under the bike next day, fooling about with a wrench. He didn't want to talk to me, he was busy. 'Aren't you going to tell me?'

No reply. I stood over him, waiting. He muttered a few words and I said what? so loudly that he had to look at me.

'I'll be finished here in an hour or so. Then I'll go. OK?'

I tidied up the front room. I wasn't sure what you were supposed to do about piss stains on your carpet, so I scrubbed it and put vinegar on. The right kind of thing anyway. The cushions didn't look very washable, but I scrubbed them too in the bath. The room was full of his odour.

I heard the bike revving outside. It sounded OK, as far as I could tell. He came up the stairs and into the flat.

'Right then.'

'Where are you going to go?'

He stood, awkwardly.

'I'm sorry I pissed your floor.'

'Yeah? What's happened to you? Don't you think you should tell me?'

'What do you mean, happened? Nothing's *happened*.'

'Look. You turn up here out of nowhere, don't know where you're supposed to be going to, and then you have some kind of a, of a, I don't know what on the floor. I don't recall that these were ever part of your repertoire before.'

He wouldn't meet my eye. He grinned at the window, at the door, as if calculating which was the better escape route. I thought I could hear next door's dog starting up.

'Look. Let's go and have a walk. Let's just get out of this flat for a while. OK?' He shrugged. OK.

We walked through the Broadway Centre. It was hard to imagine anyone quite like him appearing on the artists' impressions. It hadn't been designed with him in mind. He looked as if he were about to fall and break things. It seemed absurd that there should be dry-cleaning establishments so near him.

Haven Green. From what it is a haven is unclear, perhaps simply from the Broadway Centre. He was unsteady, tripping once on something that wasn't there, dodging an absent tree branch. There were children and dogs and grass.

We sat on a bench. He was smiling at everything, much too much smiling, it wasn't right. And he wasn't just sitting, it was more than sitting, or less, some great, uncontrollable relaxation of something that shouldn't have been so relaxed.

'What's he done to you?'

An absurdly monumental question, and it didn't really require any answer. Whatever it was, there was no recovery from it. He needed a doctor.

'He's touched by God. When he touches you, God touches you. I've seen it happen. It's happened to me. He can see it all, everything. Things you don't want seen, he can see them.'

'So why are you here with me, and not there with him?'

'Because because *because*,' this last syllable dragged out just a fraction too long, too emphasized, 'because it's started coming back, man, and I didn't want to have any more of the treatment. I had enough last time, I'm telling you.'

'What has, what's started coming back?'

'Can't you guess?'

I thought I could. Bad stuff. It was in him all right. Question and answer:

'He saw it coming back in you?'

'Yes.'

'And he treated you again?'

'Yes.'

'Like the first time he healed you?'

'No. More. The next phase, he calls it.'

Tell me exactly what he did, no, tell me exactly, no, how can I help you if you won't tell me, no-one can help me, not *him*, not *you*— His voice was rising. He was ticcing, the flies were back again. He was blinking also, wide-eyed. There were bubbles round his mouth.

'It didn't work.' My voice, not a question. 'Now you're like this.'

A haven, a refuge, a harbour. A protection. I suddenly wanted to protect him, knew that it was too late. Knew that I had to do *something*. He was

279

murmuring, ticcing, then he was still. I preferred the ticcing.

'Hey!' He sat up, and gave me his biggest, most encompassing smile, but it was fading immediately. All I could see was that he needed a doctor. And I would get him one, but first I had to find out. He seemed to be nodding off again, but this was like the sitting, both more and less than. I was anxious not to be seen with him. God help me. He was blown suddenly by a strong, bad wind coming from within, his head jerked, his neck. Wide-open eyes. But seeing what?

'Stay with me now,' I said, 'Christ!' but he'd gone. His lips were foamy, bubbly, then just foamy. No more bubbles. He took on a relaxation so complete, so total that I could see it was the end of him. His eyes were open, I could see the clouds in them. A long line of dribble drawled down his face. There were no more flies. I stood and walked away, quickly. I just left him, walked away. Like a murderer.

65

Logically enough, there is no support group for people whose partners have returned suddenly, somewhat changed, from a five-week disappearance. Fiona was trying to deal with me by herself, from first principles. She was of the opinion that I ought to 'go and talk to someone'. I was not of her opinion, naturally. I was unpredictable, moody, irritable. I was prone to outbursts of rage. I was also becoming subject to headaches. I could do no work. The *New Statesman* piece, which bore so little relation to the one I had originally written, was the only thing I'd been able to achieve since I came home. I'd been holding out, now I didn't know what I was doing. Where was what's-his-name, she'd said. Loverman? I said gone, he's gone. What did he want? Nothing.

I would walk round the Broadway Centre, scowling, muttering. I avoided Haven Green. For all I knew he was still sitting there, dead, though it was certain that by now he'd been found and taken care of. I hadn't noticed anything in the paper. I stopped seeing people, or they stopped seeing me, one or the other. Fiona refused to go out with me socially: she would accompany me to a restaurant or the pictures, but not to any occasion which demanded ordinary social intercourse. We didn't argue, she just said I had to see someone, and I refused. There was no particular drama.

I suppose it was simple vanity: I became convinced that there must be another man. That was why we were getting on so very badly. It couldn't be that I had become unbearable to be with, it had to be that someone better had come along. Five weeks wasn't a long time to find another man, granted, and she was a busy woman, yes. And she was pregnant, with my child. OK. But even so, another man there must be. Dave Barnard. He was smooth, certainly, though not tremendously interesting; he had a rather unfortunate pale-blond-to-ginger kind of complexion which was particularly unattractive round the eyelashes, and a somewhat fat face, with little side pouches, like a hamster. But he had just recently split with his girl-friend and he and Fiona had always got on well. Hadn't they been engrossed in conversation at that last party? Surely they had.

Before I quite knew what I was doing I'd found his phone number and was waiting for him to answer.

'Hello?'

'Dave? Robert.'

'Robert! How's everything?'

'Great, great, you know. So how are you?'

I was listening intently, waiting for a pause, a false inflection, a moment off guard. If he and Fiona really were seeing each other then he would surely betray the fact somehow. And if he didn't I would just ask him, so have you been seeing much of Fiona recently? The direct approach.

'I'm all right. I was trying to get to talk to you,

actually, at Ali's party, but I got sidetracked somehow.'

Sidetracked by Fiona.

'Uhuh.'

'Yeah, I was going to ask you a favour. A friend of mine, Andy Roach, do you know him? he's researching a radio programme on people who've had religious experiences, you know, revelations and faith healing and so on. And I said I'd talk to you, just to sound you out, yeah? see if you wanted to talk to him.'

'I haven't had anything like that, Dave.'

'No?'

'No.'

'I thought—'

'Is that what Fiona told you? That I'd had an experience?'

'Fiona?'

'Well, Dave, I know you were talking to her and now you come up with this shit about fucking *experiences*, and it doesn't take a genius to put the two things together.'

'OK, maybe this isn't a good time—'

'Did she tell you that as well? That this wasn't a good time for me, I'm not myself, something's got into me? I'm sure you were sympathetic. I mean you always are. Very sympathetic.'

'I'll talk to you again soon Robert.' The phone buzzed. He had hung up.

Suspicious surely, just to hang up. Trying to hide something? I paced around the flat, looking for things, evidence, letters perhaps. There was none. Fiona came home from work and I cooked, one of my renowned curries. There was too much coconut milk in it. We didn't say a lot to each other, and when we'd finished eating she said she was tired and went into the bedroom for a lie-down. I sat in the front room with the telly on. There was a phone call at eight o'clock, Fiona picked it up. Not asleep then. The bedroom door was slightly open and I listened, intently. She was saying things like no I'm fine, no really, no, there's no need. I felt desperate that she should have to be talking like this to someone, insisting that she was all right, that there was nothing wrong, when we both knew that there was. Had she been waiting for the call? Odd that it should be dead on eight o'clock. I'll ring you at eight, someone must have said, and she had retired to the bedroom to wait. There was a pause, then she said No. *Can you talk now? No.* It had to be Dave Barnard. A few more brief responses: not really, no I haven't, no I don't think so. Yes all right. Say quarter to, just to be on the safe side. Bye.

I heard her moving around in the bedroom, then she went into the bathroom. She popped her head round the door a few minutes later. Fully dressed, made-up.

'I'm off out, Robert.'

'OK.' I wasn't going to ask her where she was going. I just wasn't.

'I won't be late.'

'OK. See you later.'

'Yeah.' She hesitated. 'OK. See you.'

I listened to her leaving the house. Waited five minutes, in case she came back suddenly. I wandered round the flat, which didn't take very long, and finished up in the bedroom. Light from the back of the house lit up a patch of the curtains. Everything seemed normal. I didn't know where she kept it, but I knew it was here somewhere. Before I quite knew what I was doing I was looking for it, looking everywhere. I started to throw things around, clothes, drawers full of letters and photos and used-up biros, everything. I tipped the bed up to look underneath.

And I found it. Her diary.

Reading someone's diary is of course one of the things that you don't do in life. You only steal when you have to, you only lie when there's no good alternative, you don't read personal documents, ever. Not even if you *are* a freelance investigative journalist. Reading someone's diary can never be research, it can only be an act of invasion. Unforgivable.

I flipped through. The entries were all sorts of lengths: she was no respecter of the neat one-day-at-a-time divisions. This wasn't in daily use, clearly, but was written whenever she had something she wanted to record. Her handwriting was small without being cramped or neurotic, neat but not fussy. Sensible.

I read: '. . . these things, I don't think it even occurs to him to consider what it . . .' and slammed the book shut. It was the size of a birthday card, blue, a-week-at-a-view. A5. Re-order No 55052.

I was standing by the window, with the wreckage of the room spread before me. I sat on the edge of the bed, waiting to see what I would do next.

I found the page with today's date, no entry. No indication of where she was or who she was with. No 'DB' anywhere, no times or places or names. I turned back to the beginning. I was determined to find something.

12 February: '. . . the whole weekend. Jamie and that simpering cow Tess actually feeding each other little morsels. Vo-mit. Robert was so rude I thought I was going to have to hit him, and we had to leave early, which actually wasn't such a bad idea . . .'

I remembered that weekend. I thought she *liked* Tess. Simpering cow, huh? And I wasn't rude, exactly, I just said what was on my mind. There had been an animated discussion about Liberal politics, I recall. Well, maybe a little bit more than animated. But rude? Well, probably, actually.

I read on, skipping weeks and months, looking for something, catching disconnected phrases as they flew past like rare moths, 'all over his sleeping-bag', 'so pointless, so unnecessary', 'gorgeous big table'. Nothing about Dave Barnard, unless he was referred to in code. Plenty, though, about one 'R'. Now who, I wondered, could that be?

'R going on all day about an article. Someone stole his idea and oh boy doesn't he intend to make sure that *everyone* knows about it. I manage, *just*, to forbear from whacking him a good one.'

This, of course, was just one amongst many compelling reasons not to read diaries: you were liable to catch nasty, unflattering little glimpses of yourself, like seeing your face in a security camera from an unwonted angle. I flicked a few pages on. This was all from earlier in the year, March and April.

2 April: 'Saw Mick of all people at Pret à Manger. Someone has clearly taken him in hand, he was looking *good*. Sleeves rolled up, and showing just a hint of bicep. He's much broader in the chest than I

remembered. I don't recall him being so big, I never noticed. Little tuft of chest hair at the throat, big green eyes. He caught me looking a couple of times and offered to show me more. I told him I was a married woman, more or less, and he said I love married women. They're my favourite flavour. Have you been reading one of those new men's mags, I asked him, and he said, no, writing for one. Actually.'

Mick? Mick *Hewitt*? Fiona had been flirting with Mick Hewitt in Pret à Manger? Could this, I wondered, be another reason not to read on? In case I didn't get any little glimpses of myself, but got glimpses of people like Mick bloody Hewitt instead?

17 April: 'Dear Robert, he does make me laugh bless him. Wants me to know now that he is feeling "increasingly committed to the idea of a baby". The *idea*. I said, sweet thing, since when has a baby been an idea? and he got all sniffy on me. I think he thinks that you just decide and that's it. This platonic-ideal baby appears from somewhere and you emote about it. I think he may have been over-protected as a child. Personally I blame his mother, the estimable Clara.'

Was she going to start in on my mother now? And I'm sure I never said that, about the idea of a baby. She should have known what I meant anyway. I turned pages, some blank, some filled with the small, legible script.

'R funny all weekend. He was supposed to have flu. Never just a cold, it has to be flu. I'm supposed to run round after him and bring him tasty titbits. We spend most of the time fooling around in bed. He invents this game called twenty thousand leagues under the sea,

287

the point of which seems to be that you get the bed all messed up and then swim about on top pretending to be underwater. He forgets for a few hours at a time how ill he's supposed to be, then suddenly remembers and starts looking serious and hard-done-by. Sweet thing. I do love him.'

Days and weeks and months flipped by. 20 July: a little mark, a circle with a star in it. 23 July: 'Three days late!' 27 July: 'One week and counting.' A doctor's appointment, 2.15 30 July. 8 August, a single word: 'Yes'. So she knew a full four days before she told me. Maybe she just wanted to be completely sure. Not written big, or underlined, just: 'yes'.

We moved on. We came to the day I took the train up to Derby, 26 August.

'No call from R. Anne round, she apparently sleeping with Mark now! Unaccountable and most strange.'

27 August: 'Nothing from R. No joy from police. Where is he, the bastard? He could at least ring.'

28 August: 'R now officially missing. Absolute hell with police, etc. Just what I need. Idiot policewoman saying knowingly, ''Well dear with you in your condition, men do sometimes get scared and run off. He'll be back good as gold in a day or two, when he's had a chance to get used to the idea.'' Baby as idea again. My baby is not an idea. If he's off playing games somewhere then his timing is terrible, as usual. Bastard. Where is he?'

2 September: 'Police useless. I didn't think our law enforcers observed bank holidays, but this lot certainly seem to. Impossible to get any sense of urgency into them. They have procedures. I told them that I was

sure now that he's in trouble, absolutely certain. There is no way he would not ring for so long. They said: we're doing everything we can. We're following our procedures. I said that I was sure Robert would be enormously relieved to hear that, even if he was tied up in someone's cellar. Bad move. I'm now a suspect, no longer the decorously worried wifey. I done him in and buried him out the back. Just like all the others. Folks roundabout call me the Black Widow. It's all just too bloody ridiculous. Bastard bastard bastard. Where *are* you?'

4 September: 'What if he's dead? Wouldn't someone have found the body by now? Spoke to Angie from Missing Persons' Families Project. "Spoke" is a euphemism. She was v. good with me, calmed me down, told me to stop worrying because it wouldn't help Robert and it made me less effective. It's a long game sometimes, she said. You have to dig in for the long haul. You have to be strong. People do come back, not always, but often. There was some explanation. Nothing happens without a reason. Hold onto that.'

6 September: 'R's mother on the phone. She distraught, I distraught, absolute hell. She managing to convey her opinion that it's all my fault, for driving her baby boy away from me. We arrange to meet later in week. Not looking forward to this.'

9 September: 'R's mother all afternoon. She drinks lots of gin, and alternates between frozen incomprehension and my-poor-baby lachrymosity. She manages to thaw out sufficiently to express sympathy for me by about the fifth glass. By seventh glass she is speculating on what he might be up to. It wouldn't

be the first time he's acted funny, apparently. She comes up with a most interesting story, about him and one Kevin Salthouse.'

Kev Salthouse? *What?*

'They used to be in a gang, him and Kevin and a few others, this is when they were eight or nine or so. They were out climbing trees or whatever, then she gets a phone call from the hospital. R is unhurt, but Kevin has fallen and knocked himself out. She goes to the hospital, and when she asks how it happened, Kevin says that R made him jump off a high branch. Made you? How did he do that, she said, and Kevin says'

I knew what came next: I forced Kev to do it by making my eyes go funny and saying that he had to do it because I had already seen it, so it had to happen. Suddenly I remembered, the smell of the tree bark, Kev's podgy little eight-year-old face staring at my eight-year-old face, the new way I felt, the way my eyes felt. And I remembered others, a photographer who had accompanied me on a story about a slum landlord. The photographer's face, something not right, one eye not right. I didn't say anything. The slumlord had an assistant, to assist us off the premises. The photographer carelessly got his face into the path of the assistant's fist. The assistant favoured chunky jewellery, big rings. The photographer lost an eye. Not my fault. How could it be my fault? But I had seen it and then it had happened. Other incidents: interviewing a young mother, in connection with her common-law husband who had disappeared with money collected for an operation for their daughter. She touched my hand to emphasize a point: her hand was cold. More than just cold. I pulled away from her, from her too-white face and too-cold hands. She jumped seven storeys later that evening.

'. . . Kevin says, "Robert said I had to do it because he'd already seen it: his eyes went funny and he said he had seen it already and so it had to happen." R's mother said, honey, no-one can make you do things if you don't want to, and Kevin wouldn't say any more. He apparently had a few other accidents that summer, cuts and burns and knocks but wouldn't explain how they'd happened.'

There it was in black and white. I sat, my back wedged uncomfortably against the bed, something sticking into me. Kev Salthouse. At the end of that summer his parents had confronted mine, demanded that we be separated. Kev was having nightmares. There was something wrong with me, they said, something wrong in the head. I had forgotten all that. It had been so long ago.

If I see it, then it happens.

I held the diary. *Not really, no I haven't, no I don't think so. Say quarter to, just to be on the safe side.* The phrases hung in my head, like pieces of a curse. Fiona was leaving me, I was certain. I must have slept.

I awoke, nagged out of sleep by a quiet but persistent sound. I sat up, aching from my awkward posture, from the bits of the bed digging into my spine and shoulder. No sign of Fiona. I tried to put a name to the sound but couldn't. It was just a sound, you heard it all the time. It stopped, and I knew what it had been: next door's dog. He was barking, not loudly, but steadily and with a kind of intensity. He started up again. I got off the bed and went into the front room. There was a faint glow from a street light a few doors down, filtering through the Venetian blind. The world was asleep, except for the dog and me. He usually only got excited if there was some kind of trouble, or noise. As far as I could tell there was no trouble. There was certainly no noise, except for his barking and my breathing. I stood in the dark room, feeling tall and uneasy.

There was a shadow on the couch. A cushion. As I watched it, it came more and more to resemble the shape a small bundle would make. I heard myself saying I'm not your usual kind of client, I don't bugger my *dog*, I don't injure my *children* – would never, could never injure a child, not even accidentally, never.

No? You injured Kev Salthouse, you injured him several times, in fact you had to be separated from him because he was having—

Eight years old! I was eight years old!

It was in you then, it's in you now, and you know it.

Christ's sake, it's just a cushion –

Yes? Look more closely. The voice was one I knew, low, controlled, with a hint of a smile. Teacher's voice. A shadow behind a cushion? Is that what you see? I don't think so. Tell me what you're seeing. Tell me.

I'm not seeing anything, I don't see things, I'm not –

Tell me. Is it perhaps a baby?

I made myself look away. I looked back. Yes. A baby, all wrapped up against the cold. Except that that wasn't necessary now, because if it was a baby then it was lying far too still to be a living baby. Nothing living should be that still. If I see it, it has to happen.

The words came to me as if spoken aloud. Kev Salthouse's fall. Fuckyou's noose. Stroker's needle. The man with the headache, moaning. Whoever he was.

So was this going to happen? Our baby, a cold, still, silent little bundle? Was I going to make it happen? No, I would never, *could* never

For God's sake. What had got into me?

I went over to the sofa, the dog's bark like the wailing of women. I reached down, touched the cushion, which was cool and sleek under my fingers. I sat next to it. I picked it up. I held it, gently, carefully, in both arms, held it to my chest. I was crying, my tears fell onto the cushion. It wasn't going to happen. I knew how to stop it. I'd just been waiting for the right reason.

66

Next morning Fiona was still gone, and so were some of her things. She must have taken them with her last night. Disappeared! I laughed aloud. She must have felt it was her turn. I wasn't surprised. Sex had become impossible, since I apparently couldn't discriminate between passion and assault any more. Conversation was a minefield. Silences were deadly.

I rang her at work. She didn't try to escape the call. She was ready for me.

'Hello Robert.'

'Fiona?'

'I'm moving out for a while, Robert.'

'Why?'

She laughed, and I had to admit that I saw her point. *Why*, indeed.

'I've got to think of what's best. I've got to think about the baby, Robert. I couldn't trust you with a baby the way you are now. Could I? I'm not saying you'd do anything to hurt it, but you know you're not yourself. I worry about it all the time, Robert, and you refuse to do anything about it, and I just don't know what to do. I can't carry on the way we've been. I don't know what to do for the best.'

'OK. So when are you coming back?' I tried to speak

normally but my voice was quivery, defiant, childlike. It wouldn't behave itself. 'When are you coming back?'

'I don't know, Robert. When you're normal again.'

'I don't know how to be normal again.'

'I know.' She was being firm, businesslike, not giving an inch. I could tell it was a real effort for her. I thought I heard her voice misbehaving a little as well. She knew what she wanted to say, had presumably rehearsed it thoroughly, but that didn't make it any easier. We might not have one of the grand passions of our age, but we were accomplices, we got along. She was going to have our baby, whatever that might mean. No-one would ever write an opera called *Robert and Fiona*, but it's still hard to walk out on someone, even if it is only someone you've liked and known for a long time. Maybe even loved, on and off. It would probably be years before anyone knew her as well as I did, or knew me in the way she did. Our voices caught and stumbled on the little hooks we had between us.

'I know. Robert, you have to go and see someone. Why won't you?'

'It won't work.'

'You don't know that.'

'No; no I suppose not.' We were having a very sensible conversation. I could see her point of view perfectly. I really could. I could hear office noises in the background, phones ringing, women laughing.

'Fiona? Are you there?'

'Yes.'

'I'm really sorry about all this.'

'I know you are.'

'I'm really sorry. I don't know—' I was about to

say, I don't know what's got into me. 'I don't know how it happened.'

'I know.'

'Fiona, listen, last night, I saw something.'

'You – ?' She was nonplussed.

'I saw something. The baby.'

'Robert, you—'

'But I know how to fix it.'

'Robert. I don't know what to say to you any more. I just don't.'

'If I can fix it, will you come back?'

'You're not making any sense.'

'I'm not myself at the moment, something's—'

'Look—'

' – just gone *wrong* with me, or maybe it was wrong all the time and it's just suddenly, you know, come to the surface. He said I had a sickness, and he was right, there's something inside me.'

'We've talked about this enough Robert. I've said I'm not going to discuss it with you any more until you've gone to see someone.'

'I'm really—'

'I'm going to have to get back to work now. I'll ring you tonight. We can talk about it more then.' A concession, against her better judgement. 'But I'm not coming back.'

'Fiona—'

The phone buzzed in my ear. I listened to it for a few seconds, until the tone changed.

67

There was no danger of disappearing now; since Fiona had gone there was no-one to disappear from. Nevertheless, just in case she should come round, I left a note on the fridge door, stuck down by the frying-pan magnet:

'Just *literally* popped out for 10 Marlboro. I love you. Sorry. Everything will be all right. R.'

I took money out of our joint savings account, what she called the baby fund, what I called the slush fund. I took my small tape recorder, the one I thought of as my 007, and a sharp, serrated knife. I even turned off the water at the stopcock and emptied the fridge. I might, I thought, be gone some time. My mobile was fully charged and ready to go.

The Saab was waiting, sleek, black, hot from the early sun. I climbed in and turned over the engine, put the radio on, headed north. I was singing.

68

I picked up the signal somewhere near Leicester. *Mahog-any FM*. The programme was mostly music with occasional interviews – the spokesman for a group protesting about a proposed bypass, someone from the local chamber of commerce, a lollipop lady retiring after thirty-eight years. Adverts for car-repair firms and 'financial advisors'. It all seemed very shadowy and insubstantial, as other people's lives tend to. The presenter was called Kerry James; he sounded as if he was trying hard to disguise a north-east accent under something more 'radio-friendly'.

I parked at a greasy spoon and got the number from Directory Enquiries.

'Re*cep*tion.' The voice rose sharply on 'cep'.

'Hello? Is that Mahogany FM.'

'Yes. How can I *help* you.' Low low low HIGH low. A vacant, singsong voice, like an exotic bird.

'Can you tell me when that show comes on? With the healer?'

'Excuse me?'

'With Melissa Portmaddoch and the religious nut? Teacher?'

'Oh yes. I'll *just find* out for you.' Low HIGH HIGH low low low.

'Yellow Bird', played by a pinging metallic electronic sound. I could imagine the reception area, the framed prints of the DJs, the free car-stickers, the receptionist's swept-back hi-lites.

'Good afternoon, features editor, how can I help?' This was a man, brisk and efficient.

'Yes, I was wanting to know, when is that programme, with that guy Teacher?'

'Well he's been appearing on the Melawney Polporral show over the last few weeks, that's Thursday at seven. Are you interested in being a participant?'

'No, no I just wanted—'

'I only ask because we're having to book participant slots in advance now. Because of the demand. We've been amazed at the uptake.'

'The up—'

'So if you were interested I'd pass you along to the researcher for that show. She'd then ask you a few questions, nothing intrusive, you know, just so we can get an idea of whether you'd be a suitable prospect.'

'I see.'

'Because, I'm sure I don't need to tell you, we are attracting a certain kind of audience segment here that is not always appropriate for peak broadcasting. I'm afraid we have to screen out a good many of the enquiries.'

'Fruitcakes huh?'

'In a nutshell. Our experience in this field is very limited – this show is by way of a pilot. We're learning as we go. I'm sure you understand.'

'OK. Let me speak to your researcher.'

'Would you hold the line please?'

'All I Have to Do Is Dream'; *ping* ping, ping, ping: ping-ping-ping-piiiing, ping

'Good afternoon, Geraldine Alder, how can I help.' She was huskier, breathier, but no less efficient.

'Yes. Hi.' I wasn't ready for her. I didn't have anything to say. It was like one of Graham's auditions, except that there wasn't a script, or a sadistic director.

'You're interested in participating in the programme?'

'Yeah, OK. I mean yes, yes I am.'

'All right.' Her voice was smooth and caressing. 'I just need to take a few details. Your name please; just your first name is fine.'

'Byron.' *Byron?*

'And a number you can be reached on?'

I gave the number. I could hear her tapping the information into a computer. I could imagine her hands, slightly knotty and with chipped nail varnish.

'Now. Because of the nature of the show, I'm sure you'll appreciate that I need to know roughly what kind of issue you're going to want to raise with Teacher. I don't know if you're a regular listener to the programme?'

'No.'

'Because you see we've had some rather problematical situations arising. The last thing we want is to have to break for music. I have to be sure that you're not going to swear, for instance, or use abusive language, give out personal details – by which I mean addresses or full names. Anything like that.'

'No. I'll be good.'

'You do understand, don't you – '

300

'Perfectly. I'm cool.' *Cool?*

'All right Byron. So now I need to know, in a few words, what you're going to want to talk about. Not the whole story, that's not my business, but just as it were the subject *area*.'

'OK. Er.'

The silkiness in her voice was becoming harder.

'Is it a personal matter? Something that's happened to you?'

'Er.'

'Or something that you've done? By the way, we operate under conditions of strict confidentiality so you don't have to worry about that. We have no links with, you know, the police for instance or social services, if that's an issue. We're not here to take sides. It's really not our concern.'

Strict confidentiality. Live on air. Quite some trick, that.

'Does it involve someone else, someone you know?'

'No, no. It's me.' I'd found my voice finally.

'It's you.' Silky again, coaxing.

'It's me. There's something wrong with me.'

'Something wrong, I see.' A pause: I imagined her doodling on a memo pad. Honeycombs or paisley swirls.

'Is there any more you can tell me? Just so I've got a little bit more to go on.'

'Well – '

'Because "something wrong", that's not – you know, that's not giving me very much to go on.'

'It's hard to talk about these things – '

'Of course it is, I know it is, Byron, but you see –

from my point of view, the thing I have to think is –
you know, if you can't tell me about it now, will you
be able to tell Teacher, on the radio?'

'I harm people.'

'OK.'

I could see paisley swirls, spirals, a spoked wheel,
an eye.

'OK, do you mean you *hurt* people?'

'Hurt people. Yes.' She had something to work on
now.

'You like to hurt people? Or you just can't help it?'

'Both.'

'OK.'

She paused. She was good, this Geraldine Alder. I
sensed that she needed more. The wheel was now
surrounded by a little framework, but there was a strut
missing.

'Is there anything else you want to say?'

'Yes. Yes there is.'

'All right, and can you tell me what it is?'

'I – ' Long pause.

'OK. Is there any particular way you like to hurt
people?'

'I'm sorry, I don't quite – '

'Well, for instance, some people like to hurt people
in a – ' pen poised over the drawing, over the missing
piece, 'in a sexual way – '

'Yes. That's it.'

'In a sexual way?'

'Yes.'

'*OK.*'

Bingo. We were in business. She knew her job, this

woman. I'd probably end up the star of the show. They might even invite me back.

'Well Byron. That's all I need, and thank you for bearing with me there, and thank you for your *honesty* because, you know, that's what this programme is really about.'

She explained the procedure. They would ring me ten minutes before I was due on. If I was listening to the programme on the radio I would have to keep the sound fairly low or they'd get feedback. The rules: no accusations against named or identifiable parties, nothing that could be considered libellous or defamatory to individuals or organizations, no phone numbers, no full names or addresses. I was not to identify myself except by my first name. No foul language, no obscenity, no blasphemy. Oh, and try to *enjoy* it.

Thursday, seven o'clock. Little more than twenty-four hours away. I decided to sleep in the car. I kept the radio on late.

69

Darren from Belper, who was the turn before me, was *not* being very compelling. He had a juridical, diffident manner, and was coming across like a medieval schoolman, nit-picking, hair-splitting, needlessly argumentative.

'I thought you said just now – ' Teacher's voice, quiet, sorrowful.

'No, what I *said* was – '

Melawney wanted to wind it up: it was going nowhere. Darren was not going to cry and had no particular revelation to impart. That element of confession, of abasement, just wasn't there. I could see the producer behind the glass wall, a balding, amiable man in his early forties, shaking his head, lifting his hands to heaven. It just wasn't happening. I could see it all.

'OK Darren, we're going to have to leave it there. As always I'm going to ask you to hold the line, so that one of our trained counsellors – ' She reached for a jingle, and the computer screen in front of her gave her my name.

Mahog-any FM. A drooping, falling cadence.

'OK. We have with us now Byron, calling from somewhere near Longford. Byron? Can you hear us?'

'Yes. Hello.' Reception was good, just slightly hissy. The air was warm and still. My throat was dry.

'Right. You're through to Teacher.'

'Byron?'

There was his voice. Now that he was speaking to me directly I felt again the authority, the assertion of power.

Melawney led me through the initial phases of the conversation, then turned me over to Teacher. On Melawney's screen the words 'likes to hurt people, sexually' had popped up. They knew what they wanted.

'Byron? You wanted to tell me something?'

'Yes. Well, actually I wanted to ask you something. If you don't mind.'

'Of course I don't mind. You can ask me anything you want.'

'Yeah? OK, what I wanted to know is, where do you bury the bodies?'

'Where do I – I'm sorry, I'm not sure I heard you right – '

'Yeah you did. Where did you put him, when you took him down from that tree?'

Mahog-any FM. I could hear their voices, but the live link had been efficiently severed, presumably by the bald producer behind his glass wall. I could hear Teacher saying it's OK, it's all right, I'll talk to him, and Melawney in conversation with the producer. No-one thought to cut me off. Gladys Knight, 'Midnight Train to Georgia', someone's bizarre choice or perhaps just the nearest thing to hand. I held the phone to my ear, and then the connection was cut. I went back to the Saab and turned the radio on. When Gladys

Knight had finished, Melawney came on to apologize and assure listeners that the show – the *programme* would be continuing as normal, and they would be taking another call, but first, Teacher, you wanted to say something? Her voice was jittery. She didn't want Teacher to say anything just at that moment, she wanted to get back in control.

'Yes. I wanted to speak to Byron. If you're still listening out there Byron, then I'll be only too happy to meet you and talk to you. If you feel there are things that you need to discuss with me, ring the station back and they'll put you on to me after the programme. I feel that I recognize your voice. Have we met? I think we have. I think you weren't called Byron then. Am I right? I remember that you were troubled, fearful, and that you had to leave suddenly before we could finish what we started. I'm happy to hear your voice again, I truly am. Get back in touch. OK?' His voice, so gentle, so persuasive. 'OK?'

Melawney returned and the show's next victim popped up, and the ghastly parade of bleeding stumps limped on.

Teacher signed off with his homely prayer about being back on the road, firing on all cylinders, getting a retune, whatever nonsense it was. I rang the station.

'Re*cep*tion.'

'Yeah, I need to speak to Teacher.'

'He's on the air right now. Who's calling please?'

'Byron.'

'Byron – ?'

'From near Longford.'

'Hold the line please.'

'Memory': piiing piiing, ping-ping-ping-ping-ping, piiing

'Byron?' There he was. I could picture him, sitting in the producer's padded swivel chair. I said, 'I'll meet you, but I'll meet you somewhere neutral and I'll have someone with me. If you don't show up I'm going to the police. I have a few questions for you. Just one or two.'

'You always did have,' he said, 'as far as I remember.'

We arranged a time and a place. The only place I could think of was the kiddies' playground at the Appleby Magna Services. He said he'd be there.

'Alone?'

'If that's what you want.'

'It's what I want.'

I hung up.

70

Is that the trap there? What body part would you like me to put in, arm, leg? Head? We met under the giant fibreglass toadstool. I was fully equipped with secret tape recorder, small serrated knife, and newly-recruited witness, a photographer from the local evening paper, called Stu. I'd impressed him with my credentials, my pieces in *The Face, GQ, New Statesman*. I almost impressed myself. He knew all about Teacher, of course. I explained to him that I was after an interview, an exposé, and needed someone to take pictures. I didn't mention that in my opinion these were dangerous and unpredictable people. He would have to take his chances, like anyone else. There was the strong possibility of publication in an unnamed national monthly. He said he'd give it some thought. He rang back the next day. We drove out in the Saab.

And Teacher was there, standing, leaning against his bike, ankles crossed, arms crossed, dark, pitted face. We got out, and Teacher and Stu greeted each other, by name. I was momentarily surprised by this, then I remembered that I'd seen an article about Teacher in a local paper, I'd seen a picture, had even become somewhat obsessed with it. Now who, I wonder could have taken that picture? I remembered also that the article had been completely uncritical, almost reverential in tone, I remembered being struck by that quality about it. Teacher and Stu shook hands, and then hugged briefly. I ducked back into the car. The keys weren't there. I saw Stu hand them over to Teacher, a still, bright moment of complete paranoia, complete revelation. It's one of the last things I can remember with any clarity. The twinkle of the evening sun on my car keys, and Teacher's beautiful, gentle, mad smile.

71

Doc came in to see me. I asked him why he'd come. Why? Because you were moaning. Was I? Yes. You've been moaning for about an hour. I thought I could hear banging coming from next door. Dum da-da dum dum, dum *dum*. There's no-one next door. Are you sure? Sometimes I think I can hear things. What kind of things? Just someone moving around. I thought I heard a window break. He leaned over me and pulled my eyelids down. I'll take a look at your head, he said, while I'm here. I lay still while he unwound the bandage. Eventually the bandage started to stick against itself, where the wound was still weeping. He had to tug it a little bit, and I winced each time, though it didn't really hurt.

He looked at the wound and said I'll just clean it up, but it's getting better, definitely. I said the noises, he said what noises. From next door. Oh *those* noises. What are they, if there's no-one in that room? He said, well it's possible that you're hearing sounds from somewhere else in the hotel. Sound travels oddly sometimes, because of the – I said, acoustics? he said, yes, or just the way the building's constructed. But I heard it. Someone was banging on the wall and shouting. He sat back. Well, it could be that you're experiencing some effects, some *temporary* effects, from what's been done. I noted the passive voice, but was not at that time able to mention it because I couldn't remember what it was called. Effects? I said. Just temporary, he said, it does happen sometimes.

When will he come, I said, but he ignored me. I'd probably only just asked him that. How long will it take for my head to heal? I'd probably asked him that a thousand times as well, but it was a better question because I could pretend that I was being a good patient and taking an active interest in my progress rather than just being someone who was terrified all the time and who kept on saying the same things over and over again because I couldn't remember anything properly. And who was suffering, just temporarily, from certain acoustical effects, because of the way the building was constructed.

He said you should keep on writing your story, I said I can't, I can't see straight and I keep forgetting things. The pen keeps falling on the floor, and the paper slides about. And where I dribble, it makes the paper wet, and it rips. He said, well, what about that little tape recorder you had? You could speak into that couldn't you? It must be lying around somewhere. Where did you put it. Can't remember. Got to keep yourself busy. Keep your spirits up. Till Teacher gets here to look at you again, see what needs to be done next. I said, when will that be, soon he said. Send for the doctor, I said, my head aches. He said not to worry pal, just be cool, OK? That was hours ago, or days ago or something.

Moaning. Head aches. I had seen it, now it had happened. To me.

72

One of them came to show me something. Look, he said, you've got a letter. How could I have a letter here? I said. How could anyone know where I am? We gave her a box number as long as she promised not to tell anyone about it. Do you want me to read it to you? I said no, just give it to me. Bastard. He gave it to me, but I couldn't read it, which he knew perfectly well already, hence the little smirk. All right, you read it, I said. Dear Robert, I was so relieved to get your last letter, I was starting to get worried! What last letter, I said, I never sent any letter. We sent one for you. We don't want anyone getting worried about you now do we? You wouldn't want her to be worried would you? It was better that we write to her, while you couldn't manage it. Now you're back with us a bit more you can dictate it if you want and we'll just write it out for you and send it. You can even sign it if you like. Shall I keep on reading it? Dear Robert, da da da da to get worried! What you said gave me quite a surprise, as I'm sure I don't need to tell you, but I suppose I always suspected just a bit that you might eventually want something like this. You've always been interested in things like this haven't you, and I suppose that was just a way of trying to pretend to yourself that you didn't really believe in any of it, it was just something you were interested in. I said, I don't know if it's her style or your reading but it doesn't sound like proper English. He said, maybe it's your hearing. Maybe you're not hearing things properly. Acoustics, I said. He said, whuh? Go on with the letter, please, I said. You're reading it just fine. Dum de dum, really believe in any of it. But I'm really happy for you, that you've found something that satisfies you. I just wish it wasn't so exclusive. I wish it didn't mean that you had to leave me. Particularly now Robert, because I have some good news for you. I hope you're sitting down darling because guess what? You're a father!! She's a week old now, and she weighs nine pounds. Her hair is fair and she has beautiful blue eyes, she looks a bit like your Grandma Beale actually, particularly round the eyes. So I've called her Jessica. Your grandma cried when I told her. She said Jessica was an old lady's name, but I said that the old names were all coming back now and that it was perfect for her. She said you should be with me now, not off somewhere. But you have to do what you think is right. Please write again soon, so I know you're safe. I'll send you a picture of her. She's so beautiful. Don't be gone too long, Robert.

What did you tell her, I said. Oh, nothing much, he said. What did you tell her I said, louder, shouting maybe. WHAT DID YOU— We said that you'd decided to stay with us for a while, that you were having some changes, and that you didn't know how long you'd be gone. How long will I be gone? I said. Then: how long have I been gone? He wouldn't tell

314

me anything. What have you done? What do you mean? What have you done, to my head? Why does my head ache, and why have I got this stupid bandage on? He wouldn't tell me anything. Hold on a minute, I said, if she's just had the baby, then it must be, hold on, hold on, that can't be right. I tried to get up, to look out of the window, to see what the world looked like, but I felt dizzy and he had to help me back to bed. Do you want to dictate a letter back? he said, you could use your little tape machine. Good, that is. It's like off James Bond or something. 007.

73

They had apparently been writing to Fiona regularly, for months. Someone else had taken over these duties from Loverman, I didn't know him. He had developed quite a taste for it and had been inventing my life fluently, so he told me. He seemed proud of his work and was happy to fill me in on all the important details. In these letters I had returned to the Sons, had discovered that they could offer me what my life had so far been missing, and had asked them to take me in, which they had. It was all quite touching really. In the fullness of time I had been healed, and was now in a kind of blessed state of rebirth. I had, it appeared, no intention of returning to my former life, despite the recent birth of my child, my Jessica, and was intending to stay with the Sons of the New Bethlehem indefinitely, as a kind of associate member. Other events over the last six months: I had been having problems with my teeth, and had had to have wisdom teeth extracted, under a general anaesthetic. This had left me woozy for a few days, and it was feared at one point that I had had an adverse reaction and might have further problems, but – thank the lord! – I had made a full recovery and was better than ever. 'Adverse reaction': he must have got that from Doc.

I had apparently discovered an unsuspected talent for motor mechanics, and was now able to converse freely and with some insight on the niceties of the four-stroke OHV engine. Thus, apparently, my letters were increasingly full of technical discussions of expanding shoes and primary reduction ratios. What Fiona was supposed to make of any of this was anyone's guess. She would appear to have swallowed it all, if her reply was anything to go by. If her reply was genuine. My eyes still weren't good, and I couldn't verify the handwriting. If Loverman's replacement could generate one side of the correspondence, then why not the other? He had to do something to occupy himself through the long watches of the night and day. I doubted that the illogicality of it would have troubled him particularly.

I was getting better, clearer, all the time. My head ached less hard and less often. I was able to hold up my end of a conversation, after a fashion. Not that the conversations were much to write home about, assuming that I was capable of doing such a thing. They came to talk to me often, at all times of the day and night. They wouldn't answer simple questions, though, like what have you done to me and why. They preferred rambling, meaningless stuff about truth and intercession. Doc was very sympathetic at this time, and would stay and talk to me when I became distressed or confused, talk to me calmly and slowly, saying things as often as was necessary. He spoke about the effects of what had been done to me, and how they were temporary, purely temporary. Trust me, he'd say sometimes, would I steer you wrong? and

I'd manage a smile. That's my boy, he'd say.

I started to feel that I could remember some things, or if not remember them, then *see* them after a fashion, as if I was watching them happen to someone else. I saw bits and pieces. I would call, watch out! here he comes again! you better get out of there, pal, I would if I were you! It was like being the kind of person who goes to see the same film over and over again and who knows all the action and dialogue by heart. Here he comes! Behind you! *Watch it!* It had the same inevitability too: there was nothing I could do to change the sequence of events, all I could do was watch them as they unfolded, each time more detailed, extended, a bit more before or after, more depth of field, better sound quality. Only a matter of time before I was in Dolby Stereo.

The central thing was sitting in a chair and not being able to move. Being restrained, perhaps strapped or perhaps just drugged, though not completely. Not enough. There were two people, people I knew well, they circled me and came and went, in front and behind, very busy. They held things, carried things, brought things over to me. The atmosphere was perhaps the clearest part, very tense, expectant. They spoke, but I couldn't understand their words. There were other sounds, less well-defined, and I came to understand that they were moans, wails, screams even, and that I was making them. Then one of them came up close. Watch out! Don't let him—! Well, whatever.

I asked Doc about these little scenes, and he said, you had to have some teeth out, didn't you? You must be remembering that. No, I said, in the letters I had to have teeth out but I didn't really, did I? He just made that up so he'd have something to say to . . . to . . . to . . . Fiona? Fiona. I didn't actually have any teeth out, I can feel them all with my tongue, he said these were wisdom teeth, you wouldn't have been able to feel them properly. Then how did I know I had to have them out? How did *you* know I had to have them out, how did anybody? He said you had an X-ray, I said why did I? And he said because of your wisdom teeth. Are you talking crap, I said, or is it me? He said, don't worry about it, just relax. Anyway, I said, if I had wisdom teeth out then why is my head bandaged. You fell and banged your head, he said, when you were coming round from the anaesthetic. Why wasn't somebody holding me? They were, he said, believe me, but you kept on struggling. Why was I? You got freaked out and thought we were trying to kill you. Generals can take people that way sometimes. You had a bit of an adverse reaction. I said, the trouble is, I can't remember any of this, but I'm starting to remember something, something else, and I don't think it's teeth. Yeah? Well, take it easy man, I have to go and see someone else. I said, there were two people, and they weren't dentists. One of them looked like you. Yeah? Well, be seeing you man. Come back, I said, please, I want to talk to you. I'll be back soon, he said, try to take it easy man, you're not making things any easier for yourself. Or for us. We don't want to have to do any more, but we will if we have to. Believe me.

74

Tell me, Teacher said.

This was before the chair and the headaches, some time before that. Teacher and I were together, I can't say for sure where or when.

Tell me.

What do you want, I said, a confession? I have offended in thought word and deed, in what I have done and in what I have failed to do –

Tell me.

– and that I am most grievously sorry –

Yes. Tell me why you're sorry.

I'm sorry I ever got tangled up with you, you fucking murdering bastard.

So why did you?

I told you. It was a story. It's what I do. Didn't Stu tell you that?

So why this story?

Why any story? You sounded like an interesting freak. I'm attracted to the freakish. It amuses me.

Do I amuse you?

Amuse is the wrong word. You remind me of someone.

Who. Tell me.

You really want to know? You remind me of my

wicked Uncle Mick. He would extract confessions with the threat of violence, then punish the offences thus extracted, violently. I thought he was administering justice, I had no idea he was just a sadistic drunk with a fondness for babysitting.

And?

And? He was a bully. That's all.

Did you feel forgiven?

I felt dirty. He knew how not to mark the body. He never got found out. I saw him, quite by accident, about a year ago. He was walking with the aid of a stick. Drunk, dirty, but completely undefeated, you could still see the mean little light in his mean little eyes. He didn't recognize me.

You recognize him in me?

Let's just say I think you'd have a lot to talk about. Shared interests.

You think I want to punish you?

If I say 'yes' then *you* say – what for? Correct?

It's you who keeps on bringing up punishment.

Is that what Mr Sellars was bringing up? Punishment?

You think you saw something?

I didn't say –

What. Tell me. What you think you saw. You have to tell me.

I saw you batter the shit out of someone who was mad and vulnerable and God alone knows what happened to him after that.

After that, he was healed. He's free now.

You mean there's more? There's more than just beating the crap out of psychiatric cases? It gets more sophisticated than that?

Yes it gets more sophisticated. You seem only to be able to see violence, not mercy. There is great mercy.

Whatever it is I don't want to see it. I don't want to see any more of it.

So why did you come back?

To finish the story.

No, I think you wanted something else. You have a gift. I know and you know that this is so. It is given by God, but you don't trust it, it frightens you because you don't know how to use it. You came back so that I would take your gift away from you. Heal you of it.

My my, the things you do say.

You see this, but also you don't see it. You have talents but you refuse to use them. You won't take responsibility for them. You won't do what it is that you are required by covenant to do. I've tried to help you, and I will continue to try until I do help you. With my maker's aid. With your gift comes a sickness, and I will take that away, without damaging your gift. I won't fail you.

You mean, you're not going to let me go with my faculties intact because if you do it'll be the end of your little fiefdom here and you know it.

What is it you imagine I want to do to you? What is it that you imagine I am able to do? You sound as if I have special powers. I understood that you didn't believe in such things, not even your own.

It doesn't take special powers to beat the crap out of someone, particularly if you've got two people holding him down. It perhaps takes a special kind of *meanness* –

I'm sad to hear you talk like this. I truly am. I think when you're free, really free, you'll look back on this time and be unable to believe that you were who you are now, that you thought what you think now.

Yeah, I suppose one day I'll thank you for it, as my wicked Uncle Mick used to say. You may not think so now, my boy, but one day –

You'll thank *God* for it.

I don't see him round here anywhere.

You see what you want to see. But soon you'll really see. Soon you'll really be free. That's a promise. And then you just might start to be of some use.

To you?

To anyone.

You better finish the job off this time because once I'm out of here, then you're finished. *That's* a promise. Man.

Big talk. Goading him. I have no idea whom I was trying to impress. My voice sounded unlike itself in my ears.

I was trying to find the words that would push him into action, that would make him heal me. Take away the sight: the noose, the needle, the dead baby. I had to make him take it away.

This, I think was in his house. There was a child, a little boy of about four, he ran around a lot and spoke incessantly. Babble babble I did that and she said all over the place it was MASSIVE! Something like that, unless I wasn't hearing him right. Teacher at one point was sitting by me. The child came over and Teacher scooped him up and lifted him into the air and shook him. The child just carried on babbling, it was all green but I didn't have any and THEN! Teacher seemed uncertain quite what to do next and put him down again, carefully. There was a woman as well, she moved around very softly and pushed her hair behind her ear. She looked worried, as if she was looking for something she'd only just put down a minute ago. I saw the boy from the Burger King car park, he looked bewildered, standing at the top of the stairs. Naked. Teacher ushered him away into a room upstairs. I remember stumbling to the stairwell and bellowing up *Come on then! Do it if you're going to do it!* My rage spilled out of me, making my voice into a coarse ragged noise. *Come on then!* I wasn't there long. A few hours I think.

75

Sitting in a chair, and not being able to move. Two people, moving about, busy. Strong light overhead. I am fully awake, but prior to this I have been deeply asleep. There have been long conversations, at all times of the day and night, little sleep, broken up. I have been asleep standing up. I have dreamed about being asleep, awoken to dreams and disorientation. Techniques have been used upon me, somewhere inside me I know that, but as I sit in the chair, marvelling at my incapacity and the busyness of the two (who are not dentists, incidentally, because dentists do not wear combat fatigues and leather jackets, dentists do not have shaved-on-top-and-long-at-the-sides hair. Dentists do not *smell* like this) I cannot see the techniques, all I can see is blurriness and wanting to sleep. I want to lie still in the chair and sleep, but I must stay awake now, while the two who are not dentists move about with such urgency. They disappear behind me, they come back and appear in my field of vision. I can't see what they're doing behind me, but I can see it as well, I can see a table, it has things lying on it. Instruments. I can see that these instruments are laid out in a certain way. I have seen this way of laying things out before, I have seen these patterns before, and I must try to think where, but I can't because I am so sleepy. I wake, having dreamed that I slept for a moment. I dreamed that I dreamed something. In my dream I saw things laid out, tools, instruments. Blurry. There is a voice behind me, two voices speaking in ragged unison, unless it is just a trick of the light, no the acoustics, an acoustical phenomenon, like hearing something that isn't there, but these voices are there, they are speaking approximately together. It takes me a few seconds to puzzle out what they are doing. Then I understand: they are praying. They are saying a prayer together, all their busyness has stopped. I can relax, but only for a moment. I grip the chair, and it is indeed like being at the dentist, I grip the chair because I fear, and I fear, much, strongly, as the voices speak together, more or less, about the lord and granting aid. Intercession. The words sound strange, they do not sound like ordinary words, they are words that people never say, not usually, at least not at the dentist. I fear. The words make me fear. Then someone holds my head, from behind so I can't see him, but I can see him, he is strong, he has large strong hands. His face is tightly clenched. He closes his eyes, he screws up his face like a fist, he shakes his head, mutters words, the same strange words, muttering fast and hard, he is pressing onto my head, then he is twisting my head round, this way and that, twisting it round. I can't move my hands or my arms. I think it is about this point that I start to make the sounds, just little sounds at first, little grunts. He comes round to the front, so I can see him, but I can't since he is too close, all I can see is a patch of his jeans, my head is pushed into his leg, his thigh. His hands are moving over my head, his fingers are gripping my head, digging into my head, all over my head. The other one is standing behind and I can see him, I know who he is, he is he is. I know who he is. The one with the fingers pulls his hands away and moves away, my face is no longer pushed into his thigh, I sleep and wake and hear sounds from behind me, from the table where the things are. Where the things are laid out. Then he is behind me again and he is calling out words now, shouting, calling things out and I call out as well, I call out as loud as he does, louder, I'm yelling, and his voice rises as well, we're yelling like a pair of maniacs, there is a lack of control, of good order. Things are wild and strange, like in a dream, just before you wake up, but I do not wake up so this, presumably, is not a dream and thus, presumably really took place. Things continue, howling and wildness, and he is back on my head again, in my hair, what are you doing there I yell at him and he is yelling his fearful words, get away from me, get away from my head, what are you doing up there? The other one comes and I feel my hair being cut away in a small area, right down to the bone, then I smell something and something is rubbed against my cold scalp, it's freezing, all the yelling stops for a moment, except mine, that continues in the new silence, what are you doing up there you murdering bastard, get away from my head you murdering bastard, get away from me, get – well the words aren't important I suppose, and probably there are no proper words now, just as it were the shapes of words, the sound of words but no real words, my words have become strange like his, stranger, because they are just noises, grunts, howls, as I shake myself, try to shake myself free, but just shake myself so that I and the chair rock against the floor, tapping against the floor. I set up a rhythm, rapid, counterpointing the non-words that I am yelling, I'm a one-man band, I got rhythm. Man. The other one grabs my head now, he locks his elbow round my neck and I think he is going to strangle me, then he loosens off and I can breathe and make my sounds again. My head is braced, but I am still knocking against the floor, and my legs are going, everything's going. The one who was digging about in my hair is back, he has taken an instrument from the table where the things were laid out like surgical instruments in an operating theatre. These are not surgical instruments, though, these are tools, laid out like in a garage. He is behind me, so I can't see but I can and what it is is a drill, a hand drill, he has the drill to my head, and there are no words but there are sounds and rhythms, and now there is the little whining sound as he turns the drill, slowly, into the little frozen patch on my scalp, like a frozen lake in a park, he is drilling through the ice, and under the ice? Is there anything under the ice? Are there slow fishes trawling the dim blue waters, their blank faces circling endlessly by, waiting for the thaw? Strange, the things you remember: I recall that the skull is thicker in some places than others, and so I'm thinking, is this a thick bit or a thin bit, how long will it be bone he's drilling through? The whine and the little scrape as the skull parts to let in the drill bit, is it even clean? Does that matter? I'm not making any sounds now, just rocking the chair, tapping out my panic rhythm, rocking the chair, rocking the chair, my face is now clenched like his was earlier, my jaw is clamped shut, my eyes screwed down so hard they hurt. Is there pain, is this worth that? He stops drilling for a moment, and I wait. The other one relaxes his hold on me for a second. Then the drilling starts again, and the grip returns, and now there are sounds to make again. I don't know if anything comes out. I hear moans, howls, screams. I see slow fish, circling round the deep blue frigid waters, circling round with blank black eyes. Big slow fish. Blind.

76

I don't know what's inside me now, it frightens me. Something got in, something got out, I don't know. There is damage. Sometimes I can see, most of the time I can't, often I don't know if I'm seeing or not. I see clouds, just clouds, much of the time. I watch them. The damage is localized, not extensive, which they say is fortunate. But it is severe. Unsurprisingly, it is in the part of the brain that is responsible for vision, the occipital lobe. A deep, messy lesion. They can't fix it. Brain tissue is apparently unique, in that it cannot regenerate itself when damaged. I will never see again, in any sense of the term worth using. So no more nooses, needles. No more dead babies. If I can't see it, then it can't happen. We've got it out, stopped it, Teacher and I. He did a more thorough job than he intended. I am free of it. Healed.

How did he find that exact part, the visual cortex, the occipital lobe? Did he use a book, like an owner's manual for a bike? Or did the lord simply take his hand and guide the drill to that spot? I won't ever know now. He got it right anyway. Bang on.

My days are strange. There are discontinuities, vast smooth rolling interruptions, windy, like travelling at high speed, through a black wind, howling.

Black. There won't be any improvement.

I got away, though, I crawled away from him. I remember it. I remember the taste of soil in my mouth as I escaped. I remember it clearly, as if it were a dream. The police found me. I made a report, a complaint. They are conducting an investigation and there have been some arrests, though my testimony is mostly uncorroborated and evidence scarce. The damage to my brain, which is their best evidence, sadly makes me less than ideal as a witness. Juries are apparently deeply sceptical about witnesses who drool and can't always remember their own names. I can't imagine why. They're trying, though. Teacher was detained, questioned, released, is being watched. They say they'll get him. Just a matter of time. Now I'm in a proper bed in a real hospital and the doctor is a real doctor. I think. He has no discernible smell, other than soap and tobacco. He speaks in real words, not frightening, mad ones. He talks about scans and percentages and things that are dull and undramatic and soothing. He has a loud, confident voice. He looks right, as far as I can tell, which isn't very far. I can't be really sure, being really sure about things is probably not in my range just now. I saw my Grandma Beale, a young girl, swinging from a low branch, her dress riding up, her little legs kicking out. God was smiling on her. She was smiling back. And someone put something into my arms, a baby, a little girl apparently, even younger than the girl swinging in the tree. She's called Jessica, the voice said, isn't she beautiful. Yes. I said, though I couldn't see her. Yes, she's beautiful. She's so little. Something trickled down my face. From my eyes. I held her for a moment. Is she alive? I said, is she alive, oh Christ, she isn't dead? Of course she's not dead, silly, said the voice, she's perfect and beautiful. I saw her dead, I said, though I suppose I couldn't have, not really. I must have been mistaken. Sorry. My face was wet with tears and they took the little girl from me. I'm sorry I said, for leaving you, for not loving you enough, for being so afraid, for chasing after all those other things, impossible things. Sorry. Don't cry she said, you'll be better soon. Will God smile on me? I said.

He's smiling on you now, the voice said. Can't you see? You've just got to be brave. Sleep now. Dream dreams.

THE END

SHEEP
by Simon Maginn

'Too small for human bones (unless they were children's) . . .
He dug faster . . . The sheep stared at him with their dead
eyes, innumerable pairs of flat, black little eyes. They were
starting to jostle each other . . .'

James, a builder, and Adèle, a promising artist, arrived in west
Wales hoping that a change of scene would help them come
to terms with the death of their daughter. Together with Sam,
their young son, they settled into Ty-Gwyneth, the ramshackle
farmhouse which James had been commissioned to repair. Its
former occupants, they were appalled to discover, had fallen
prey to drugs, madness, incarceration and murder.

During the course of his renovations, James dug up some very
odd-looking bones. Sam had a fall and saw something which
inexplicably linked the present to the past. Adèle's painting
became stranger and stranger – and so did Adèle. Could the
house's history be influencing their lives? In the disastrous
aftermath of supper with Lewyn, a nearby farmer, James
decided to investigate the contents of the freezer . . .

'The best début novel I have read since *The Wasp Factory*'
Peter James

0 552 14122 4

VIRGINS AND MARTYRS
by Simon Maginn

A woman's arm is found washed up on Brighton beach. The palm of the hand has been pierced, possibly by a nail. There is a wedding ring on the appropriate finger, and from the lividity of the flesh it is clear that the ring has been put on after death.

Daniel, a graduate student struggling to finish his dissertation, moves into a house in Hove owned by a polite and inscrutable skinhead. Wendy, the former occupant of his room, has vanished, leaving few traces: some shredded paper, a hank of hair. But gradually Daniel begins to feel Wendy's presence all around him, guiding him to shelves in the university library where crumbling books about decomposing corpses and sacrificial virgins are kept. And curiously, Daniel finds himself unable to eat, even to buy food. As he becomes thinner and weaker, his mind is dominated by sinister visions of a starving Wendy and of his own hand, wet, dead, and with a neat hole piercing its palm . . .

'A name to watch'
Ramsey Campbell

0 552 14249 2

AFTER THE HOLE
by Guy Burt

'POWERFUL, ATMOSPHERIC AND EERIE . . . HE IS A
BORN STORYTELLER'
Evelyn Anthony

It was the end of term at Our Glorious School. Most of the
pupils were preparing to return home; some were going away
on a geography field trip. But for five members of the sixth
form, it sounded more fun to embark upon what their friend
and mentor Martyn called 'an experiment with real life' – to
spend three days together in The Hole, a windowless cellar
room in an unfrequented part of the school buildings. Martyn
was to lock them in, and in three days he would come and
let them out again.

At first, it all seemed quite a laugh – eating and drinking,
jokes and banter. Solid Mike and dependable Liz, Geoff with
his secret supplies of booze, irritating Frankie and delicate
Alex – what a story they would have to tell when Martyn
came to release them! How surprised and admiring their
friends would be!

But three days passed, and Martyn did not return . . .

After The Hole is a dark and menacing first novel, written
when the author was still at school. Compulsive and claustro-
phobic in quality, it has been compared to John Fowles's *The
Collector*.

'AN ASTONISHINGLY ASSURED DÉBUT . . .
GENUINELY SHOCKING'
Mark Morris

0 552 99531 2

A SELECTED LIST OF FINE WRITING
AVAILABLE FROM CORGI BOOKS
AND BLACK SWAN

THE PRICES SHOWN BELOW WERE CORRECT AT THE TIME OF GOING
TO PRESS. HOWEVER TRANSWORLD PUBLISHERS RESERVE THE RIGHT
TO SHOW NEW RETAIL PRICES ON COVERS WHICH MAY DIFFER FROM
THOSE PREVIOUSLY ADVERTISED IN THE TEXT OR ELSEWHERE.

14144 5	**POSSESSED**	*Thomas B. Allen*	£4.99
14054 6	**THE DOLL'S HOUSE**	*Evelyn Anthony*	£4.99
13817 7	**EXPOSURE**	*Evelyn Anthony*	£4.99
14168 2	**JIGSAW**	*Campbell Armstrong*	£4.99
09156 1	**THE EXORCIST**	*William Peter Blatty*	£4.99
99531 2	**AFTER THE HOLE**	*Guy Burt*	£5.99
99532 0	**SOPHIE**	*Guy Burt*	£5.99
13947 5	**SUNDAY MORNING**	*Ray Connolly*	£4.99
14227 1	**SHADOWS ON A WALL**	*Ray Connolly*	£5.99
99602 5	**THE LAST GIRL**	*Penelope Evans*	£5.99
12550 4	**LIE DOWN WITH LIONS**	*Ken Follett*	£4.99
12610 1	**ON WINGS OF EAGLES**	*Ken Follett*	£5.99
10050 1	**THE DOGS OF WAR**	*Frederick Forsyth*	£5.99
13990 4	**THE FIST OF GOD**	*Frederick Forsyth*	£5.99
13598 4	**MAESTRO**	*John Gardner*	£5.99
13840 1	**CLOSED CIRCLE**	*Robert Goddard*	£4.99
13562 3	**TAKE NO FAREWELL**	*Robert Goddard*	£4.99
13869 X	**MATILDA'S GAME**	*Denis Kilcommons*	£3.99
12433 8	**A COLD MIND**	*David Lindsey*	£4.99
13489 9	**HOOLET**	*John McNeil*	£4.99
14122 4	**SHEEP**	*Simon Maginn*	£4.99
14249 2	**VIRGINS AND MARTYRS**	*Simon Maginn*	£4.99
99391 3	**MARY REILLY**	*Valerie Martin*	£4.99
14145 3	**MANCHESTER BLUE**	*Eddy Shah*	£4.99
14290 5	**FALLEN ANGELS**	*Eddy Shah*	£5.99
14143 7	**A SIMPLE PLAN**	*Scott Smith*	£4.99
10565 1	**TRINITY**	*Leon Uris*	£5.99